Dear Reader,

I've never been very good at talking about my feelings. Guess I'm not much different than most men I know. I'm not easy with my feelings and sure don't explain them well, but I'm honest, and I told Katie right up front that I wasn't interested in anything permanent. I'd messed up my first marriage, and I had two kids to think of now.

But when I found out that my discipline had deserted me as far as Katie was concerned, there just wasn't anything else to do but marry her. That's how I live. Anyway, I didn't think our marriage had a chance, and with that attitude it was touch and go. Our story just goes to show that sometimes miracles happen, even to good ol' boys like me.

Best of luck to you,
Reno Martin

Oklahoma

CURTISS ANN MATLOCK

A Time and a Season

Published by Silhouette Books New York

America's Publisher of Contemporary Romance

For Jim,
my very own maintenance man.

Thanks.

SILHOUETTE BOOKS
300 East 42nd St., New York, N.Y. 10017

A TIME AND A SEASON

Copyright © 1985 by Curtiss Ann Matlock

All rights reserved. Except for use in any review, the reproduction
or utilization of this work in whole or in part in any form by any
electronic, mechanical or other means, now known or hereafter
invented, including xerography, photocopying and recording, or in
any information storage or retrieval system, is forbidden without
the permission of the publisher, Silhouette Books, 300 E. 42nd St.,
New York, N.Y. 10017

ISBN: 0-373-45186-5

Published Silhouette Books 1985, 1993

All the characters in this book have no existence outside the
imagination of the author and have no relation whatsoever to
anyone bearing the same name or names. They are not even
distantly inspired by any individual known or unknown to the
author, and all incidents are pure invention.

® and ™ are trademarks used under license. Trademarks recorded
with ® are registered in the United States Patent and Trademark
Office, the Canadian Trade Marks Office and in other countries.

Printed in the U.S.A.

Chapter One

Voluminous storm clouds, ranging in color from hazy purple to deep blue, almost black, tumbled across the sky. The wind rose, tossing Katie's hair wildly, battering her body. She tried to walk, but the wind pushed her back, taking her breath away. Suddenly, in the distance, she saw the dark shape of a swirling funnel cloud snaking toward the earth. She opened her mouth to scream, but no sound came out. In minutes the tornado would be upon her, and there was nowhere to run, nowhere to hide.

It came to her then that she was dreaming. She struggled to wake from the horrible nightmare, but couldn't quite make it. In the next second the scene of her dream changed. The storm was gone and Katie stood safely upon a wide plateau, knee-deep in prairie grass, a bright blue sky above her, a gentle breeze ruffling her hair. From the slope below, a man approached. Closer and closer he came, ever slowly. Katie watched him curiously, growing impatient with his leisurely pace. Then he was there before her, but all she could see were his eyes, the darkest shade of brown she had ever seen. They regarded her somberly, speculatively. Then their light changed to one of exceeding warmth and gentleness. Katie was drawn by that warmth, knowing here she was safe, she was at peace from the storm.

She awoke with a start. The dream had been so vivid, the man so real. As she stared into the darkened room, the dream faded, but not the spell it had cast. Intuitively, she felt something ahead, something waiting to happen.

Sitting up to switch on the bedside lamp, Katie shook away the portentous feeling, dismissing it as leftovers of the dream. The night had been like many others of the past months. She'd tossed and turned, finally falling into a deep sleep around five-thirty in the morning. Checking her watch, she saw it was now eight. The room's darkness was caused by heavy drapes drawn tightly across the window.

An imploring whine came from the side of the bed. Katie stretched out a hand and ruffled the fur of a huge black Labrador retriever, who rested her chin against the sheets and looked up expectantly.

"You can't fool me, Sam," Katie scolded. "I know you were on the bed last night. Your black hair is a telltale clue." Sam was short for Samantha. She was a dog who at times thought she was human. Many mornings Sam was not only lying across the blankets, but had her head on the pillow as well. Katie had given up trying to teach her to stay off the bed.

Reaching for the telephone, Katie rang room service for an English muffin and coffee. She slipped on a robe, opened the door a crack for the waiter, then sat cross-legged on the bed, again reaching for the phone and dialing a long-distance number from memory.

"Hello." A familiar woman's voice on the other end answered.

"Hi, Celia. I hope I didn't wake you. I wanted to catch you before you and Ray left for church."

"Katie! No, no, you didn't wake me. And it's about time you called. The assignment was to take three days at the most. What have you been doing? Ray's storming about expenses again. He says he's not paying you for a vacation," Celia scolded, running all her thoughts together as usual. Ray Whitney was the owner-editor of the magazine Katie worked for; his wife, Celia, was coeditor. "We were getting a bit worried," she added gently.

"Don't be. I'm fine. I'm bringing a bag of fresh pecans from the Anderson orchard as a bribe for Ray's forgiveness. And I ran across another article I thought would be great. Have we done anything on raising sheep lately? Mrs. Anderson put me on to her brother, who raises them. I already have the piece half finished and with pictures."

"Sheep?" Celia sounded as if she'd never heard of the animal. "I didn't think they had sheep in Oklahoma. Isn't that cattle country?"

"You've seen too many movies, Celia." Katie chuckled. "Look, I'm just north of Chandler. I'm coming home today, so I'll see you Tuesday morning. I want a day to rest and get the apartment in order."

"Chandler..." Katie heard the rustle of paper in the background. "I can't seem to find it on the map— Oh, here, it is. That's quite a way to travel in one day, Katie," Celia said doubtfully.

"It is one full day's driving. I want to come home, Celia."

"If you say so... Wait a minute." Celia spoke to someone at the other end, and Katie picked up Ray's muffled voice. "Katie," Celia said, "Ray says there was something on the radio just now about a winter storm approaching, so you be careful."

"I will," Katie said, and hearing a timid knock, looked over to see the waiter with her tray. She motioned him in, but he looked with obvious uncertainty at Sam, who was blocking the way. "Celia, I have to run now. Room service is here. I'll call you when I get home."

"Okay, and please call your Aunt Claire. Now! She has called me three times this week."

"I will, I promise. Bye."

Replacing the receiver, Katie called Sam to her side. The waiter stepped into the room, leaving the tray on the desk. Handing the young man a sizable tip, Katie shut the door and turned to Sam. "You frightened him, you know that?" Sam sniffed at the tray. "None for you, my friend. You'll have to be content with dog food. We'll stop later and get a big brunch."

Then she sighed. What was she doing carrying on whole conversations with a dog?

Pouring a large bowl of dry dog food for Sam, Katie switched the motel radio to an easy-listening station, which was the only place she might catch a weather report on an early Sunday morning. Sitting cross-legged again on the bed, she spread the muffin thick with butter and jam, pleasantly surprised to find the motel served real butter. She loved the stuff.

Katie enjoyed eating, and nibbled constantly. As a rule her nervous energy burned the food as fast as she ate, but sometimes she did have to count calories in order to stay in a size seven jeans, which she was determined to do. Slender, but not thin, Katie filled her jeans fully. However, this was not a morning to conserve, and, finishing one half the muffin, Katie spread the other half thick with the remaining butter.

She had splurged on room service this morning, splurged on the whole trip actually. She had been gone ten days and had spent every night in a nice motel. Usually on these trips, always accompanied by Sam, Katie stayed at a moderately priced motel or camped in her van, which, though old and somewhat battered, she had modified comfortably for camping.

But she needed this trip, she rationalized, even if she no longer had much savings. And her small travel expense account would defray some of the cost.

Katie Garrett was a staff writer for a "back to the land" magazine, a publication that contained articles on homesteading, organic gardening, home building and home cooking. Founded ten years ago, the magazine was still small, serving mostly the rural Ozark region of Arkansas and Missouri, but had begun expanding to other states in the past year.

This trip she had been concerned with researching an article on growing pecans and a feature on a remarkable woman, Annie Anderson. Katie had thoroughly enjoyed the lively old woman and was proud of her article. She hoped Ray would be pleased and that maybe she would get a raise.

Katie poured the last of the coffee and reached for the telephone again to make the call to her Aunt Claire and Uncle Will.

After getting through the hellos and being fussed at for not calling sooner, Katie said, "Don't fret, Aunt Claire. I'm coming home today."

"I don't think you should, Katie," Aunt Claire said. "There's bad weather coming down from the northwest. Your Uncle Will's leg has been acting up and the chickens' feathers are fluffing out. I think this will be a bad one."

Katie smiled at her aunt's folk superstitions. "I want to come home. It's only a day's drive. I'll beat the storm."

"You're a Garrett through and through, stubborn as Will. Take care, honey. I'll hold you in my prayers. Call us when you get in. I'll be waiting."

"Yes, Aunt Claire. And thanks. Love ya."

Pushing aside the heavy drapes, Katie looked out at the sky. Bands of heavy gray clouds stretched across low and wide, making it seem much earlier. The sky darkened even more to the west as cloud built upon cloud. Again Katie felt the uneasiness settle upon her like a blanket. Raking her fingers through her long auburn hair, she shook her head as if to throw off the feeling. She wanted to go home—today. She wanted to see and feel the security of her own place. Not that she could ever really call it home. Not the home she had known for all the years of her life. That home was gone, like her father and mother. Gone forever. But the apartment was hers, and the bed the same one she'd had from childhood. She wanted to go home.

She took soft faded Levi's and an ivory fisherman-knit sweater from her suitcase and, while dressing, caught the weather forecast. It didn't sound too bad, at least for Katie's purposes. Cloudy, much colder, but no rain or snow expected until later afternoon or evening. By that time, she should be nearly home and a good deal ahead of the storm approaching from the Rockies. And contrary to her dreams, tornadoes were highly unlikely in early February.

Pulling on cowboy boots of fine-grain leather, she straightened her pant legs. Covering the fancy stitching of the boot tops always seemed a bit of a shame to Katie. Western boots were in vogue, but she had been wearing them long before they became a fad, and would still be long after. She simply liked their comfort.

Katie had her own style of dress, born of a natural instinct for knowing what looked attractive on her. She chose clothes not only for how they looked, but for how they felt against her skin. In the winter she loved natural woolens; cotton and wool flannels were a favorite. In cooler temperatures she rarely wore dresses, but come summer, cotton-blend skirts and dresses were practically all she wore.

After making sure she hadn't forgotten anything, Katie loaded the van and, with Sam at her heels, went to settle the motel bill. The same young man who earlier had brought her breakfast tray manned the desk in the quiet lobby. He smiled easily, not bothered now by Sam, with the tall registration desk for protection.

"Heading home?" he inquired as he added her bill.

"Yes, to Arkansas."

"Weather is closing in, but going east you should be okay."

"I think so," Katie said as she wrote the check. "Which is the best way to the Interstate?"

"Take a left out here on Route 66 and go a few blocks down to State Highway 18. Take it south. It's small and a bit rough, but no traffic to speak of, especially today."

Outside, Katie tightened her coat around her neck and tugged a knit stocking cap down around her ears. The wind picked up and seemed to go right through the thickness of her clothes. Sam took a morning ritual run in the small lot bordering the motel grounds. Then Katie gave out a summoning whistle, impatient to start home.

As she shifted gears and pulled the van out onto the highway, a shivery chill shot down her spine. There it was again, the feeling. Then it was gone, disappearing as quickly as it had come. Katie looked at the sky in apprehension. Sam licked at Katie's hand, then rustled around restlessly, seeking the perfect position.

The Garrett family, especially the women, were known to be fey, at least by family lore. Katie had a strong sixth sense and often relied on this sense of knowing, this intuitiveness... But not today. Today she only wanted to get home. Besides, very often this same intuitiveness fooled her and nothing happened as expected. And if she hurried she could beat the storm anyway. She wouldn't take all the interesting back roads as she usually did. She would drop down to the

Interstate for a while, then cut away and head northeast to her home town of Porterville, Arkansas.

By eleven o'clock, Katie and Sam were well into eastern Oklahoma and looking for somewhere to have a late breakfast, or lunch—anything. Katie was starving. A small café at the exit of the Interstate had looked inviting, but was closed.

She had taken the Interstate, then exited at a promising state highway heading northeast, a quicker and more interesting way home. Or so she thought. At the moment she questioned the wisdom of that decision. The weather forecaster still predicted cold and partly cloudy until evening, but that didn't account for the icy rain and mist repeatedly falling on the van windshield. For the last hour Katie had been forced to drive more slowly, even while on the four-lane Interstate.

Topping a hill on the somewhat winding road, she felt a tickling rise from the tiny hairs on the back of her neck and again a chill shot through her. Something was wrong. The road noise of the van had changed. There came a harsh grinding sound from somewhere in the depths of the truck. It grew louder. Wide-eyed, Katie stared at the dashboard, lifting her foot from the accelerator. The grinding culminated in a popping sound. The engine continued to purr gently, but the van steadily lost power and coasted down the backside of the hill.

Katie gunned the engine. It roared, but no power made it to the wheels. With the road now beginning to patch with ice, she guided the coasting van to a stop, the right wheels off the blacktop. The grassy shoulder was too small for her to pull completely from the road; moreover, it dipped dangerously into a deep gully.

Pulling the emergency brake, Katie stared tight-lipped at the steering wheel.

"Damn!" she swore aloud, hitting the steering wheel with her fist and receiving a definite look of reproach from Sam. "Don't look at me like that, Sam. I don't need to be corrected at this moment."

That feeling this morning—it hadn't simply been an overactive imagination after all. She should have listened to her instincts and not been so muleheaded. But thinking of "should haves" wasn't helping now, and neither was her sixth sense.

"In any dark situation, look for the bright spots," her father, Renfrow Garrett, used to say.

Katie looked at the sky. Not a bright spot was to be found there.

Mentally she surveyed the situation. At least the engine continued to run, and with it the heater still functioned. One bright spot.

She could either get out and walk to the nearest house—and who knew how far that would be—or she could wait for help from someone passing by. Watching the cold drizzle hit the windshield, Katie opted for the latter alternative and switched on the emergency blinkers. Stopped on the downside of a hill was not exactly the safest position to be in, but there was nothing that could be done about it at the moment. Someone should be along soon, coming home from church or *something*. At least she fervently hoped so.

Her stomach let out a muted growl, and Sam raised an eyebrow. Katie thought longingly of scrambled eggs and hash browns, then shrugged in Sam's direction and stepped to the back of the van, rummaging for something to snack on. While she was back there, two cars whipped past, one right after the other.

Katie watched in disgust as the cars disappeared down the road. The drivers probably couldn't see her in the back and thought the van empty. To make matters more aggravating, all she could find to munch on were stale corn chips and water from a thermos. Usually she had at least a few cans of soft drinks in the cooler. Master and dog shared their meager fare, waiting.

Forty-five minutes later they still waited. One other car had whizzed by, not even slowing. Sam napped comfortably in the back while Katie drearily watched sleet hit the windshield and slide down in silver streaks. She vaguely considered getting out and raising the hood as an added indication of trouble to passersby, but decided icy rain falling on an open engine wouldn't help matters. She kept the van warm by turning on the engine at ten-minute intervals. It ran now, a smooth rumble as always, but for some unfathomable reason no power made it to the wheels.

Looking at Sam peacefully snoring, trusting her master to take care of things, Katie too felt drowsy. She switched off the motor. With the fuel gauge registering only a quarter of a tank, gas was at a premium.

Slipping off her woolen ski cap, she ran slim fingers through her long silky hair, allowing it to fall comfortingly across her cheeks. She reached for a blanket and spread it over her legs, settling as best she could in the driver's seat. She didn't dare lie on the built-in bed for fear she'd fall asleep. *Now I feel like sleeping,* Katie thought wryly.

They'd wait a bit longer, and if no one came, she and Sam would just have to get out and walk to the nearest house. That prospect looked less and less inviting with sleet hitting ever more thickly against the glass.

Katie slowly opened her heavy-lidded eyes. She was freezing, her teeth chattering, her legs stiff and cramped. Struggling to focus her eyes, she checked her watch and was startled to find she had slept nearly two hours. Large chunks of sleet hit the van and a thin film of ice coated the windshield.

Hearing a motor running, she smeared the fog collected on the inside of the windshield and tried to peer through the ice-covered glass.

She watched as a pickup backed slowly toward the van. A man alighted from the cab and, pulling the brim of his Western hat low against the sleet, walked quickly toward the van.

Issuing a sigh of relief, Katie tried to quiet her chattering teeth and rolled down the window to speak to him.

The man was of average build, wide-shouldered and solid. His hat, pulled low across his brows, left his eyes in a dark shadow and unreadable. The rust-colored Western-style sport coat he wore was fine for a night on the town, but hardly adequate for the present pelting of sleet. He hunkered before her with both hands pushed deep into his jeans pockets, and Katie sensed an air of annoyance from the tight thrust of his jaw.

"What's the trouble?" he asked, his voice deep and smooth.

"The van broke down a while ago," Katie had to pause to get full control over her shaking voice. "The engine runs, but the wheels won't turn."

The stranger rather grunted and reached for the door handle. Katie tried as quickly as possible to scoot to the passenger side to give him room, but was hampered by sharp pains shooting across her frozen feet and up her legs. She grimaced and turned her face, unwilling to have the man view her discomfort. Mentally she berated herself for ever being foolish enough to fall asleep.

It never occurred to her to be wary of this stranger. She was too grateful for help and was already anticipating warmth and a hot meal.

It did occur to Sam, if only for a second. The dog placed her large paws and the front half of her body upon the console between the stranger and Katie, sniffing curiously. The man gave a half-smile and ruffled Sam behind the ears. Sam's tail picked up tempo back and forth, signaling her approval.

"It's freezing in here. Why didn't you keep the engine running for heat?" the man asked, more as an accusation than a question.

"I did for a while, but the gas began to run low. I turned it off and accidentally fell asleep," Katie admitted sheepishly.

The man gave a small grunt. "Well, let's give it a try," he said, turning the key. The starter whined a bit, but refused to turn over, protesting the cold. He tried again. The starter gave a grating sound, slower and slower as it drew on the weakened battery. Just when Katie's heart had nearly hit bottom, the engine started. It coughed and balked, but then purred gently.

Katie watched as the man moved the gearshift through the gear settings one by one. Nothing. Leaning back against the seat, the man thoughtfully stroked his thick mustache.

"Lady, I'm sorry, but it appears your transmission has gone out."

"Oh." Katie let that word sit there a moment while she chewed her lower lip. Conscious of almost uncontrollable shivering, she clamped her hands firmly between her knees. Then she asked, "How far to a gas station or garage where I can see about getting it repaired?"

"I don't think there's anything open today within a radius of twenty miles. Even if there were, in this weather it could very well be difficult getting someone to come out. Are you headed somewhere nearby? I could give you a lift."

Katie shook her head, her eyes focusing on the icy rivers running down the windshield. "No, I was heading home... to Arkansas." Suddenly she felt very tired and wished to be back home, curled snug and safe in the familiar green easy chair in the old kitchen. The kitchen which was no longer hers, a secure and comforting way of life which was gone.

"Would it be too much trouble to drive me to the nearest motel? Is there one not too far away?" Her voice echoed fatigue, and the man turned his head sharply in her direction.

"Look, my ranch is just a couple of miles up the road," the man said. "I have a tow chain in the truck. I can tow your van to my place and call a buddy of mine who owns a garage over in Tyne. See what he says about looking at your van."

Katie shook her head. "I couldn't let you go to all that trouble."

"It's not that much trouble. I was on my way home, and it's over seventeen miles up to Tyne and the nearest motel. I'd just as soon stop at my ranch for warming up and a bit to eat. And you don't want to leave your van sitting here all night. No telling what may happen to it."

The man was right. Leaving the van in this dangerous position on the road was asking for trouble, especially with the visibility so poor. She chewed her lip again and pondered her choices, which were few. She just wished she could see this man's eyes better and be able to tell from their expression if he really felt as agreeable as he was trying to sound. But, she thought again, her choices really were few.

"Okay," she agreed finally.

The man's jaw appeared to soften, and he nodded his approval. Turning to step from the van, he stopped and extended a hand to Katie. "Name's Reno Martin."

"I'm Katherine Garrett—Katie," she said. His grip was firm, his large hands work-roughened.

Zipping her coat to the neck and pulling on her sock hat and gloves, Katie followed Martin from the van, wanting to be of some kind of help. Actually, there was little Katie could do, but she felt guilty sitting in the dry cab of the van while this Good Samaritan worked out in the frigid air to help her.

The outside cold hit her face, causing her to suck in a sharp breath. The moisture raining from the gray sky was pure sleet now and in the icy stillness it made a crackling sound rather like crisp rice cereal. Shaking from strain and hunger, Katie felt her limbs weaken and leaned on the front of the van for support.

"Get back in the van," Martin ordered.

"I just want to see if I—" Katie began, but was cut short by the stranger's gruff voice.

"Just get back in the van. No need in us both getting frozen."

Ordinarily Katie would put up an argument against being ordered around, by a stranger at that, but at the moment she just didn't feel like it. She climbed back in the van, grateful to ease into the seat and rest her shaking legs. Sam nudged her arms, then licked her cheek.

"Oh, Sam," Katie sighed, hugging the dog's neck and burying her face in Sam's soft fur.

A fine mess her stubbornness had gotten her into this time. For all she knew, this Reno Martin was a thoroughly wicked character who drank himself senseless and raped defenseless women. Katie chuckled at her imagination. She really didn't believe it and Sam seemed to take to him. But Sam took to everyone, and Katie had been wrong before.

"You'll have to protect me, Sam," Katie mumbled, and she thought again, *I really don't have a choice.*

Martin finished with the tow chain and came around to the window. "We'll have to take it slow. The ice is building on the road, but we only have to go a couple of miles. Watch the chain. Try to keep it taut and just brake lightly if need be. Okay?"

"I've got it. I've done this before," Katie assured him, not wanting him to think her completely helpless.

He seemed about to say more, but simply tapped the door with a gloved hand and said, "Good."

Switching on the wipers, Katie cleared the windshield of the thin, watery ice. With a watchful eye on the tautness of the chain, she guided the van to follow the pickup before her, keeping a light hand on the steering wheel. The wipers made a rapid thumping sound as sleet and now the beginnings of snow pelted against the glass. Her neck and shoulder muscles ached with tension as she strained forward in the seat for a better view. Visibility was getting worse.

Though the going was slow, it took less than ten minutes to reach the dirt turnoff for the ranch. A rough timber archway, with the name Martin burned across the top, emphasized the drive and a deep wood flanked both sides. Rutted and patched with ice, the drive headed uphill. Martin shifted to a lower gear, trying to keep the pickup at a slow and steady pace.

As he neared the top of the incline, the pickup's left tire spun on a patch of ice, sending the truck sideways and then backward, pulled by the weight of the van. The truck barely missed hitting a tree.

Katie, her pulse beating in her ears, hit the brake to keep from dragging the pickup farther, creating a slack in the chain and allowing room for Martin to straighten it.

Carefully he began again, this time successfully topping the rise and pulling the van into a large clearing. He drove the pickup on into a two-car garage whose door was already open.

Katie braked the van just outside the garage behind the pickup and the tow chain drooped to the ground. Slumping forward, she rested her arms and forehead on the steering wheel. Whining softly in concern, Sam nuzzled her neck.

Katie was exhausted. She hadn't even energy enough to open the door. She felt so cold, a bone-gripping kind of cold. Her feet were numb and her legs and arms ached. First

her teeth began to chatter and then she began to shake un-
controllably all over. It made her angry. She wanted to stop,
tried to, but couldn't.

She heard the door open and felt a cold blast of air. Then
strong arms were dragging her from her seat.

"I'm okay," Katie said through chattering teeth, pushing at the hands. "I just needed to rest a minute." She half
opened her eyes and took a step, but her legs buckled. Her
mind spinning, she began to sink into darkness. With an
iron will, she fought hard to hold on to consciousness.

Chapter Two

Quickly Reno Martin's strong arm wrapped around Katie's waist and saved her from collapsing. With his support, the two made their way toward the house. The ground crunched under their feet and sleet pelted them from above. Katie was practically hauled up some stairs and across a wide veranda.

She felt, saw and heard everything in blurry confusion, as if in a foggy mist. Her nostrils picked up the musky scent of after-shave mixed with that of stale whiskey. The cool leather of Martin's coat rubbed her cheek and his warm breath fanned her forehead. The door was yanked open before them and several voices spoke at once.

"Daddy, Daddy. Oh, a dog!" Sam's tail brushed past with several thumps against Katie's thigh.

"It's about time, Reno. What in the world do you have here?"

Gently, Katie felt herself lowered into the folds of a great chair. Warmth touched her face, and through half-closed eyes she caught the flickering of a fire and the soft sheen of wheat-colored braids.

"I'll get a blanket, Dad."

"Yes, babe, and some hot coffee."

"Sit, Reno. You're in need of warming, too."

"You're too bossy, Maggie."

"Yes, I know. At least give me your coat."

Someone's hands removed Katie's boots, then her hat and coat. Rough hands, the stranger's hands, Katie thought. They rubbed her own rapidly, then rubbed at her feet trying to increase the circulation. A blanket was tucked all around her shivering body.

Able to focus at last, she looked directly into eyes of the deepest velvet brown—warm, penetrating eyes, clouded now with concern. As she watched, they became even darker; so dark a distinct pupil disappeared. Katie felt herself claimed and drawn into the depths of those brown eyes, into the vibrant warmth she sensed there, lost in remembrance of another time.

With startling clarity, the morning's faded dream flooded back, and Katie recognized those eyes. Surely it was impossible...he couldn't be... She blinked, trying to clear her thoughts, bring herself back to the moment. Reno Martin was calling to her.

"Miss Garrett...Katie? Is that warmer now?" As he spoke, Reno rubbed her hands rapidly, scraping her soft skin with the roughness of his. "Here, take a sip of this."

As if she were a child, he held a cup to her lips, and Katie obediently sipped from it, grateful for the liquid's warmth all the way to her stomach. It was coffee, hot and delicious.

"Here, Reno, let me do that. Take a cup of coffee yourself." Such a raspy voice spoke.

Reno rose from where he had knelt before her and Katie followed him with her eyes. Then the coffee cup was once more raised to her lips, and Katie heard again the gravelly, raspy voice. "Ah, there now. You're doing fine. Let's take just a bit more of this coffee."

Katie took another swallow of the hot brew and, with a sigh, allowed her head to rest against the chair back, feeling her strength slowly return. Smiling wanly at the tiny old woman who held the cup and to whom the raspy voice obviously belonged, Katie managed a hoarse "Thank you."

The old woman smiled in return, her face crinkling into wrinkles. Platted gray hair formed a crown atop her head, and she sat on a stool close to Katie's knee, regal as a queen. "You're welcome, my girl," she said, patting Katie's hand. "And now, you look able to manage this cup. I'm going to see about getting you all some hot food." Stiffly she straightened from the low stool and headed from the room.

The chair enveloping Katie sat in front and just to the left of an enormous rock fireplace. Running her eyes over the wall, she noticed it wasn't a true fireplace at all, but a large wood stove, its doors open wide for immediate heat. The wall behind was made of stones, varying in size, shape and color.

Across from Katie and on the right of the stove sat another giant chair, at the moment containing Reno Martin, a young girl and a much younger little boy. Sam lay at their feet. All four pairs of eyes radiated curiosity and concern.

Katie's gaze fell to Sam and that was all the dog needed for an invitation. Wriggling over to her mistress, she laid her head upon Katie's lap. "Hi there, girl," Katie crooned softly, stroking the dog's satin fur.

"Feeling better?" Reno asked, his gaze studying her carefully.

"Yes, much." Katie was struck again by the rich brown of his eyes. Their look of concern softened at her answer.

The children were obviously Reno Martin's children. They both favored the man quite a bit, though the girl less than the boy. The young girl sat on the arm of the chair, leaning against her father, her arm around the back of his neck. It was her hair, light brown and hanging in braids to her waist, that Katie's vision had picked up earlier. The girl's dark blue eyes somberly studied Katie.

The little dark-haired boy, maybe four years old, scrambled from Reno's knee and came to pet Sam. The boy looked a miniature of his father, with added freckles and a boyish exuberance.

"Your dog sure is neat. What's her name?" he asked.

"Samantha—Sam for short," Katie answered, glad to find her normal voice return. "And she likes little boys, too." The small boy's smile widened and he snuggled closer to the dog.

"Katie, these are my children. That little ball of fire at your feet is Joey and this quiet one here is Summer. Kids, this is Katie Garrett."

"Hello," the two children said in unison.

"Hello," Katie said.

"Honey," Reno said, addressing Summer. "Take my cup on into Maggie and help her finish getting the meal on the table."

Silently Summer nodded, slipped from the chair and padded gracefully from the room, her fluid movements like that of a sleek cat. From the room behind her, Katie heard the rattle of dishes and soft murmur of voices.

Reno leaned his head back, closing his eyes. Sam sprawled at Katie's feet and Joey stretched out beside the dog, bringing his face very close and whispering and stroking Sam's back. It was quiet, peaceful, and Katie felt her strength returning as she warmed.

She was embarrassed to have acted so fragile and feeble, alarming everyone. What in the world had gotten into her anyway? Stubbornness, pure and simple, Katie thought, remembering her determination to get home. For the moment, however, the strong homeward urge had abated, replaced by mellow complacency.

Turning her gaze to Reno, she studied his face, the strong jawline, the way his dark hair curled slightly on his forehead and brushed the collar of his shirt. The color was between brown and black, with traces of gray at the temples. He had a thick mustache, the coarse dark hairs tinged also with gray, and shaped to droop longer at the corners of his mouth. Maybe he could be described as handsome, but more probably his attractiveness came from inside, from a male strength he exuded.

In repose for the moment, his face had an almost haggard look, Katie noticed for the first time. A stubble of beard shadowed his chin and cheeks. Deep circles showed under his eyes, and numerous lines fanned their outer corners.

His eyes fluttered open and Katie found herself again staring into their depths. The strong sense of recognition struck her anew as she watched a smile begin, first in his eyes, and then spreading to his lips. Caught staring with so frank a curiosity, Katie blushed and quickly averted her eyes to the flickering fire.

Several minutes later, Reno rose. "Think you could eat something now?" he asked, reaching out a hand to help her up.

"Yes, definitely, but first I'd like to use the bathroom."

Joey piped up. "I'll show her, Dad. Come on, Katie." The small boy grabbed Katie's hand, pulling her toward the back of the house, Sam at their heels. Depositing Katie at the bathroom door, Joey let go of her hand and announced cheerfully, "I'll get Sam some food and water, too."

The bathroom was all male—plain, decorated in varying shades of dark blue. Several bottles of after-shave and cologne sat atop the counter and a masculine robe hung on back of the door. There was no feminine clutter in sight. Katie wondered about a Mrs. Martin.

Katie found a washcloth and towel to freshen her face. She didn't have a brush, but managed to use her fingers to comb her long thick hair somewhat into its usual semblance of order. When she emerged, she felt much renewed, projecting the life and confidence of the old Katie. And somewhere along the way, in her mind, Reno Martin was no longer a stranger, but had become "Reno."

All except Maggie were seated around a large round oak table when Katie entered the dining area. At her step, Reno looked up, smiled a welcome and stepped around to hold a chair for her.

"Maggie has baked us up a real treat—some of her delicious homemade biscuits," he said.

The older woman placed two gingham-covered baskets on the table and Reno held another chair for her. "Let me introduce you to our Maggie... Maggie Latimer." Reno bent to kiss the older woman's cheek softly. "Maggie, this is Katie Garrett," he said with mock formality.

"Don't try to make up to me, Reno Martin." Maggie brushed him away with a wave of her hand. Reno winked at Katie, his eyes twinkling merrily. "Katie and I have met," Maggie said. "Have plenty of biscuits, Katie. You're a mite thin. Wait for prayer, little man." This she said tapping Joey's hand as he reached for one of the round golden breads.

Maggie bowed her head and everyone followed suit while she said a short prayer. Upon Maggie's "Amen," they all dug into a meal of homemade soup, biscuits, butter and jam. Soon the table was rowdy with talk. It reminded Katie of her own family and how it used to be when her parents were alive and how it still was when her aunts and uncles and the many cousins gathered together.

"You said you were heading home, Miss Katie, to Arkansas. What brought you to Oklahoma and traveling in such nasty weather?" Reno asked.

"I was over in Chandler doing research on pecans for an article I'm writing. I'd just finished up, and after a week away I wanted to get home." Katie smiled ruefully. "I should have known better. I knew the storm was coming."

"You didn't know you'd break down, though," Summer said.

"No... I guess not," Katie said, thinking of her earlier premonition.

"An article." Reno looked curious. "For a magazine?"

"Yes. I work for *Country Times*. It's what they call a backwoods publication, articles on country living and that sort of thing."

"I've seen it... have a few issues around here somewhere," Reno said. "Maybe that's why your name seems so familiar... your face, too."

"I don't think I've ever had my picture in it, but maybe I've just forgotten."

"Bet you were over there talking to Annie Anderson," Maggie said.

"Yes. Do you know her?"

"I did... a long time ago, when she first married." Maggie stared into space, remembering. "She and her husband were always crazy over pecans. Haven't seen her in forty years. Heard she did real well with pecans, though."

"Do you travel a lot?" Summer asked, looking at Katie.

"I have lately." As she answered, Katie wondered at Joey's quietness. She was amused to see him, out of the corner of her eye, discreeting slipping bits of biscuit to Sam, who sat quietly under the table.

"Then you're not married, Miss Garrett?" Summer asked. Katie was struck by the young girl's voice. It was soft and sweet, but somehow not like a child's at all.

"No, I'm not. And please, call me Katie."

"You must not even be engaged or even have a steady, traveling all over like you do," Summer continued, questioningly.

"There are such things as personal questions, Summer," Reno interjected as a mild reprimand.

"It's okay, Reno," Katie said, easily using his given name. Reaching for a third biscuit, she said, "These are delicious." Then she smiled at Summer. "I'm able to travel right now because I don't have anyone at home. I did live with my parents, but my mother died when I was nineteen and my father passed away last November. Traveling is something I'm really enjoying—for the moment."

"Our mother is dead, too," Joey said somberly. Katie wasn't exactly sure what to say to that, but before she could say anything, Joey brightened. "But we have Maggie and Grandma. Do you have a grandma?"

"No, but I have an Aunt Claire and she is an awful lot like your Maggie," Katie said with a grin.

"Hand me the phone, sweetheart," Reno told Summer as she refilled his coffee cup. "I need to give Ted Carter a call to see about getting Katie's van fixed as soon as possible."

"He ain't there."

Reno glanced quickly toward Maggie, who had spoken. "What?" he said.

"I said, he ain't there," Maggie repeated in a superior tone.

"How do you know?" Reno said, his voice low.

"Because I called his house this morning looking for you when you hadn't come home." Maggie raised her eyebrows and looked at him accusingly.

The children quieted, their eyes moving from Maggie to Reno. Sensing the undercurrents, Katie wished she were not in the middle of what appeared to be a private family affair.

"Well, where is he?" Reno asked with a resigned sigh, ignoring her barb.

"Sue said he had gone up to Tulsa with his brothers. She didn't expect him back until late tonight. With this weather, I imagine it won't even be tonight."

Reno looked to Katie. "Guess I'll have to get in touch with him tomorrow morning, Katie. There probably isn't anything Ted could do this late in the day anyway." Reno's mood had seemed to turn sour at Maggie's veiled criticism. Katie nodded as he rose and reached for his coat at the back door. "I've got to check a few things in the stables. Sonny slacks off on the job when I'm not here to keep after him. I'll only be a few minutes, then I can drive you into Tyne and the motel."

"Not this evening you won't," Maggie stated, looking out the window. "I felt the wind pick up half an hour ago. This norther is here."

"It's snowing! It's snowing!" Joey shouted as all eyes followed Maggie's glance. Engrossed in conversation throughout the meal, none of them had noticed the growing storm. A thin white blanket covered the ground. Tips of dead grass and dark bare patches still showed, but large flakes were falling heavily. Night was coming early as thick gray clouds blocked the late-afternoon sun.

"And underneath that white layer is ice—thick ice," Maggie said. "You know these February storms as well as I do, Reno. Everything comes to a standstill. No one is going to travel on a night like this. You and Katie happen to slip off the road, you two would be out there all night."

Uncertainly, Katie looked to Reno. "But—" she began, and Reno cut in.

"Maggie's right, Katie. It could be pretty dangerous between here and Tyne. And frankly, I'm not up to handling whatever might arise or to spending another night away from my own bed."

"You can have my bed," Summer offered to Katie.

"Yeah, Katie's going to spend the night. Yeah!" Joey sang while hopping up and down. "Can I go out in the snow now, Daddy? Can I?" Sam rose to her feet, wagging her tail, her big bulk following Joey around.

"Sure, get your coat and you can come with me."

So, Katie decided, she really didn't have much say in the matter. The weather and Reno's practically refusing to take her decided all for her. And she was rather glad. There was much more warmth in this family house than there would be alone in a motel room.

Reno opened the door to leave and Maggie called after him. "Wait right there, Reno. You can walk me home."

Katie glanced at the older woman in surprise. "You don't live here, Maggie?"

"Oh, no, honey. I live up yonder in that cottage." Maggie pointed out the window to a small house several hundred yards on up the dirt drive.

"Forget it, Maggie. You're staying here, too," Reno commanded. "I'm not risking you, or me, getting a broken leg trying to get you home." Maggie opened her mouth to reply, but Reno raised his hand. "Listen—for once."

"Harrumph," was all Maggie said, then turned to clearing the table.

Reno and Joey, with Sam tagging along behind, went out; a cold blast of air blew in when they opened the door. Maggie left Katie and Summer to finish cleaning the kitchen while she rested on the couch.

"Don't pay Maggie's bossiness any mind," Summer said. "It's just her way."

"I could tell. It's part of her charm, I would say," Katie said.

Summer smiled at that.

Katie wiped the table, then stepped to the window and peered outside. Back from the house stood a large barn, its double doors open wide. A spotlight above lit a wide circle on the outside and bright lights shone yellow from the inside. In the growing dimness, Katie could just make out corral fences extending to the east. A giant elm near the back of the house, its trunk and branches now shadowy black, blocked any further view in that direction.

"We raise horses," Summer said, stepping beside Katie. "Breed, raise, some training."

They both watched Joey sliding on the icy ground in the glow from the barn, turning his face to catch the falling snowflakes.

"Joey can't remember ever seeing snow," Summer said. "He's only four, well almost five—next month."

"And how old are you, Summer?"

"Eleven. How old are you, Katie?"

Katie started at the bold question, then smiled. Turnabout was fair play. "Twenty-eight," she answered.

Summer nodded, then wiped a knife and placed it in a drawer, seemingly deep in thought.

Katie knew her family would be worried, so after finishing up in the kitchen, she placed a collect call to the Garrett farm.

"Katie!" Uncle Will answered and called to Claire in the background, "Claire, it's Katie."

"Now, I'm all right, Uncle Will," Katie hurried to assure him. "But I can't make it home tonight."

"Where are you, Katie girl?"

"Still in Oklahoma. The van broke down on the road. A Mr. Martin stopped to help me and I'm staying with his family for the night. The storm is upon us."

Uncle Will didn't say anything, and Katie heard him hissing explanations to Aunt Claire and her aunt's voice demanding to be allowed to talk. Katie smiled, picturing the two.

"Katie?" Claire's voice came on the line. "Are you okay? Do you have a comfortable place for the night?"

"Yes, Aunt Claire, very comfortable. The Martins have made me feel very much at home."

"That's so nice of them. I've been worried. Did you break down about noon?"

"Sometime around then. Why?"

"I had a feeling. I've been worried ever since," Claire said.

"If you could feel the van breaking down, why didn't you feel my being rescued?" Katie asked with logic.

"I don't know...too worried, I guess. Clogged everything up," Aunt Claire passed it off vaguely. "Now, dear, when do you think you can get the van fixed and get home?"

"Tomorrow, I hope. It may depend on what's wrong with the van. And the storm, of course." The line crackled loudly.

"Katie, I'm having trouble hearing you. What did you say?"

"A day or two, Aunt Claire," Katie said louder. "Please call Celia and Ray and let them know."

"I will, dear. Don't worry. If you end up staying longer, please call again. I'll rest easier when you're home," Aunt Claire said, and Katie heard Will in the background.

"Quit fussing over the girl, Claire," he said, then took the phone. "Katie, we'll see you when you get home. Thanks for calling."

Katie hung up as Summer came into the kitchen. "Was your family very worried?" Summer asked.

"Yes. That's what families are for, isn't it?"

Summer smiled. "Yeah, I guess so."

"It's good to know there's someone at home who cares enough to worry," Katie said thoughtfully.

The young girl looked at her closely, and Katie noticed she'd spoken her thoughts aloud, betraying a moment of sadness. Ache at the loss of her father stabbed at unexpected times.

Throwing off the feeling, Katie said, "I need to get some things from the van for the night. Want to help?"

"You bet!"

The porch light lit their way a few feet out and they reached the van by holding on to each other and sliding. It was downhill. Getting back to the house with the things was another matter, however. Katie and Summer slipped and fell repeatedly, laughing and giggling. Katie felt like a child again, and with a special friend, in a special winterland world, with the snow falling soft and silent.

Reno appeared on the front porch. "What the hell..."

"Daddy! We're in need of rescuing." Summer giggled.

Reno, in sturdy hiking boots, stepped down carefully. Grabbing Summer under the arms, he lifted her off the ground with one arm and Katie's small suitcase with the other, making his way back to the porch. Katie rose to her feet, trying to follow, but Reno growled, "Stay there!"

Depositing Summer and the case on the porch, Reno returned for Katie. Putting his arm around her as he had Summer, he gripped her just under her breasts. Even through her thick jacket and sweater, Katie's skin tingled. Again she caught the scent of him, and involuntarily her senses stirred. Every fiber of her being was vitally aware of this rugged man who now unceremoniously hauled her toward the porch and solid ground.

"My banjo," Katie called. She still had hold of her cosmetic case, but had left her instrument case behind on the ice. She pulled around, almost upsetting them both.

"I'll get it," Reno said shortly. He walked with her toward the house, hardly allowing her feet to touch the ground. Then he went back for the banjo. Standing again on the porch, he thrust the case at her and said, "I suppose you couldn't go one night without that thing. And what were you two doing out there? You could have broken your necks trying to haul that stuff up."

Katie had barely known the man several hours and here he was barking at her like he'd known her for years. Her anger rose, and she surveyed her mind for a hot retort. Then she noticed again Reno's fatigue, his reddened eyes and the stubble of beard even darker than before. Reconsidering her words, she lost the opportunity to say anything as Reno turned and strode into the house.

Summer touched Katie's arm. "Please forgive Daddy, Miss Katie. He's very tired . . . you know how men are," the young girl said with a worldly air. "He's not usually so rude."

Katie looked at the young girl who stared up at her anxiously. Then she smiled, pushing the anger away. It would do no good to upset the child.

"It's okay, Summer. Come on, let's go in out of the cold."

Chapter Three

Clunking up the stairs with the cases, Summer led the way to her room, explaining to Katie the plan of the house as they went.

"Daddy's bedroom is that one in the back hall next to the bathroom. The whole house is sort of built around the wood stove. The hot air rises from the stove up the openness of these stairs. That's why the stove is in the middle of the house instead of on an outside wall like most conventional fireplaces. Daddy designed and built our house himself." Obvious pride reflected from the child's voice.

Summer treated Katie to a tour of the upstairs, which contained the children's bedrooms, a loft play area and a large bathroom, complete with plastic boats, fragrant bath powder and strewn towels. Summer's room was extra neat; not like the bedroom Katie remembered having as a child of eleven.

"May I see your banjo, Katie?" Summer asked.

"Sure." Katie smiled, laid the instrument case on the bed, and flipped up the two catches.

Joey, with Sam close on his heels, entered the room and plopped himself on the bed. "Is that what Dad was yelling about?" he said.

Summer ran her fingers over the wood and down the strings on the neck of the instrument. "Gee, it looks old." Then she blushed. "I mean it's beautiful, but like an antique."

"It sure is scratched," Joey offered.

Katie grinned at the two. "It is old. It was my father's . . . from when he was about twenty."

"Can you really play it?" Joey asked.

"Of course she can play it, dope," Summer said. "Why do you think she carries it around?"

"Yes, I can play. My father began teaching me when I wasn't much older than you, Joey." Katie removed the instrument from its case and lightly picked out half a tune, then covered the strings with her palm. "But not tonight. We don't need to be making a bunch of racket. Your father is tired and so am I."

"Come on, Joey. Move it," Summer ordered, shooing her brother from the bed.

"Okay. Come on, Sam," Joey complied good-naturedly. "Let's go play cars."

Summer, playing a good hostess, folded down the bedcovers and fluffed the pillow before leaving. Katie grinned as the young girl walked demurely from the room and hollered after Joey, taking two stairs at a time. Summer was at that in-between age. Part of the time she mothered Joey and her own father and at other times she was pure child again.

Katie luxuriated in the warmth of a relaxing bath, then decided her thin flannel gown and matching robe were sufficiently high-necked and proper enough to wear downstairs. Standing before Summer's dresser mirror, she was brushing her hair when Reno's reflection appeared, his dark gaze appraising her. Slowly Katie turned, her cheeks reddening under such close scrutiny.

Reno's hair was damp, perhaps from a shower, and his bare feet accounted for Katie's not hearing him approach. Dressed in faded jeans and a plaid flannel shirt, he leaned one arm against the doorway.

"The door was open..." he began. "I just came up to make sure you have everything you need."

"Yes...yes, Summer has seen to that, thank you." Katie wondered at the depth of those brown eyes and the way they made her feel.

"I'll say good night, then. Maggie told me to tell you they were all having a snack downstairs." Reno turned to go.

"Reno...I'd like to thank you for all you've done for me."

He shrugged. "No big deal...Good night."

Tapping the hairbrush against her palm, Katie watched him leave, contemplating the attraction she felt in his presence. And there was attraction there, deep attraction, no doubt about that. Why? Reno was handsome enough, but it was more than looks Katie felt drawn to. Oh, who could analyze attraction, Katie thought with a sigh, and she tossed the brush to the bed. Once again she remembered the dream and wondered. Did he feel the attraction between them, or was it simply a mirage on her part?

Katie found Maggie, Summer and Joey congregated in the kitchen.

"Thought everyone could use a snack with our dinner being so early before," Maggie said. She had prepared what she considered a snack: scrambled eggs, bacon, home-canned peaches and more biscuits.

The four of them ate heartily, as if they had not eaten all day. The wind buffeted the house and the window glass radiated the outside cold, but inside, the kitchen was cozy and warm with companionship. Talk was easy, laughter abundant. Again Katie was struck by the familiar ease she felt with the children and even Maggie. A few short hours ago, she'd been determined to get home, but was stopped in her tracks by a force beyond her control. And somehow, for some unfathomable reason, she felt almost as if she were home.

Katie slept one of the most peaceful nights she'd had in months and woke refreshed and eager for the new day. As usual, strange bed or no, she had to push Sam off her legs.

Ruffling the dog's fur, she scolded, "Sam, this is Summer's bed. You shouldn't be here."

Shivering in the cool room, she rubbed moisture from the glass and peered out the window. Everything outside was a muted gray and white and the wind still buffeted the house and rattled tree limbs.

It didn't appear she would be going anywhere today either. Strange, the thought didn't upset her. It was nice to be stuck here, as it were, sheltered from the world for a while.

Hearing voices and laughter, Katie guessed everyone else was already up and perhaps waiting breakfast. Dressing quickly in gray wool flannel trousers and a soft blue sweater, Katie brushed her auburn hair and hurried downstairs, Sam at her heels.

Stepping from the last stair and pivoting around the corner, she ran right into a solid male chest. A warm, bare chest, faintly tanned and covered with sparse dark hairs which formed a ridge to his navel. Instinctively she reached out to steady herself, her eyes fixed on Reno's broad frame, her heart beating rapidly. His waiting arms caught her. The sensation which leaped between them shook Katie, and she raised her eyes to his in wonder.

Heat flickered in his brown gaze. His grip tightened upon her arms and his eyes moved to her lips. Katie swayed toward him, drawn by a magnet of warmth. In anticipation her breath caught in the back of her throat as she saw his head move almost imperceptibly down to meet hers.

Joey's voice broke the spell. "Daddy, when can I go out? Can I go out with you? Katie, can Sam go out with me?"

Immediately Reno let Katie go and turned to look at his son. "Have some breakfast first, son, then we'll see. And I imagine Sam is going out right now. Am I right, Miss Katie?" Reno, smiling at her, still had hold of her hand.

"Yes. Yes she is," Katie said, flustered. "Dogs always have to go out first thing in the morning, Joey. But maybe Sam will be willing to go out with you later as well."

"Go let Sam out the back door for Miss Katie, Joey," Reno said.

"Okay." Joey beamed at being given the honor. "Come on, Sam."

"Katie," Reno said, buttoning his shirt, "the storm is still with us. Radio reports are urging no travel unless absolutely necessary. The roads are thick with ice, though crews are sanding now. It looks like you're stuck with us another day. I'm awfully sorry."

"Oh, Reno, your family has made me feel very welcome. I hate imposing so much."

"It's no imposition. I think my family is finding it all a bit like a party. Naturally, Summer is thrilled to be out of school." Reno inclined his head toward the window. "There's no need to phone Ted Carter's garage yet. He couldn't get out here anyway. By tonight this thing should be wearing itself out and break up. We'll try to get you out of here tomorrow." He took Katie's elbow. "Now, come on to breakfast; I smell sausage. As you can see, our family does love to eat."

Katie found she couldn't feel sorry about the storm at all. She tried to act serious, but happiness kept bubbling out. She wasn't worried one bit about the van; she was concentrating on now, this unique space in time.

Glancing at Reno, Katie found his eyes upon her, thoughtful but, other than that, unreadable. There was nothing in his manner or tone to indicate he felt any more toward her than a gracious host to a guest.

After breakfast, Katie again placed a long-distance call to Porterville, first to the magazine offices and, getting no response, then to the Garrett farm. Aunt Claire answered.

"The storm has hit here too, dear," the older woman explained. "The wind took out half that old apple tree by the garage last night."

"That must be why I couldn't get an answer at the magazine. I tried there first."

"Oh, yes. The roads are terrible. Everyone is urged to stay home," Claire said. "Is there something you need me to tell Celia or Ray?"

"Just tell them to expect me when they see me. Two, maybe three days. I just can't be sure, Aunt Claire, but I'll get home as soon as I can."

When Katie hung up, Reno stood at her elbow, handing her a cup of coffee.

"Folks worried about you?" he asked.

"No, not any more," Katie took a drink of the coffee. "My aunt said the storm has hit hard there, too."

"Umm . . . I caught the early-morning news report on television. They mentioned Arkansas. Whereabouts is your hometown . . . Porterville?"

"Yes. It's a small town in the hills, middle-northern part of the state."

"Do you come from a big family?"

"Not exactly." Katie shook her head. "I'm an only child, but I have three sets of aunts and uncles, numerous great-aunts and uncles and hordes of cousins. The town of Porterville is all interrelated somehow. Uncle Will, my father's brother, and his wife, Claire, have always considered me part of their brood. Aunt Claire tends to hover like a mother hen.''

"Does that bother you?" Reno sipped his coffee and watched her over the top of the cup.

"Sometimes ... But it's because she loves me and cares. How can I fault that? I've learned to put up with it, to humor her.''

"Sounds like you have a nice family,'' Reno said.

"Yes, they are,'' Katie said. "And how about you? Did you come from a big family?''

Reno shook his head. "No. Just me and the kids—and Maggie.''

Joey came in, pulling on Reno's pant leg and holding up a miniature pickup for his father's inspection. "Daddy, can you fix the wheel? I was driving on Sam and it just came off.''

"Driving on Sam?'' Reno chuckled.

Katie grinned. "With our big family, Sam's used to being overrun, so to speak, by children.''

After the minor car repair, Reno braved the weather to care for the stock, but the rest of the day they all spent cuddled in the warmth of the house. Katie played several games of rummy and Uno with Summer, then read books to Joey. Maggie sat by the fire, knitting on a sweater for Summer, sometimes dozing. Reno, bent over papers, worked at his desk.

Just after noon the wind and snow stopped, but the air remained bitter cold. Relenting to Joey's pleas, Reno took the boy outside, but only for fifteen minutes. "Too cold,'' Joey came in chattering. And after her morning session of slipping and sliding, Sam, pampered dog that she was, refused to budge from her space by the wood stove.

Maggie occasionally grumbled about wanting to go home, complaining of sleeping on the couch the night before, but

Reno remained adamant in his refusal to take her up the slippery hill to the cottage.

"I had enough trouble caring for the horses this morning. And if you don't like the couch, you should have taken me up on the offer of my bed last night. Since you like a firm mattress, maybe you should try the floor," Reno said, a teasing twinkle in his eyes.

"You shouldn't talk to an old woman that way, Reno," Maggie said.

"It's your old part I'm thinking about."

Maggie gave out her characteristic "Harrumph!" and they all stifled a giggle.

"Reno, Summer tells me you designed and built the house," Katie said. "If you wouldn't mind showing me around, I might be able to get an article out of this. Might as well work while I'm here."

"I didn't actually design it. I got most of the ideas from different magazines and put them together. Built, yes, with the help of two friends." The subject was evidently a favorite of Reno's, because with little more prompting he led Katie around, explaining the floor plan and building methods he had used.

On the stairs he explained the plan for total heating with the wood stove.

"The hot air rises to those vents," he said, pointing to the ceiling in the middle of the house above the staircase, "and a fan circulates it down again to the rooms of the lower floor, keeping a more even heat throughout. For cooling, we left the shade of the elms, and again we can use the fan to circulate the air. We do have a central air conditioner, too," Reno added with a grin.

Katie wanted pictures, but Reno refused to make the trek to the van for her camera. And he refused to let her go, either.

"I have to have pictures to go with the article," Katie argued. "Or it isn't any good at all."

"You can get them later, when things begin to thaw out," he said. "Next time, maybe you'll remember a writer has more need of a camera than a banjo."

Katie glared at him, but refused to say more.

Late in the afternoon, almost dusk, Maggie announced, "Reno, the wind is coming from the south. Take me home."

They all paused, listening. The change could be felt, imperceptible, but there all the same; the storm had broken, warming begun.

"Maggie, the ice is still there," Reno said.

"Reno, I want to go home," Maggie stated stubbornly.

Reno sighed, but rose to pull on his boots.

Joey went along, chattering, whooping and hollering, as he slid on the ice and snow. Katie had come to realize Joey was a chatterer, the house silent without him. Katie and Summer watched the trio's progress up the hill, Reno guiding Maggie with a strong arm. They made it safely, Reno and Joey heading for the barn, instead of the house, on the way back.

"Katie, now would you play some on the banjo?" Summer asked eagerly.

"Sure," Katie said, rising to go for the instrument. But Summer jumped up.

"I'll get it for you."

Summer brought the instrument case from upstairs and Katie removed the banjo, tuned the strings a moment, then launched into a slow love ballad. Summer watched with bright eyes, as if it were magic. Katie smiled. She had watched her father in much the same manner. From the ballad she played into an old and popular hymn. Summer sang softly.

Katie was picking a modern tune of toe-tapping quality when Joey came running into the room. Still dressed in his boots and coat, he began to clap to the beat and stomp his feet. Summer threw back her braids and joined in, tapping her hands on her knees.

When Katie ended the fast-paced tune with an exaggerated flourish, the children begged for more.

"Please, Katie," Joey urged, his brown eyes so like Reno's, wide with childish appeal.

"First you need to get out of those wet things," Katie admonished, tugging at his coat.

When Joey's coat was hung and his boots set to dry by the stove, Katie sat in one of the enormous chairs and played again. She was in the midst of a second rousing bluegrass melody when Reno entered. Catching sight of his frame in the hall archway, she stopped, fingers in midarc.

"What's all this?" Reno said, a wide grin across his face.

"Oh, Daddy...you can plainly see what it is," Summer said logically. "Katie is playing her banjo."

Katie cast an uncertain look toward Reno, suddenly shy before him.

"Well, come on, Miss Katie," Reno urged.

Katie smiled, lowering her eyes, then began a slow, lovely ballad; upon ending the tune, she started right into another, faster melody. Faster and faster she picked, and by the end she was out of breath. Rising to the resounding applause of Reno and the children, Katie made an exaggerated bow.

"More, more," Joey shouted gleefully.

"You don't think that's enough?" Katie teased.

Joey shook his head, grinning widely. Giving herself a moment to catch her breath, Katie then began a real high-stepping old bluegrass tune, a childhood favorite. Summer and Joey joined hands and danced around the living room. Watching them, Katie was reminded of the musical parties in her own home long ago, parties still a tradition in the Garrett clan today.

Soft light from the table lamp and flickering fire warmed the timber beams and polished wood floor. Katie closed her eyes, allowing herself to feel the music as it flowed from her fingers against the banjo strings. It flowed up and out, filling every corner of the room.

When she finished, Katie found Reno's eyes, warm and bright, upon her. He stared at her a long moment, then said, "Okay, kids. You've had a chance. Clear the way for me and Miss Katie."

With a few quick movements, he moved the large braided oval rug from the middle of the floor. Next, he put on a record of pop-country sound and turned from the stereo, asking in mock formality, "Katie, will you do me the honor?"

Placing her hand in his, Katie played along. "Thank you, sir."

Reno smiled down at her and Katie felt her heart tug. His eyes, sparkling from the effects of having a good time, flowed over the length of her body, lingering momentarily at her breasts before returning to meet her gaze. Katie blushed, but met his eyes with an equally bold look.

At that, Reno threw back his head in a full laugh and whirled Katie around the room, two-stepping to the rapid beat of the music. After a moment Summer and Joey joined in and the four of them flowed to the upbeat country sound.

The song ended, but Reno continued to hold Katie, and when the next tune, a slow love ballad, began, he pulled her close. His cheek rubbed the side of her hair and his hand felt hot upon the small of her back. Closing her eyes, Katie easily followed his steps, moving her body with his. Tiny sparks of heat flickered through her body as her breasts rubbed his chest, her thighs brushed his.

The music ended, and Reno stepped away. Katie, conscious of the children watching with rounded eyes, hoped her face didn't betray any of her feelings.

After a pause, another toe-tapping tune began and Reno reached for Summer. Katie had to run after Joey, but, giggling, she caught and lifted him into her arms and whirled his small frame around the room.

"Enough. I've had enough," Reno breathed, flopping into one of the big chairs when the record ended.

"So have I," Katie said. "Oh, Joey, you're much heavier than you look."

"Thirty-five pounds," Joey announced proudly.

"I don't doubt it," Katie said.

"I'll make us a snack," Summer said. "Is anyone real hungry, or will popcorn and drinks do?"

"Popcorn sounds fine, Summer. Maggie has fed me these two days until I'm about to burst," Katie said, rising to help. Summer waved her away. Katie, still getting her breath, sat back gratefully.

"Well, I want a peanut butter and jelly," Joey said, following his sister into the kitchen.

"You do know how to pick a banjo, Miss Katie," Reno said. "And I'm glad you brought it in last night. It's much more fun than a camera."

Katie inclined her head. "Why, thank you, Mr. Martin."

"You must have learned the art at an early age to be able to play so well," Reno said, kneeling before the stove to feed the fire more wood.

"Yes. It's sort of a tradition in our family. My father used to start up playing the guitar or banjo, people would drop in, and soon we'd have a party." Katie ran her finger lovingly over the strings.

"Your father died in November, you said. Was it sudden?"

"No. He had leukemia," Katie said. "We found out about six months before he died. He refused to go through with any kind of treatment and was quite healthy until the last month. He was in his sixties and had lived a good many years without Mom. I think he wanted to go with her.''

"Do you live with your aunt and uncle now?''

"Oh, no.'' Katie laughed. "Aunt Claire would like me to. She thinks I shouldn't be gallivanting, to use her expression, all over the countryside as it is. I love her, but couldn't live with her. I have a small apartment in town.''

Minutes later, Summer entered with a tray bearing a huge bowl of popcorn and four soft drinks. Quickly Katie rose to help the young girl with the tray, which seemed nearly bigger than she was. Joey perched on the low stool beside Katie's chair and munched on his peanut butter and jelly sandwich.

"Can Katie play some more, Dad?'' Joey said, giving his father a wide-eyed look, seeking to charm a yes answer. Reno only smiled at his son's efforts.

"Not tonight, bud. When we finish this popcorn, it's time for bed. The weather will clear tomorrow. Lots of chores for you and me, and we have to see about getting Miss Katie's van fixed.''

When the last kernel of corn was eaten and thirst sufficiently quenched, Reno ushered his children off to bed. Katie was touched when both children favored her with a goodnight kiss. Joey even stopped to kiss Sam, who gave an answering thump of her tail against the floor.

While Reno was upstairs with the children, Katie gathered the empty glasses and bowl and carried them into the kitchen.

"Come on, Sam,'' she called, waiting for the big dog to lumber to the back door. Stepping to the sink, she washed the few dirty dishes and was just finishing up with the popcorn pan when Reno entered.

"You don't have to do that. You're our guest, not a maid.'' He stood close, leaning against the counter.

"Oh, I don't mind. And I don't feel much like a guest after these last days. Your family has made me feel very welcome," Katie answered. Vitally aware of his nearness, she lowered her lids, not daring to meet his gaze.

"Yes," Reno said quietly. "You do fit in as more a part of things than a guest."

Their eyes met then, steadily, each questioning the other. Katie knew he was going to kiss her, and she wanted him to, ached for him to. Her eyelashes shielded her eyes as she focused on the strong line of his jaw and his parted lips beneath his thick mustache seconds before they were pressed to hers.

His lips were warm and gentle, touching her fleetingly, testing, then pulling back. His rough hand stroked across her cheek and moved to the side of her neck. Katie neither opened her eyes nor moved, willing her body not to follow its natural inclination to press toward him. She was afraid to, afraid of the sensations beginning to boil deep within her.

Reno let out a sharp breath from deep in his throat. Covering her lips again with his own, he massaged sensuously, demanding her response. Seemingly of their own accord, Katie's lips parted, welcoming Reno, giving to him. Her composure began to slip as desire welled up within. Her head whirled and she raised her hands to press against the hard expanse of Reno's chest. His taut muscles trembled slightly beneath his shirt. She could feel his desire, though he remained in tight command, standing next to Katie but not pulling her to him.

Deep in the recesses of her mind, her brain registered Sam's bark, demanding to be let in. And common sense urged her to break away, but she couldn't. Reno's lips were sweet and warm. She wanted more, so much more.

Slowly Reno lifted his head, letting out a long breath. "Sam's getting impatient." A bark sounded again.

"Yes," Katie murmured, self-consciously keeping her eyes averted from his, trying to bring her heartbeat and breath back under control. She opened the door and Sam entered, shaking snow from her black fur. "Oh, Sam. Why in the world would you roll in it?"

Reno nonchalantly handed her a towel, and Katie briefly brushed the dog dry. Handing the towel back to Reno, she met his gaze, searching his face. There was no more invitation there. Katie didn't know what she would have done if there had been.

"I think Sam and I will say good night now," Katie said.

Reno inclined his head slightly. "Good night."

Katie left Reno propped against the kitchen counter. For a long time she lay awake thinking of the attraction she felt for him, her body throbbing. It could lead nowhere, she cautioned herself, except into a one-night stand. After all, the van would be repaired and she would be heading home to Arkansas. Even if that took several more days, two people didn't develop a meaningful relationship in such a short period. And Katie was not the quickie, one-night-stand type. Still, it was tempting. There was something very appealing about Reno Martin.

Chapter Four

Reno watched Katie leave, his eyes moving over her body from her compact shoulders to the roundness of her rump. Then he bent and pulled a beer from the refrigerator, returning to slouch in one of the great chairs by the fire.

He was irritated with himself for kissing her. Didn't he have more sense than to start something he couldn't finish? It was her lips. He had looked down and seen those lips, so red, and not from lipstick or chapping.

It was those lips he had first noticed when he'd found her in the van. Then her eyes . . . large, round doe eyes. She wasn't really beautiful, but a woman who caught and held a man's attention. Her name fit . . . Katie . . . gentle, but with a fiery side.

It was a good thing he'd come along when he did on Sunday. She'd been out in the cold long enough and was sort of strung out. She hadn't liked it though; his ordering her around, doing things for her. Reno chuckled. No, Miss Katie was a pretty self-sufficient woman.

Thinking of the expanse of double bed waiting for him, Reno pictured Katie upstairs and sighed. Damn, that bed was lonely with just himself in it. Hell, it had been lonely when Lynn was alive.

Thoughts of Lynn rarely flitted through Reno's mind anymore. After four years, he'd finally worked through most of the anger, disappointment and guilt, which, for a time, had threatened to engulf him. There were the kids to consider. He couldn't be wasting time on negative emotions and wasn't a man to worry over past regrets. He had changed his life to be just what he wanted, buying this land and building a home.

Reno didn't often think of himself as lonely. He kept too busy. It was only at night sometimes, when he sought sleep and the bed felt twice as big. Some nights he would just throw himself down on the couch. At least it didn't feel so empty.

Once in a while Joey would patter downstairs and wake him with whispers of being afraid. At those times, Reno gathered up his young son and together they settled down in the double bed. It didn't seem so empty then . . .

Reno got up for another beer and, with a second thought, pulled two from the refrigerator. He had been drinking way too much lately, but the alcohol helped him to sleep when these moods came upon him.

He was thirty-four and calmed down considerably from what he had been eight or ten years ago. He and Lynn used to party all weekend then, blowing money as fast as he made it working the oil-field crews.

Taking another drink of beer, Reno thought again of his overindulgence. Drinking and Diane. Another thing he had been overdoing lately: seeing too much of Diane Holt. She was beginning to get ideas. And, hell, he wasn't being fair to the woman. She needed to be out looking for a man to marry. It occurred to Reno that that was exactly what Diane was doing. He needed to break it off. His intentions were not in the marrying vein.

Besides, Maggie was nagging at him. And she was right. He wasn't setting a very good example, with Summer growing up so much now. Summer had a fairly good idea what went on those nights he didn't come home, dragging in the mornings after, resembling a runover dog.

Summer. She turned twelve this year. Not much more and she would be in her teens, as beautiful as her mother had been. Summer's resemblance to Lynn startled him at times. But it was only physical; inside, Summer was so different it was hard to believe she even came from Lynn, from himself for that matter.

Summer was never rowdy, not a demanding kid, but a person who always thought of others. And calm, so damn calm at times Reno felt himself the child and Summer the parent. Nevertheless, Reno and his daughter shared a strong bond.

Joey was a different story. He was easy for Reno to understand because the two were so much alike, outside and in. And like his father, Joey carried a charming wild streak, which Reno would have to try to train in the right direction.

Reno's pride in his children went deep. They and his ranch were the main reasons for most decisions he made, for life itself. Still, he occasionally felt a giant void in his life. But it wasn't a void to be filled by a woman, not permanently anyway. He wasn't cut from husband-type cloth. Marriage to Lynn had taught him that.

Looking across the firelight to the other great chair, Reno pictured Katie as she had looked only an hour ago. Funny how she seemed so familiar, not like someone he could count the hours since meeting. Almost in surprise, he realized how much he had enjoyed the carefree musical time of the evening.

It had tickled him, thrown him off somewhat, when Katie caught him surveying her so frankly and paid him back with a daring look of her own. She appeared a small woman, but holding her in his arms, Reno had felt the firm strength of her muscles. His blood grew warmer remembering the way her thick mass of hair caught the firelight—auburn hair, betraying the fiery side of her nature.

Okay, boy. Go slow here, Reno admonished himself silently. This was no fly-by-night woman. There was a permanence about Katie. And permanence in a woman was just what Reno avoided religiously.

Leaving the empty beer cans lying on the floor by the chair along with his boots, he stoked the wood stove for the night. He slipped from his clothes and carelessly tossed them across the end of the bed, accustomed to Summer's picking up after him. With the help of the beer, sleep came easy.

Katie came downstairs early in the morning. It was still dark. The fire glowing brightly behind the glass doors of the wood stove showed her way to the kitchen. There was a light on above the sink and a pot of coffee hot upon the burner of the coffeemaker. After letting Sam out, Katie poured herself a cup and turned off the light so she could see out the window.

The barn was well lit inside and out, indicating Reno's presence. Two horses pranced in the nearest corral. The deep darkness of night was fading as the sky lightened toward the east. A figure emerged from the barn, reached down to pet Sam and walked slowly toward the house. With a twinge of anticipation, Katie self-consciously stepped from the window to sit at the table.

Reno's steps scraped heavy on the porch just before he entered the side door. He stood still for a moment, then switched on the overhead light and looked at Katie in surprise.

"Well, good morning. Thought you were up when I saw Sam. Do you always sit in the dark?" He was bundled in a sheepskin jacket, gloves and cowboy hat, but he only removed the gloves to pour a large mug of coffee.

"I like the dark, its peace and quiet," Katie said. "You look pretty cold."

"Umm," Reno answered, sipping his coffee. "The ice is still here, but the melt has started. Everything feels heavy and wet." He drank deeply of the coffee. "We'll be able to get your van to town today—later this morning." He moved to the back hall and lifted Katie's coat from among the others on the coatrack. Holding it out, he said, "Here, put this on."

She regarded him questioningly. "Why?"

"Just come on." Reno shook the coat. "It's a beautiful morning to see the outdoors."

"Cold," Katie grumbled as she slipped her arms in the coat.

"Yes, that too." Reno chuckled as he tugged on his gloves, indicating Katie should do the same. They both stepped outside. Reno had cleared the steps, but from there on, the ground was ice and snow. "Be careful," he warned, taking a steadying grip on her upper arm.

The earth resembled a winter wonderland, the winter-night darkness lifting, the sky turning pale toward the east and promising to be crystal clear. Frozen whiteness of snow clung to the tree branches, fence rails, even the electric wires. There was no breeze, only a hushed stillness.

Katie stopped, drinking in the beauty. "Oh, my," she whispered. Reno grinned down at her, his eyes revealing the enjoyment he too felt at the sight. The horses Katie had seen earlier pranced into view in the nearby corral, their breath steaming in the crisp air.

Reno guided the way across the faintly melting ice toward the barn. Stalls lined either side of the long building, and now and again a horse poked his head through the opening, blowing and twitching its body. The dirt-packed floor was scattered with straw; the musky odor of warm animals mixed with hay filled the air. Reno had turned off all the lights except for one at the far end of the building. It was to this that he now led Katie, stopping at the last stall, its slat door open.

Katie heard a faint high-pitched crying as Reno reached for a battery-powered lantern and stepped into the stall. Following, Katie saw the object of attention. Curled in a pillow of straw in the corner was a mother calico cat and her newborn litter of kittens, all jet black. Delighted, Katie knelt close, not daring to touch them, for they appeared only minutes old.

"Martin Ranch has some new occupants. Thought you might like to see them."

"They're so tiny," Katie said. "I never can get over how small animals can be born. How many?" The little balls of black fur were squished together on top of one another, sleeping or nursing, kneading at their mother's soft stomach.

"I'm not sure," Reno answered wryly. "But enough...we always have more than enough."

Suddenly the mother cat arched her back, her teeth bared, hissing and spitting. Katie and Reno turned to see Sam backing from the doorway, wary of the cat's wrath. They both chuckled and stepped from the stall, Reno switching off the lantern and replacing it on the hook.

"Come on. I'll show you a bit of the ranch and we can watch the sunrise," he said, taking Katie's hand and leading through the back door of the barn.

Careful of the snow-and-ice-covered ground, they walked to a near corral and leaned against the top rail, brushing off snow and breaking ice to make a comfortable place for their arms. Several smaller corrals and one long one stretched up an incline toward the east. Sparse trees showed as black silhouettes against the horizon, now turning coral with the rising sun.

Bordering the house and corrals on the north was a thick wood, the tree's darkness in sharp contrast to the bright crystals of snow formed over every branch. The early-morning sun rays sparkled off the ice, highlighting the whiteness.

"How big is your ranch?" Katie asked.

"Sixty acres. A lot more that I need for my purposes," Reno answered. "Our place here sits about in the middle of those acres. I prefer not to have a bunch of neighbors crowding around me."

"Except for Maggie?" Katie said, raising an eyebrow.

"Except for Maggie. I bought this section from Maggie Latimer about three years ago. She and her husband lived and farmed this land for most of their lives, but he died and it was getting harder and harder for Maggie to even keep up the cottage. She sold me this section at a good price, keeping a small section for herself, with the provision I maintain her home for the rest of her life. Maggie and I understand each other and find the arrangement profitable all around."

Katie nodded, reading between the lines what she had observed in the last two days. Between Maggie and Reno's family was more than just money and land—a sharing love also. "Where are the horses?" she asked. The corrals were empty except for the two horses she had seen earlier.

"Those two," Reno replied, inclining his head, "and ten more in the barn, my own and several we board. We sold quite a few the past fall and hope to expand this year. We breed, raise and train—for pleasure riding, show, rodeo and work." He gave a half-grin. "The work horse has not been totally replaced by the pickup truck. And racing is up-and-coming in Oklahoma since the state passed a pari-mutuel racing bill. Horses are a growing industry in this country again. We're small, but we're going to grow, too."

"We?" Katie said.

"Though they're young, the ranch belongs to Summer and Joey, too. And I have a friend who wants the job without all the responsibility—Sonny Jackson. I couldn't do all this on my own. When things get hopping around here, we hire all the male help we can get."

"Male help?" Katie teased. "You mean females aren't allowed?"

"No female has ever applied. It's a thought, though. Maybe if I had some feminine help around, male help wouldn't be so hard to keep." Reno grinned. "You're sure full of questions, Miss Katie."

Katie blushed. "Habit from my job, I guess."

The two fell silent, watching the sun become a full red ball above the horizon. Katie thought of her father, his love of the early morning. An ache opened up within her as she felt the sudden sense of loss.

Sensing Reno's eyes upon her, Katie turned and gave him a half-smile, wondering at the look of concern reflecting from his gaze.

"Let's go in. You're cold," he said.

For the first time in several years, Katie found it natural to want to share her feelings. "No," she said with a small shake of her head. "It's just that I was thinking of my father. He loved the mornings, watching the sunrise." Katie's eyes brimmed with unshed tears.

Reno pulled her to him, and she rested her head against his chest. The tears slipped quietly down her cheeks, but she didn't sob.

"When he was dying, I couldn't seem to help him. Not just because he wouldn't let me, but because of something going on within myself. I don't know...changes, a rest-lessness. Dad could see it, even understand it, but said I would have to find the answers on my own. For the first time in our lives we were unable to help each other. I think it caused him great sorrow."

Reno held Katie, quietly stroking her hair for a long minute.

"I think you two did more than you know," he said. "You shared."

Katie looked into his brown eyes. "Yes," she said finally.

With the tips of his work-roughened fingers, Reno wiped the tears from her cheeks. "Come on. We've stood long enough in the cold."

As they walked around the barn and toward the house, Reno kept a supporting hand on her elbow. Katie felt the touch warmly even through her several layers of clothing.

Sausage sizzled on the stove, and Summer, dressed in a soft-pink sweater and faded jeans, was in the act of placing bisuits into the oven when Reno and Katie stepped in the back door.

"Umm, babe, that do smell good," Reno said, shrugging out of his coat and helping Katie with hers.

Summer looked up and smiled. "There's still no school today, Dad. It was on the radio. Hi, Katie." Summer poured two cups of coffee, handing one to Reno while Katie reached for hers. "Sonny called about ten minutes ago. He's going to be late. His truck slid into the ditch when he was pulling out of his drive."

"I didn't count on him getting here anyway. At least not until noon. It will probably melt enough off the roads by then," Reno said. "Where's your brother?"

"Upstairs getting dressed. He wants to get out in the snow."

At that moment Joey entered. "Daddy, Daddy, will you go out with me?" he asked eagerly.

Reno grimaced. "Now, Joey?"

"Yes, now, before it all melts away."

A smile lit Reno's rough face. "Okay."

The two left, and Katie began helping Summer with the breakfast.

"Why anyone would want to go out and get cold and wet is beyond me," Summer said with a shake of her braids.

Katie laughed. "I like snow. A bit of it. And I've had my bit for the morning."

To Katie, the breakfast Summer prepared was more of a feast: eggs, biscuits, cream gravy, several jams and oranges—all Reno's favorites.

"Do you always make a breakfast like this, Summer?"

"Most mornings, yes. Oh, it varies. Sometimes pancakes or hash browns," Summer said. "I have to get up earlier. School, you know. But Daddy likes it, and then we all have this time together."

"I do believe you spoil your father," Katie commented, watching Summer not only pour Reno a cup of coffee but sweeten it as well and place it beside his plate.

Summer grinned. "I know. Maggie says that, too. But Daddy likes having someone do for him. Just like Maggie's growling—it's his way." She stepped to the back door, calling for Reno and Joey.

Throughout the lively and talkative breakfast, Katie watched Reno. He did like to be waited on. By the end of the meal, Summer had gotten up three times—twice to refill his coffee and once to fetch him a bottle of honey. But Reno never failed to state his appreciation, commenting on how delicious the breakfast was more than once.

Again Katie was struck by the contrast between his rough male features and the way he could be so gentle. Reno was equally at ease with both of his children, though the young ones themselves were quite different. Joey was active and boisterous; Summer, quiet and demure.

Once, Katie allowed her gaze to rest upon him rather long and Reno, sensing, glanced toward her. Immediately a veil was pulled across his features, his expression turning cold and guarded. Baffled, Katie looked away and turned her attention to the children and thoughts of getting her van underway again.

The sun was high after breakfast and already beginning a melting job on the ice and snow. The steady drip of moisture from the roof and trees became more rapid. While Katie and Summer cleared the dishes, Reno telephoned his friend with the repair garage, making arrangements for the van to be towed to town later in the morning.

"Ted says he'll be out in two or three hours with a tow truck," Reno told Katie as he hung up. "The roads should have the ice pretty well melted and beat off by then. This type of hit-and-run storm often happens in Oklahoma at the end of winter. Sort of Mother Nature's last punch. By afternoon there will be little trace of it left."

"Thank you, Reno, all of you—for everything," Katie said. "I'm not sure what I would have done if you hadn't come along."

"No trouble," Reno said, brushing aside her thanks. "We've enjoyed having you here."

"We sure have," Joey put in. "Even Sam has liked staying here." The small boy munched on a jellied biscuit, breaking off a piece for Sam, who was sitting near his knee, awaiting dropped crumbs patiently.

"Joey, you're getting crumbs all over. We're done with breakfast now, you know," Summer scolded.

Joey jumped up and threw the rest of the biscuit to Sam. "Can we see those kittens now, Dad?" Without waiting for an answer, he scampered off to get his coat.

Reno turned to Katie. "Well, Miss Katie, I have a few things to attend to outside. I'll drive you into town when Ted comes for the van."

"There's no need, Reno. I'm sure I can hitch a ride in the tow truck." Katie's heart sunk unexpectedly at the thought of leaving.

"You haven't seen the Carter Garage tow truck. I have a few errands to run in town anyway, and Summer and Joey will want to go along. The storm brought them a break in routine. They will want to milk it for all it's worth."

Summer helped Katie gather her things, and then the two of them spent the rest of the time waiting on the tow truck going over the spring catalog, studying the latest styles. Katie was surprised to find that Summer, at such a young age, sewed many of her clothes. Katie herself couldn't sew beyond mending a torn hem or replacing a button, and she admitted as much to Summer.

"But I can crochet and knit," Katie said.

"Maybe I could show you about sewing and you could teach me crocheting and knitting," Summer said.

"It is a wonderful idea, but, I'm not going to be around very long," Katie said gently.

"Oh, yeah." Summer lowered her head, her eyes returning to the colorful catalog page again.

Wanting to ease the child's disappointment, Katie said, "Hey, let's exchange addresses so we can write each other. And anytime I get back this way, I'll stop in to visit."

Summer brightened somewhat and brought paper from her father's desk. As they were writing the addresses, there came the crunch of wheels on gravel and the sound of a powerful engine. Through the large front window, the two saw a tow truck pull into view. Quickly Katie gathered her purse, carefully depositing in it the Martin address, and walked outside with Summer.

Ted Carter was a thin, wiry man of few words. He simply nodded at Reno's introduction to Katie and in ten minutes had the van hooked to the tow truck, ready to go. "I'll call you," he said, getting into the cab.

As the van disappeared down the dirt road, Katie looked to Reno. "How does he know where to call me?"

"There's only one place to stay in town—Tyne Motel," Reno answered. "He seems kind of odd, but Ted Carter is a master mechanic. He'll do good by you, Katie." He strode to the porch for Katie's luggage and placed it in the pickup bed. Whistling for Sam, he slammed the tailgate behind her. "What do you say we take Miss Katie to lunch, kids?" The suggestion met with loud enthusiasm.

Katie sat next to Reno, the children to her right. As Reno had predicted, the icy covering over the land was melting fast. Except for deeper patches of hardened snow here and there, everything now just appeared wet, as if a drenching rain had recently fallen.

Katie wondered if it was her imagination, or if Summer had somehow maneuvered to have her and Reno sitting close. Considering the thought a silly notion, Katie dismissed it. But she couldn't as easily dismiss the sensations she experienced as her thigh brushed up against Reno's. And she was sure her awareness of the man sitting beside her was written all over her face.

She found it difficult to keep her mind on Joey's jabbering and questions. Her thoughts drifted back to their kiss of last night, feeling again the sweet pressure of Reno's lips on hers. Growing warm between her legs as well as on her face, Katie couldn't help glancing at Reno. His eyes met hers, then he returned his attention to the road, a slow smile creeping across his face.

Thoroughly embarrassed, Katie looked firmly ahead.

The town of Tyne was old and small; the kind with a main business district built around a town square, park benches and a statue in the middle. The Tyne Motel and Restaurant sat on the outskirts, looking uncommonly modern next to a host of older buildings.

Opening the wide plate-glass door to the restaurant, Reno said, "This place is known for its homemade soups, Miss Katie... and peanut-butter pie."

"Yeah, Daddy," Joey chimed. "I want a big piece of peanut-butter pie."

"Peanut-butter pie?" Katie raised a curious eyebrow. "I've never heard of such."

"Guess that's because no other restaurant makes it," Summer said. "Maggie had a recipe for it once, but now she can't find it."

Reno winked. "Give it a try.... Live dangerously."

While awaiting a hostess to seat them, they stepped aside for people paying the cashier. Suddenly Joey darted away, almost tripping an elderly gentleman, and went directly toward a silver-haired woman. He hugged her around the skirt. Summer followed her brother and was wrapped in a warm embrace by the woman. Reno said something under his breath, his jaw tightening, and placed a hand on the small of Katie's back, propelling her forward.

"Hello, Millicent," he said. Not Milly, but *Millicent*, very proper. And the name fit. The woman was elegance itself, dressed as she was in a gray wool suit and a blouse of pure blue silk. Her expressive hands were carefully manicured and bore several diamond rings.

"Hello, Reno." Even the woman's speech managed to sound elegant. "Such a treat to run into the children. It has been some time."

Katie saw Reno's jaw working as he and the other woman surveyed each other coldly.

"I have the day off from school today, Grandma," Summer said, looking uncertainly from Reno to Millicent.

"And Daddy brought us here for peanut-butter pie," Joey said.

"Is that so?" Millicent smiled from one child to the other.

Embarrassed by the tension and hostility she could sense but not understand, Katie was grateful for Reno's supportive hand still resting on the small of her back.

"Millicent, this is Katie Garrett," Reno said. Katie almost wished he had said Katherine.

"How do you do, Miss Garrett. It is Miss, isn't it?"

"Yes, it is. Hello." Katie extended her hand, and the older woman clasped it lightly for a few seconds. The jeweled hand was cold.

"Daddy found Katie out on the road Sunday and brought her home," Joey said. "She has a great big dog."

Millicent's cold eyes shot up to Reno. "Is that so?" she said for the second time in two minutes, her icy gaze flickering from Reno to Katie.

"Katie's van broke down in the storm not far from our house. Daddy helped her, and Maggie thought it best Daddy didn't try to drive Katie to town with the roads being so bad and all," Summer explained. Then, switching the subject, she asked, "Grandma, may we come and visit the weekend?"

"Why, of course, sweetheart." Millicent looked pointedly at Reno, then turned to Joey and said in a silken voice, "Would you like that too, Joey?" Joey smiled and nodded his head. Millicent raised an eyebrow to Reno.

"It's fine with me. Summer will call and let you know what time Saturday morning," he said.

The hostess approached, waiting patiently. Millicent surveyed Katie vaguely. "Nice meeting you, my dear. Reno, good day." Reno touched the brim of his hat and Millicent rather waltzed out.

Reno grinned sarcastically as they followed the hostess to their table. "And that, Miss Katie, was my mother-in-law."

"So I gathered," Katie replied dryly.

Lunch was pleasant, with Reno and Katie both relaxing in the warm glow of the children's natural joy. The peanut-butter pie was all that had been promised. Joey polished off a piece of his own and the last bit of Summer's, managing, as a small boy will, to spread some on his shirt.

Dabbing at the pie on Joey's elbow and chest, Katie caught smiling glances from the woman in the next booth. Suddenly she saw in their group what the woman did: a family. Again Katie was struck by how natural it felt being with Reno and his children. And she felt the warmth of their caring in including her. It was a feeling she dreaded leaving behind.

Chapter Five

When Katie registered at the motel, there was a message from Ted Carter. "Already?" She looked questioningly to Reno.

The clerk pushed the counter phone toward her. "Ted said it was important. You can use this phone if you like."

Katie dialed the garage number and Carter answered. "Yes, Miss Garrett. There's a problem about the van. You need a transmission all right, and I'm having a devil of a time finding one. I can't believe it. A common make and everything. Now, don't you worry. I will get one. It's just going to take time."

"How long do you think?" Katie asked.

"I'll try to get one this afternoon; get it installed tomorrow, first thing in the morning. Nothing to putting it in. We simply yank yours out, slip another in and fasten her down. Now, I did locate a brand-new transmission, but like I said, no sense spending the extra on a van of that year...no slight intended, ma'am. And a rebuilt one will do just the same."

"Yes, you're right, Mr. Carter. And if I had money to burn, I wouldn't be driving that old thing."

Seeing Katie's puzzled frown, Reno motioned for the phone. Katie waved him away, but Reno took the receiver from her hand. Katie glared at him and Reno ignored her, speaking to Carter. "What's the problem, Ted?"

"Now, like I was just telling your lady friend, I'm having trouble getting that transmission."

"You mean Wright's up in Muskogee didn't have one?" Reno asked.

"Nope. But there's a shop clear into Tulsa that's gotta have one. I'm going to call there directly. Don't worry, Reno. We'll get her fixed up."

"I'm not worried, Ted. And thanks."

Reno turned to Katie. Her eyes regarded him hotly. "Hasn't anyone ever told you it is rude to grab a phone from a person's hand?"

"Just trying to be of help," Reno said.

"Well, did you find out any more than I did?"

"Nope." Reno took Katie by the elbow, steering her from the lobby and the clerk's prying eyes. "I just wanted to make sure."

Katie bit her tongue against a snappy reply. Reno was simply being Reno: taking charge.

While Summer and Joey waited in the cab, Reno unloaded Katie's cases from the truck bed. Pulling the key from the doorknob, he handed it to her, saying, "Here. Keep this on you. You don't want to get locked out."

She stood at the door, with Sam at her knee, and waved to the children as Reno backed away. Barely, she could hear Joey say, "'Bye, Sam! 'Bye, Katie!"

Practically slamming the door shut, Katie stalked across the room and plopped on the bed. *Damn, damn and dou-*

ble damn! she thought. What did he think? That she was a complete imbecile who couldn't handle anything? Imagine grabbing the phone right out of her hands. Then that business with the key. And he hadn't said anything about seeing her again. She had certainly tried to give him time, making a lot out of looking around the room, checking to be sure she had everything. Surely he could have said "How about dinner" or something. Instead he had seemed in a hurry to get her unloaded into the motel room and be off.

"Oh, Katie, don't be a fool," she said aloud. Sam lifted her head from the carpet and Katie pulled a face at the dog. "I know, I'm talking to myself again," she said, adding silently, *It's sure going to be a long afternoon.*

Reno pulled from the motel parking area unnecessarily fast, sending gravel flying. Summer lifted a curious glance, but said nothing. Joey started with his round of questions.

"Daddy, why didn't Katie come out and stay with us again?"

"Just because, son."

"Well, what about Sam? It's awfully small, that motel room."

"Sam is fine. She's with Katie."

"Will Katie come and visit, Daddy?" Joey asked.

"Katie will be leaving tomorrow, Joey," Summer answered, and Reno felt her close inspection.

Suddenly Reno whipped into a driveway, backed out and turned around.

"What are you doing, Daddy? Did you forget something?" Joey asked, studying his father quizzically.

Reno, grinning, reached over and ruffled his son's hair. "Yes, I forgot something. I forgot to ask Miss Katie to dinner."

"Oh, good. She going to come to our house?"

"No!"

"Can—"

Summer reached over and cut Joey short by placing a hand over his mouth. "Will you shut up for two minutes?" The two giggled and wrestled playfully as Reno pulled to a stop in front of Katie's room and hopped out, placing his Western hat firmly upon his head.

Three long, quick strides and he was in front of the door. Hesitating only a fraction of a second, he knocked firmly. *What in hell do you think you're doing?* flashed through his brain, and then the door opened and Katie stood there, auburn hair slightly awry as usual.

Her expression was one of startled surprise, and Reno grinned down at her, his gaze lingering slightly on her full, red lips. He leaned an arm lazily against the doorframe.

"I forgot. Will you have dinner with me tonight?"

At first she just blinked, then a smile came, beginning in her green eyes and spreading to her lips. "Yes, I'd like that."

"Good," Reno said, already stepping away. "I'll pick you up at seven."

Once more Katie stood and waved to the children as they drove away. Summer, openly grinning, said, "I like Katie, Daddy."

Reno smiled back. "Oh, you do, huh?"

"Yes, and she sure is pretty."

"She sure has a neat dog," Joey said, and they all laughed.

"Summer!" Dressed only in jeans and socks, Reno stomped through the hall, yelling, "Summer! Where the hell are my black dress boots?"

Coming from the kitchen area, Summer answered placidly, "Right here, Dad. I just buffed them up a bit. And here's your shirt."

"You buffed— What in the world? I don't need that fancy shirt, Summer. It's only dinner." Reno realized he was snapping unnecessarily. He was irritated. He'd promised himself to stay away from the woman and now here he was taking her to dinner.

"It's not all that fancy, and you look very handsome in it."

"Oh?" Reno grinned down at his daughter and bent to kiss her cheek, cupping her chin in his rough hand. "Summer, thank you for the shirt . . . Okay, I'll wear it, but I repeat, it is only dinner," he said, studying her seriously. Summer nodded solemnly.

Reno knew Summer wanted him to marry again. He'd tried talking to her, explaining that he wasn't planning to marry again—ever. But how did you explain a thing like that to an eleven-year-old? Especially a girl, your own daughter, who you hoped would someday find a nice young man to marry.

Also, he couldn't fully explain it to Summer without sounding critical of Lynn and ruining what he hoped was a good remembrance the young girl had of her mother. If she had much remembrance at all. Summer rarely spoke of Lynn.

It was good for the kids, having Maggie living so close. Good for Maggie, too. Hell, even good for him, Reno thought as he left the three of them preparing tacos for dinner. With Maggie to look after Summer and Joey, Reno had considerable freedom and could rest easy that the children were well cared for in his absence. And the children gave to Maggie as well. Her life would have been pretty lonely without those little ones.

In a strange way Maggie and Reno helped each other through lonely times. Reno grinned to himself. Sometimes being around Maggie reinforced his vow to remain single. She was an outspoken woman; she said what she thought and made no apologies. Reno could talk to Maggie, a bit more than to most people. As a rule, he was a right close-mouthed man.

It was dusk, the streetlights lit, when Reno rapped on Katie's motel door. Immediately the door swung open and she stood before him, her face pale in the dimness, her green eyes wide, expectant.

Smiling down at her, Reno said, "Sorry I'm late. It's a bad habit of mine."

Katie smiled in return and stepped back for him to enter. "No matter. I'm just ready myself."

She stood before the mirror fumbling with a small gold loop earring. Reno's eyes narrowed as he watched her movements. Her hair flowed full and soft to her shoulders and he could see pink skin showing through the translucent whiteness of her blouse. Her trouser-type slacks were of deep navy velvet, fitting smoothly at the waist and across her hips.

"There, I got it. I have the devil of a time with these things." Katie sighed and turned quickly. Catching Reno's hard stare, she smoothed her pants, saying, "Is something wrong? Did I over- or underdress?"

"No, you look just fine," Reno said, his voice rather clipped. He didn't intend to encourage her with a lot of compliments. To soften his manner, he smiled and picked up a sweater coat lying on the bed. "This the coat you're wearing?"

"Yes, thank you." She hesitated a moment before stepping beside him.

As she slipped into the sweater he held out, Reno caught the musky fragrance of perfume and freshly shampooed hair. He was suddenly glad to be with her. It was a strange feeling, and along with it came a vague sense of warning.

"There aren't a whole lot of restaurant choices in Tyne," Reno said as he held the door for Katie and she slid into the high seat of the truck. "That's why I thought we could drive over to Muskogee. It's only abut thirty minutes or so. There's a place over there that serves a fantastic steak-and-shrimp dinner. Okay by you?"

Katie simply nodded. It didn't matter where they ate. She was pleased and excited simply to be having dinner with him.

"Did Ted call about the transmission?" Reno asked.

"No. I was wondering, but hated to bother him. I figured when he had something to tell me, he'd call."

Reno nodded. "He probably won't think there's any need to call you until the van is finished. He'll have it tomorrow, as promised."

They both lapsed into a slightly strained silence. Except for the dashboard lights and truck headlights against the road, it was dark. Katie sat, her hands lying calmly in her lap, feeling anything but calm on the inside. She wondered what Reno was thinking and what it was about the man that attracted her so. He wasn't a huge man, yet he seemed to fill the cab with his presence. A unique maleness emanated from him. Katie found her thoughts straying to a more intimate vein and was glad Reno could not clearly see her face in the dark.

The host of the restaurant greeted Reno by name and led the way to a table far in the back of a series of dimly lit rooms, an atmosphere of intimate privacy. Reno ordered a bottle of wine, telling the waiter to hold dinner for the moment.

"So, Miss Katie, you were quiet as a mouse on the drive over here." Reno smiled. "This morning you were full of questions. You have stayed at my house, even seen the details of its structure, shared meals at my home and played with my children. Yet I know hardly anything about you. Except I have noticed you eat a powerful lot for such a small woman."

Katie grinned. "Yes, I do. My father used to say 'body of a dachshund, appetite of a Great Dane.'"

The waiter returned with a bottle of wine in a bucket and two stemmed glasses. He expertly removed the cork, handing the bottle to Reno, who said, "Thank you. We'll order . . . say, in fifteen minutes."

Handing a glass of the sparkling amber liquid to Katie, Reno touched his glass lightly to hers. "Now, let's hear a little about Katie Garrett and how she grew into a distinguished roving writer."

"Well, distinguished is stretching things a mite." Slowly Katie sipped her wine, running a finger over the fine moisture collecting on the outside of the glass. "I got the job simply because I was in the right place at the right time: just out of high school and in need of employment. Unlike many of my contemporaries, I didn't care to move off to Memphis or Little Rock to find my fortune. Of course, it's not the 'in' thing—it wasn't then, either—but the fact is, I got along wonderfully with my parents. I enjoyed living with them and loved the old home town. I contacted the magazine when it was also just beginning in life, and I've been with them ever since."

"And how long is ever since?" Reno questioned.

"Ten years. Is that a roundabout way of figuring my age, Mr. Martin?" Katie teased. "I'm twenty-eight." It was difficult to tell in the dimness, but Katie could almost swear Reno blushed.

"I must admit I was curious. Watching you with Summer and Joey, well, you're like a child yourself." His lips twitched into a smile. "Then other times you're a very mature woman, all woman. It's confusing."

Katie shook back her hair and laughed, then regarded Reno more seriously, though a faint smile remained. "Perhaps I'm confusing because I find you confuse me, my feelings I mean." Her heart thumped as she stared into his dark eyes.

Reno raised his wineglass to his lips and spoke before taking a drink. "Yes, Miss Katie, I would definitely say sparks get to stirring the air whenever we are together."

The waiter appeared and Reno sent him away, saying they would wait a bit longer. With Reno's gentle, encouraging questions, Katie continued to talk of herself, her parents and her life in rural Arkansas. She was even able to speak of her father, touching briefly on the months of his illness. Little by little Katie felt the strain between them slipping away.

"I'm not exaggerating about my father, Reno," Katie was saying when the waiter returned for the third time. "Once he got a letter delivered to the house with no more address on it than 'Tall Tale Garrett, Porterville, Arkansas.' Even the post office knew who that had to be." They both chuckled, and Katie looked at the waiter sheepishly. She felt quite tipsy, having had several glasses of wine on an empty stomach. Her face felt hotly flushed, and she wondered absently if her hair was doing its usual own wild thing.

Reno gave the waiter their order and then escorted Katie to the restaurant's lavish salad bar. His guiding hand placed upon the small of her back began a caressing motion as they were obliged to wait in line behind several other couples. Katie was conscious of extreme warmth, not only from his hand but from his entire body positioned very close.

Reaching for a plate, she stepped away several inches, seeking to dampen immediately the flickering of desire Reno had ignited with his touch, also blaming the excess of wine she'd consumed for her feelings. Busying herself with the salad makings, she avoided his dark gaze.

Relaxing once more at their table and enjoying the expertly prepared food, Reno and Katie drifted again into easy conversation. Reno spoke now of his own childhood, which had not been all cake and cream, as he put, but then again, not so bad. Orphaned at the age of twelve, he and an older brother, Dave, had been placed in an orphanage.

"We were never adopted. People rarely want older boys, especially ones as rough and rowdy as we were. But the children's home wasn't such a bad place...no storybook horrors here. We were loved and fondled over along with about twenty other kids." Katie noticed Reno's eyes take on a faraway look as he spoke, remembering. "Mr. Weaver, the home's handyman, sort of took Dave and me under his wing, teaching us all kinds of things; repairing cars, tractors, mowers, carpentry, even how to work with horses at his own place a couple of miles down the road.

"Dave died when he was sixteen—pnuemonia complications. I stayed at the home until I was seventeen, mostly because of Mr. Weaver. You had to leave when you turned eighteen anyway. With Dave gone, there didn't seem much use hanging around."

Reno spoke honestly, factually, with no bitterness or regret, his manner not one to evoke pity.

"So you ended up here. The proud and distinguished owner of a rapidly growing horse ranch," Katie said.

Reno grinned at her mocking of his earlier comment. "So it goes—in a roundabout way. Did a hitch in the army, roustabout with an oil crew, now rancher. And unlike you, I will accept the term 'distinguished.'" Inclining his head in her direction, he said, "And I bow to you, Miss Katie. You must be one talented interviewer to unlock all my ancient history."

It was on the tip of Katie's tongue to ask one more question—about Reno's wife. But she resisted. If he had wanted to speak of her, he would have. And Katie didn't want to pry into feelings Reno might prefer hidden. Perhaps he found the subject too painful. Along with the compassion she felt for Reno, Katie uncomfortably recognized a sharp jealousy.

"Now it's my turn to play the interviewer," Reno said. "Tell me, from whom did you inherit your wild mass of red-brown hair? It's almost the same color as my best riding horse."

Tossing her head and raking a hand through her long mane, Katie assumed a mock superiority. "It is said in the Garret clan that I bear a remarkable resemblance to Great-Aunt Agnes. I take this as a compliment, as she was supposedly a great beauty. A family portrait of Agnes taken when she was about seventeen bears this out." Katie lowered her voice in a conspiratorial tone. "The only thing the family never cares to talk about is the fact that Aunt Agnes ran off to San Francisco and became the madame of a thriving bordello."

Reno nearly choked on his after-dinner coffee, then threw back his head and laughed. It was a good sound—free and full of life. With every touch of Reno's gaze, Katie felt herself being drawn closer. And she liked it. She didn't want to turn from the warm fire building within.

Reno had enjoyed several cups of coffee and Katie two small pots of tea when Reno slid back his chair. "Ready to go?" he asked.

Katie nodded, slipping into her sweater coat with his assistance. His hand brushed against her shoulder, and a tremor shot through her body. Did he notice? Inside she was quaking. She wasn't ready to go, wasn't ready to face him at the door of the motel room. Not wanting to part from him, Katie wasn't at all sure she could handle the consequences of asking him to stay.

In the restaurant lobby, Reno paid the check, then turned to Katie. His eyes were very hard and bright, though his face remained expressionless. Hot tension enveloped them. Wordlessly, Reno placed a possessive hand to the back of her waist and guided her to the truck, helping her in on the driver's side. Slipping across the seat, Katie settled only inches from him. Once out on the open road, Reno slipped his arm around her shoulders and drew her near.

"Reno...I—" Katie began uncertainly, but he cut her off. "Shush. For now." he said.

Katie relaxed against him, feeling her own neck pulse beating against his arm. What was she going to do when they reached the motel? Was there really any question? She wanted Reno Martin as she had never wanted a man before. She wanted to lie next to him, feel his lips against her own again.

But, damn it! She wasn't a one-night stand. If she gave herself to every desirable man she came across, pretty soon there would be nothing left of Katie. She wanted no part of that kind of life.

Her eyes strayed to the strong line of his jaw. Reno wasn't just any man. Somehow he touched her as no one ever had before. And she wanted him.

I don't know what I want, she thought. *How could I? I only met the man three days ago.*

Katie sensed turmoil going on inside of Reno as well, but made no move from the shelter of his shoulder. He lifted his hand and softly stroked her neck, just below her ear. Tingling sensations flowed downward and gathered deep within Katie's abdomen, and it suddenly became exceedingly hot in the truck cab.

It seemed all too soon that they pulled to a stop in front of her motel room.

The outdoor lighting lit the truck cab plainly. Katie's eyes fluttered downward, not daring to look at Reno. He shifted toward her and cupped her face with his left hand, bringing his warm lips to hers, massaging with gentle pressure. Katie's heart raced madly, her breath nonexistent as she clung to him.

When he raised his head, she buried her face in his neck, inhaling the powerful male scent of him. "Reno...I have to explain . . ." she began, struggling to straighten her whirling thoughts. What did she have to explain? What she felt, when she wasn't even sure what that was?

She drew back and faced him fully as he ran his hands in a stroking rhythm up and down her back. "Reno, I've just met you. I'm not accustomed to jumping into bed with a man I hardly know simply because it feels good. No matter how badly I want to."

Reno's fingers played softly across her forehead, pushing at wisps of hair. "I know. I knew from the first. But Katie, I can't offer more. I'm not a man who wants to get involved—ever."

Katie was grateful for Reno's honesty, respected him for it and would not have expected or wanted less of him. He caught and held her eyes with his, their dark questioning filling Katie with heat. She could no more pull away from his embrace than stop her heart from beating. She wanted Reno. That was all that mattered at this moment. Reading the answering desire in her green eyes, Reno pressed his lips once more to hers, demanding, as he parted their moist softness with his tongue.

Katie's palms pressed to his chest felt the ripple and strength of his muscles. She moved her hands across his shirt, longing to feel his skin.

Dragging his lips from her mouth and across her cheek, he kissed with feathery softness down to the hollow of her neck, his breath hot upon her skin. A tremor shook her shoulders and raced down her spine. Automatically, Katie arched her neck. Startling flames of heat shot through her body, pushing away all thought except her need and desire for him.

Reno reached for her hand and led her from the pickup to the motel doorway. Taking the key from her shaking fingers, he unlocked the door and pushed it wide, allowing Katie to enter first. She switched on the lamp, and her side

vision noticed Sam rising for a greeting. Turning, she saw
Reno still standing in the doorway. His thick brown hair fell
across his forehead and his hard eyes regarded her. He made
no move to enter, and Katie stared at him quizzically, silence growing heavy in the air. At last Reno broke the silence.

"I think we'd better stop things right where they are."

Katie took a step toward him. "But why, Reno?"

"Look, Katie, this sort of thing isn't for you. You're not
a woman to be used for one night of a man's pleasure."

"I'm an adult woman, Reno." Katie's anger flared, her
body aching in need of him. "I can decide what I want on
my own. And I didn't happen to think of it solely as *your
pleasure.*"

"I don't reckon I did, either. But I have a feeling what's
happening between us is about to lead me where I don't
want to go. You're a beautiful woman, Katie, and I thank
you much for a most enjoyable evening."

With that, Reno reached over and pulled the door softly
closed. Katie, chilled, stood rooted to the spot. She heard his
receding steps, the gun of the engine and the crunch of
gravel as the pickup pulled away.

In bewilderment she slumped to the bed. Sam padded
over, laying her head in her master's lap. Katie stroked
Sam's silken fur and noticed the dog's expression seemed to
mirror her own confusion. Undoubtedly, Sam had picked
up on the tension in the air and also didn't understand Katie's unusual lack of attention.

Padding to the door, Sam wagged her tail. Katie pulled
her coat tight against the cold, opened the door and walked
into the crisp night air with the dog. The dark clearness of
winter sky stretched above and stars sparkled like jewels.
Sam took off across the gravel parking lot and Katie followed more slowly behind. She breathed deeply, needing the
freshness to clear her mind and cool her body. The term

"unfulfilled passion" passed through her thoughts. She grinned wryly. The muscles of her arms, indeed her whole being, physically ached, touched by a terrible void.

It was then the inkling began. She must be falling in love with Reno. Surely it wasn't possible. She had only met the man...what, sixty-eight, seventy-two hours ago? Hours that could be counted. But, Katie conceded, emotions rarely existed on a timetable. She was falling in love with him. Her thoughts were concerned for him and his feelings first, before that of her own. Reno had wanted her as much as she had wanted him. Some hurt, something which touched him deeply, could be the only reason for his turning and walking away from her tonight. And perhaps because he cared for her, too.

The hot anger of rejection Katie had felt when Reno had closed the door on her now vanished with these thoughts. She knew Reno felt as empty right at this moment as she did herself. She longed even more to give of herself to him, to comfort him in some way.

What caused Reno to shy away so? Was she such a threat to his freedom? Did she remind him of his wife? Did the remembrance of the wife he had lost still hurt him? These and other thoughts converged in mass confusion upon her mind as Katie called Sam back to the room, changed clothes and fell exhausted into bed, too tired even to remove her makeup. Surprisingly, she fell into an immediate, though not peaceful, sleep. Dreams, filled with distorted colors and pictures, caused her to toss and whimper occasionally. Earlier than usual, Sam jumped onto the bed and lay close, wanting to be of some help to her distraught mistress, but not knowing how.

The shrill ring of the telephone jarred Katie from sleep. Rolling to her back, she opened her eyes to pitch dark, not certain if she had dreamed the telephone's ring or not. It rang a second time, the sound loud and piercing. Alarm shot through her as she struggled to find the receiver on the bedside table in the dark, her body stiff from tense sleep.

"Hello," she managed, her voice still heavy with sleep.

"Hello. Are you awake?"

Reno, his voice low and husky. It occured to Katie he was the only one she knew who would call. Aunt Claire and the Whitneys didn't even know where she was.

"I am now."

Did she detect a hint of a chuckle? He said, "Well, good. I've been awake for hours, thanks to you, Miss Katie." Reno paused, and Katie remained silent, sensing he had more to say. "Look, I have a cabin over on the Illinois River, just northeast of Tahlequah. It's beautiful, peaceful. I can bring a couple of horses and we can ride. Come there with me today."

It was Reno's turn to wait as Katie considered. She heard the faint sound of his breathing at the other end of the line, and her own heart beat wildly within.

"Okay," she said, simply, quietly.

Reno let out an audible sigh. "I'll be there to pick you up about seven-thirty."

"I'll be ready."

"Wear something warm," he cautioned, and the line clicked dead.

Chapter Six

Reno replaced the telephone receiver gently so as not to make unnecessary noise that would waken his small son sleeping beside him. He sat up slowly, throwing long bare legs silently to the floor. Joey stirred, but remained in a deep, peaceful sleep.

Stepping around the bed, Reno bent to pull the covers around the boy's small frame, placing a soft kiss on the angelic face palely illuminated by bright moonlight. Fatherly pride swelled within, and Reno grinned, thinking of the many expressions, few of them angelic, usually found on his active son's face.

After tossing and turning part of the night, Reno had slept maybe two hours when Joey had come padding down the stairs and into the bedroom. Reno had stirred, settling the youngster close under the blankets, then found himself totally awake, no chance of more rest. His thoughts were irrevocably drawn to Katie.

Katie Garrett with the moist, tender-red lips and mass of wild hair. Well, so much for his resolve to stay away from the fire, Reno thought, gathering a robe and heading for the shower.

It was six o'clock when Reno slipped into a sheepskin-lined suede jacket and stepped out into the frosty morning. It being late winter, the stars still shone brightly, but deep darkness was lifting. It promised to be a clear day. He walked quickly up the dirt road to Maggie's cottage. His boots crunching on the cold ground and the crowing of a rooster were the only sounds disturbing the early-morning quiet.

A light shone from Maggie's kitchen window. Reno had counted on this. Maggie kept odd hours, the spry old woman requiring little sleep. Her ears were as sharp now as the day she was born. Before Reno could even rap at the back door, he heard her muffled voice call, "Come on in, Reno." As expected, Maggie, fully dressed, sat in a well-used rocker, reading.

Waving away her offer of coffee, Reno said, "Could you keep an eye on Joey? I'm heading over to the river for the day. Sonny will be here around eight-thirty or so. Joey will probably spend most of the day with him anyway."

"Humph. I don't trust that harebrained Sonny to watch Joey all that well. I reckon I'll keep an eye on the both of them. Like as not, Sonny will spend a couple of hours up here with me lazing over a big lunch." Maggie pushed her wire-rimmed glasses farther up her nose and surveyed Reno closely. "You taking Katie with you?"

Characteristic of the old woman. She wanted to know something, she just asked. Reno grinned slowly, used to Maggie's ways. "Don't you ever worry about prying, Maggie?"

"No, I'm too old to worry about it. Guess you are taking her, if you're going to hem and haw. Nice cabin you have up there on the Illinois."

"Yep. I'm taking a couple of horses. I plan on being back maybe just after dark." Reno turned to go.

"You don't want the kids to know about Katie, do you?"

He turned back to her, his face unreadable. "I'd rather they didn't. Summer can get hurt. She has notions about me marrying again and she might get the wrong idea."

"Reno, the child is the smart one. Sometimes it's like that. God's plan, I suppose." Maggie paused, rocking slightly.

Reno kept still, a stony expression turned toward the cabinets. Respect for the older woman was the only thing stopping him from shutting the door upon her speech.

"It takes two to make a marriage, Reno," Maggie continued. "It wasn't all your fault yours wasn't so good. This Katie is something special. Maybe with her, you might find you like the marriage bed. It beats changing beds the way you do now. You might think on it."

Reno opened the door. "I'll have Summer send Joey up before she leaves for school."

Maggie nodded, continuing to rock peacefully.

Twenty-five minutes later, Reno had the gear loaded and the horse trailer hooked to the pickup, horses inside and grained. Entering the kitchen, he found Summer sitting at the table, her face still flushed with sleep.

"Good morning, pumpkin." Reno pulled off his hat and gloves, tossing them to the table, and bent to brush his lips against his daughter's cheek.

"Good morning, Daddy." Summer yawned, stuffing her hands between her knees. "I heard you come in last night. Ten o'clock is kinda early. Didn't you have a good time with Katie?"

"We had a fine time," Reno said blandly. Summer regarded him curiously. "Really, babe—a good time. Katie was just tired; so was I.'' Then, changing the subject, ''I'm going up to the river for the day. I need to get away for a bit.''

This wasn't unusual for him, and Summer didn't question it.

''Oh. I saw you loading the horses,'' Summer said.

''Figured Uncle Jake might want to ride with me,'' Reno said as explanation for two horses. It wasn't an out and out lie. Reno often took the bay for Jake Miller, nicknamed Uncle Jake, a retired rancher who lived close by. All the same, Reno avoided his daughter's eyes. ''Don't bother with a big breakfast. I'm leaving in a few minutes. I'll grab something on the way.''

He went to the bedroom to check on Joey. Reno never left his children without a parting look, as if to leave a piece of himself while away. Joey lay sprawled in the middle of the bed, one leg thrown clear of the blankets. He would wake soon. After stoking the wood stove to keep the morning chill from the house, Reno stepped back to the kitchen to take his leave of Summer. She now appeared wide-eyed, taking milk from the refrigerator. Shooting her father a smile, she lifted her lips for a quick kiss.

Putting his arm around her shoulders, Reno held Summer to him for a moment. ''Maggie's expecting Joey before you go to school.''

''Okay... Daddy?''

''Yes, babe.''

''Will Katie be leaving today?''

Reno stiffened, but carefully kept anything from showing on his face. ''I imagine so. Her van should be repaired.''

''I wish I didn't have to go to school so I could see her... say good-bye,'' Summer said. ''I hope we see her again. You like her, don't you?''

"I like her fine. When have you known me not to like a beautiful woman?" Reno teased.

"We exchanged addresses and she promised to visit when she gets back this way again," Summer said, following him to the back door.

Reno simply nodded. "I'm off. I'll be back around dark, or soon after."

It was almost seven-thirty when Katie stood before the mirror brushing her long mane, tying it loosely with a leather strip into a swinging ponytail. She had dressed snugly in a thermal cotton undershirt, covered by a soft-blue flannel shirt tucked neatly into slim denims. She had also taken the precaution of wearing thick boot socks.

Reaching for the telephone, Katie dialed the motel office. "This is Miss Garrett in room twelve. I'd like to leave a message, please." She paused while the person on the other end presumably grabbed a piece of paper. "Ted Carter, Carter's Garage should be phoning sometime today. Please tell him I'm out for the day and will see him first thing in the morning. Yes . . . Thank you very much."

As she hung up, Katie heard the crunch of tires on gravel outside and knew instinctively it was Reno. Without waiting, she opened the door. He looked surprised at her abrupt appearance. A slow grin spread across his face.

"Ready?" Reno asked.

Katie nodded, turned to the room for her coat and purse, whistled for Sam and pulled the door locked behind her. "You did know I couldn't leave Sam cooped up in the room all day?" She shot a questioning glance toward Reno.

"Didn't even think about it. But no matter. You are more than welcome to join us, Sam," Reno said, speaking directly to the huge dog, who wagged her tail in friendly reply.

The pickup was already warm from Reno's drive into town. Settling Sam to the far side, Katie slipped into the small space left next to Reno. He smiled and squeezed her hand. Katie felt like a woman in love and looked forward to what the day would bring. If this was to be the only day they would have together . . . well, then she would savor every bit of it. Somehow, deep inside, Katie felt she may never have another day like this one in all her life.

"I left a message for Ted. Told him I'd see him tomorrow," Katie told Reno as he shifted into gear and made to circle the motel so he wouldn't have to back the horse trailer.

Reno nodded. "He won't worry about it."

Reno drove through town and on its outskirts pulled into the parking area of a small café. Reaching under the seat, he retrieved a tall thermos. "I can just bet Miss Katie is more than ready for some breakfast."

She grinned. "I was hoping you would mention something about food soon."

"Just sit still. I'll grab us some sausage-and-egg biscuits and we'll eat on the way. Sam eaten yet?"

"Yes, I fed her earlier. But you'd better get her one anyway."

"Ah . . . like mistress, like dog."

Katie took a playful swing at Reno's arm, but he was quicker and gripped her wrist in his strong hand. Slowly he bent to kiss her softly, then instantly let her go. "I'll just be a few minutes," he said. Katie watched him walk quickly into the café, the warmth of his kiss still tingling her lips.

After about ten minutes he returned, carrying a bulging bag and the thermos. "Reach into the glove compartment. There should be a couple of mugs in there."

Katie found the mugs and poured them both piping hot coffee, juggling the mugs until Reno carefully pulled the pickup and trailer onto the road again. They drank the hot brew in companionable silence before digging into the biscuits.

"Here," Reno said, handing Katie a half-eaten biscuit. "Give this to Sam. I'm full."

Katie took the biscuit and munched on it absently.

"I said give it to Sam. Geez, how do you manage to stay so small, Miss Katie?" Reno teased.

She regarded him with a guilty grin, then handed the rest of the biscuit to Sam.

Katie enjoyed the scenery as the pickup sped smoothly along the state highway. The land rolled alternating meadows and woods, divided by barbed-wire fencing and settled with farms, ranches and country homes. The early-morning sun turned the eastern half of the sky a bright orange, bathing the pickup cab and everything else in a golden light. With the added warmth of the sun rays, Katie shrugged off her coat for more comfort.

"By the end of the day, we won't need our coats," Reno commented.

"Oh, everything is so beautiful." Katie sighed. "I love the morning sun."

"On a full stomach," Reno teased.

"Definitely!" Katie laughed.

"The cabin up here sits only on two acres, but right beside the river," Reno said. "I own it in partnership with a friend, but I'm the lucky one. He's a lawyer over in Tulsa and can't seem to find much time to spend up here except a couple of weeks in the summer for the family vacation."

"You come often, then?"

"As much as possible. I haven't been up since the first of winter, though—too much going on about the ranch this year. I bring the kids when the weather is nice. Joey I have to watch real carefully. He's learned to swim some, and last summer he kept heading for the water—whether anyone was around or not."

Katie smiled at the obvious warmth in Reno's voice when speaking of his children. "It can't be easy being both mother and father," she said. "You manage quite well."

"It's a little harder with Summer than with Joey. Her being a young girl at times has me unsure of exactly what to say or how to act. Earlier this year they showed a film at school about the female cycle. Summer knew all about such things, of course, living on the ranch as we do with the animals. But there were details a young girl would have to be concerned with and that she just had never been exposed to. She came home all excited about it, feeling like she was really growing up." Reno smiled wryly. "She wanted to talk about it. I tried, I felt pretty stupid. So I sent her up to Maggie."

Katie smiled knowingly, remembering her own experience with learning. "There's more to come, Daddy. Soon she'll be dating. There will probably be hordes of guys. Summer is a beautiful young girl."

"Hey, don't rush things!" Reno protested. "Surely another three or four years."

"Summer seems very mature for her age," Katie said. "What about her grandmother? Isn't she a help when it comes to the feminine side of things?"

Reno raked a hand through his thick hair. "You probably noticed yesterday, I'm not one of Millicent's favorite people."

"I caught some undercurrents," Katie admitted.

"Millicent Stephens is the pillar of local society. At least she believes she is. She didn't like it when I married Lynn." At the mention of the name, Katie looked at him sharply, but remained quiet. Apparently, Reno hadn't noticed this was the first time he'd mentioned his wife. Continuing, he said, "Horrified at the prospect of me being the sole parent to her grandchildren, Millicent began proceedings to take Summer and Joey away from me. Finally her lawyer convinced her it would come to nothing and she dropped the case."

"But why? You provide for the children such a wonderful home, love, everything they could want," Katie said.

"I didn't have the ranch, the house, when Lynn died," Reno explained. "I was working long and erratic hours in the oil fields. Plus, Millicent wants Joey and Summer instilled with her own values—values I don't happen to agree with. And for them to move in what she considers a proper society. When she dropped the case, I agreed to let the kids visit. After all, she is their grandmother. But I'd rather Maggie for a role model." Reno chuckled. "Remember what I said about the school film?"

Katie nodded.

"Summer spoke to Millicent about it and Millicent told her to be quiet. Well-brought-up young ladies didn't speak of such things."

Katie chuckled, too, then pressing Reno's arm, cried, "Look, look!" Up ahead, alongside the road, a doe and her fawn stepped from a thickly wooded area. Reno slowed for Katie to get a good look as the animals appeared to freeze. Feeling Reno's eyes upon her, Katie turned. "What is it?"

"What I said before," Reno answered. "At times you're like a child. You get such a kick out of simple things. I've almost forgotten what that feels like."

Ten minutes later, Reno slowed the truck and pulled onto a dirt road bordering the edge of a plowed field in which the grass-green sprouts of winter wheat were beginning to show. He hopped out to open the barbed-wire fence and Katie carefully shifted into gear, guiding the truck and trailer into the fenced area. Back again behind the wheel, Reno slowly drove over the rutted road, still soft from the recent snow and rain.

"All this land, about eight hundred acres, is owned by a farmer, Jake Miller," Reno said, swinging his arm to indicate its vastness. "He used to keep some cattle and horses, too, but he's pretty much retired now. I met him when the company I worked for at the time sunk a well on some of Miller's property. With a bit of talking, I got him to sell two acres down on the river."

"Seems like you know an awful lot of people," Katie observed.

"I make it my business to know certain people," Reno said.

The truck bumped along the edge of the field and on into a winter-brown woods. The only green appearing among the leafless cottonwood and elm trees was an occasional scrub cedar and mistletoe parasite high in the bare branches. Sunlight lit upon the treetops from the east and the light filtered down to the forest floor. Continuing down the dirt road another mile, Reno pulled the pickup to a stop in a small clearing near the side of a weather-darkened log cabin. The morning sun shone upon the cabin roof and made bright patches upon the ground not shaded by the wood.

Reno opened the door and stepped out, turning to take Katie by the hand. She pulled on her coat and buttoned it high. A deep chill hung in the still air, the sun too new in the day to provide sufficient warmth. Except for the chatter of birds, all was quiet. Sam alighted behind her, pausing to sniff the air before padding away to investigate the area.

"What do you think?" Reno called, stepping to the trailer for a quick check on the horses.

"When you said cabin . . . I don't know what I expected, but nothing quite like this."

Satisfied the horses were fine for the moment, Reno took Katie's elbow and led the way into the cabin. Their boots made a scraping sound on the pine boards of the porch, which stretched the length of the front. The screen door creaked in protest as Reno drew it open, reached through and opened the solid wood door, allowing Katie to enter first.

The room they entered was long and dim. At one end, toward the south, stood a massive rock fireplace, a timber beam mantel above. In front of the fireplace sat two cushioned wing-backed chairs reminiscent of the ones in Reno's living room. The room also contained a large wooden table-and-chair set, a rocker and Colonial-style cabinets, complete with modern countertop and set-in gas range. Built along the west and north walls and meeting in the corner were two sets of bunk beds. The room was rustically warm, but now had that empty dead feeling a house gets when it has gone quite a while without human habitation.

"You don't lock the door to safeguard all this?" Katie asked.

"If anyone gets way back here and wants in, they'll find a way. We figure we'd rather have them just step in instead of breaking out windows or down the door."

"Makes sense," Katie mused.

"We have this room, with these bunks," Reno said, stepping to a door on his right, "and in here is a bedroom for privacy. The only problem is this room can get pretty cold, separated as it is from the fireplace—our only source of heat."

Katie followed him and looked into the room to see a chair, a dresser and an old-fashioned double spool bed covered with a brightly colored quilt. She looked from the bed to Reno, but he had turned his back to her, walking away.

"But like I said," Reno continued, "my lawyer friend, Bill Turner, only gets up here in the summer, so he and his wife don't worry about heat. When I come up and it's a bit cold, I use one of the bunks or bed down there in front of the fire." Nodding to a door which stood ajar on one side of the fireplace, Reno said, "Through there is the back porch and bathroom. Figured you might want to make use of it before we start off. A bit harder on a woman out in the woods all day than on a man," he teased.

Katie grinned wryly. "I've always thought what a bum rap Mother Nature has placed upon the female sex in many ways."

"Ah, but how wonderful the differences." Reno laughed. "Go on now. I'll get the horses unloaded."

Several minutes later, Katie emerged from the cabin, pulling on her gloves. The day promising to be warmer, she decided against her woolen hat, but did keep her coat buttoned all the way up, if only for the time being. Reno was in the process of saddling the horses.

"Hand me that blanket," he said, nodding toward the truck bed. The color of the horse he saddled closely resembled that of Katie's own hair.

"Is this the horse you spoke of? Your favorite one?"

"Yep. Conti Color. One of the first horses I bought." He checked the cinch, then stepped beneath the horse's neck to saddle the other, a gentle-looking bay, for Katie.

"Have you seen Sam?" Katie asked, looking around, her eyes searching the forest.

"Sam's a Lab, isn't she? Take a guess," Reno answered, inclining his head toward the river.

Katie whistled, and moments later the black dog appeared from the direction of the river, her thick coat dripping. When only a few feet from the group of humans and horses, she stopped to shake vigorously. "Oh, Sam." Katie laughed as water sprayed everywhere and the horses snorted, shying away.

"Some dog you got there, Miss Katie." Reno smiled, his eyes resting on her warmly. Katie's own green eyes locked with his. Reno and Katie were at ease, close. Though he had gloves on and she several layers of clothes, Katie's senses tingled at Reno's touch as he helped her into the saddle.

Reno led a trail through the trees, Sam bounding along, now beside, then behind, sometimes in front. Enjoying her surroundings, Katie remained quiet. Riding as they were, single file, talk would have been difficult.

Soon the path opened onto clear rolling ground of winter-tan native Bermuda and buffalo grasses, no barbed-wire fencing in sight. Reno turned to look at her and, grinning, bent low and spurred his mount to a run. Catching the sudden spark of freedom, Katie did the same.

The sun's brightness caused her to squint and the cool clear air blew past her ears, whipping her hair, as Katie enjoyed the exhilaration of speeding across the open ground. She strove to flow with the bay's movements and to keep to the same ground Reno traveled before her, realizing he knew the area and its danger spots.

They galloped thus for three, maybe four, miles. Then Reno reined his horse to a stop near a stand of trees and what appeared the rough, jutting ground of a creek bed. Reining the bay in close by, Katie threw her leg over the saddle and jumped down beside him.

Laughing, she shook back her windblown hair, pulling free of the leather strap now barely holding it. "Oh, I enjoyed that!" Katie gasped for breath. "I don't ride that much, you know. I'll probably be terribly sore tomorrow."

"You did fine," Reno said. "But I thought it best to stop on this side of the wash. Didn't care to have you trying to jump the bay and one, or both, of you ending up with broken necks."

Allowing the horses' reins to drop free, Katie and Reno walked along the creek bed for several feet. Katie turned her face skyward to the sun. "Ah, that sun feels great. Do you suppose spring is just around the corner," she said, not really asking a question and Reno remaining silent. Unbuttoning her coat, Katie stuffed her gloves into the pockets, then raised her hands to secure her hair once more into the leather strap.

"No, don't." Reno stopped her by taking one of her hands. "It looks beautiful hanging down and all over like that." The words were stiffly said, as if he were unaccustomed to saying the word beautiful or to making a compliment. Perhaps he didn't even mean it as a compliment, just as a statement of how he felt.

Katie shrugged in acquiescence, pleased Reno kept a firm hold on her hand. They walked slowly alongside the crooked creek bed which cut through the land from the northwest. Here and there trees grew on either side, their roots bared and gnarled by rushing water during heavy rains. At places, the sides of the creek seemed almost to have been sliced by a shovel, so steep and clean were the cuts made into the earth by the water. Now, on this balmy winter's day, only a small stream gurgled over the creek's rocky bottom.

"Does your friend, Mr. Miller...does he own all this land?" Katie asked.

"Yep...which was another reason I wanted a cabin up here. It's hard to find enough land to really ride on anymore without running into modern society and fences. Oh, Miller has fences too, has to, but his landholdings are vast. You can ride through plenty of country without coming upon other people's property—and sometimes trouble. He's been very generous allowing us the use of his land." Reno grinned. "Part of the deal when we bought."

"As you said, it helps to know the right people."

"Yep."

Mounting up once again, the two allowed the horses to set the pace and followed the meandering creek to the west about five miles, part of it through timber, until they approached a blacktopped state highway. Here they carefully crossed the creek and continued back the way they had come, stopping again where they had before, this time on the far side of the wash.

Reno sat leaning against a fallen tree, long since dead, its bark peeled and the wood bleached white by the weather. He raised one leg and Katie propped herself against it, facing him. Now and again her ears picked up the sound of a woodpecker hammering in a nearby tree.

The horses nibbled the dry grass several yards away, lazily fanning their tails. It was an uncommonly still day for Oklahoma. Basking in the sun's warming rays, Katie and Reno slipped off their coats.

"Tell me, Miss Katie, why is it you're not married?" Reno asked.

"Umm, guess I just never found the right person." Her eyes flitted across his face, drawn up to the deep shine of his dark hair.

"A lot of people don't find the right person. That doesn't prevent them from marrying," Reno observed.

"That's true," Katie agreed. "I don't know why I've never married. I'm certainly not some kind of women's libber. Neither have I felt I *had* to have a man to live. But I do feel men and women go togther, to share a life. I believe it's the way God set up the whole world. Look around . . . male and female pairs of everything—horses, dogs, fish, birds, plants. Sometimes, even on the same tree, there are flowers that can be distinguished as male and female. And every male and female of every species, work together to make their life easier, better, and to further life itself."

"That is very profound thinking." Reno grinned.

"Perhaps." Katie blushed, then said in mock haughtiness, "And I want you to know I have had several chances. Things just never worked out somehow. Perhaps I'm a perfectionist, an old-fashioned dreamer, but I want to feel about a man the way my mother did for my father. They had a certain magic which lasted thirty-one years."

"Some people aren't meant for marriage." Reno leaned his head back against the dead tree and gazed at the blue sky.

"Maybe," Katie said. She wanted desperately to ask Reno why he was afraid of involvement, but somehow she felt it would be better just to listen. He wanted to tell her something; she could feel it.

"I'm one of those people, Katie." Reno's eyes searched her face, and he gently brushed her cheek with his hand. "I see you look at me with those green eyes, so trusting, so eager." Katie only blinked, waiting. "Look, I'm a widower, but if Lynn hadn't died, we'd be divorced. When we married, it was great. For about a year. Then it seemed we each wanted our own way, and neither would give in. We separated four times."

Katie had not been prepared for this. Somehow in her mind, she had pictured Reno's wife as incredibly beautiful and Reno so in love with her he was unable to forget. For a moment she was unable to say anything, then, "What was Lynn like?" she asked quietly.

"She was beautiful. Summer resembles her a lot. She liked to sing and dance and party, liked to stay on the go. I found that great at first. Hell, I was a rough rounder from the oil fields. I was making top money, and we blew every bit of it just living high. Then Summer was born and I began to change. I remembered the kind of home I'd always wanted as a kid, the kind I wanted to give Summer, then Joey when he was born. A father working regular hours; a mother in the kitchen baking cookies. Lynn had other ideas."

Reno paused, staring at the ground while gathering his thoughts. "I've always been headstrong about anything I've ever wanted. I tried to make Lynn fit into a role that I wanted her to play. When I bought the land from Maggie and announced to Lynn I'd quit the oil company and we were moving to the country to build a horse ranch, she had a fit. We had a big argument and Lynn drove off in a rage. She was too distracted to pay attention, and crashed into a semi.''

"Do you blame yourself for her death?" Katie said.

"No. Not anymore. I did at first, but it was really an accident. We just had a fight, like many we'd had before. What I have learned is my decisions, my life, my mistakes affect so many other people. I made a mistake when I married Lynn. I was crazy for her, thought it was love for life, but it wasn't. There are few 'loves for life,'" Reno said with a bitter twitch of his lips. "If I make another mistake like that one, Summer and Joey will be the ones hurt the most."

"But Reno, you deny yourself and the children so much life has to offer by worrying about making a mistake. As you said, you have learned more about yourself, more about what you want out of life."

"Well, mistake in marriage is one thing I don't intend to repeat," Reno said. "I hadn't even thought along this vein since Lynn died...till I met you. I could feel those green eyes pulling me in. Good grief, I haven't even known you, what, but three days? And here I am talking about marriage."

"No," Katie said. "Talking about not marriage."

Reno smiled and Katie caught the spark of desire flare in his eyes. Instantly she felt her own body respond.

"And I do believe we have done enough talking," he said huskily, lowering his head to hers, his lips hot against her own. His hand pressed the back of her neck, holding her firmly. Then he broke his lips away and held her to him, stroking her hair gently. Katie cuddled into him, burrowing her nose at the base of his neck.

"You smell good," Reno said.

"It's soap."

"Well, it's good."

"My aunt makes it."

"Umm."

The minutes they sat thus were heaven for Katie. She could feel Reno's warmth and the tight control in which he held himself. She wasn't sure if it was his heartbeat she heard or the pounding of her own blood in her ears. Desire stirring deep within her made her press herself even closer into his arms.

Inwardly, she knew exactly what she was doing. She was hoping to break down Reno's wavering reservations. She tried to push the thoughts aside. *I shouldn't do this, think like this. I hardly know him.* But in her heart, she felt she did. Her heart did not question.

Finally Reno moved, pushed Katie away and stood up, pulling her up beside him. "Let's head back," he said gruffly.

Chapter Seven

In the clearing of the cabin once more, they unsaddled their mounts, Reno stowing the gear in the bed of the pickup again.

While he formed a rope corral for the horses, Katie wandered down closer to the river, following along behind Sam. The carpet of leaves beneath her feet muffled her steps. Soft rustling came from the brush as small animals, rabbits, squirrels, or the like, scurried away at her approach.

It was no wonder Reno loved coming here. The place formed a restful retreat. The river at this point was perhaps a hundred and fifty yards wide, smooth at the moment, and bordered on both sides by trees. The river, the woods, the expanse of farmland surrounding the cabin area all combined to give it a feeling of isolation from the bustling business of the world. Katie felt the earth almost talked to her. A holdover, perhaps, of ideas from her Grandma Garrett, her mother, too.

Sam brushed against her knee and Katie bent to ruffle the dog's ears, removing a few sticks here and there gathered from the animal's morning jaunt in the woods. Sam's ears perked and her tail picked up tempo. Turning, Katie saw Reno approaching.

"You'll have to check her good for ticks when you get back," he said. "They winter over easily in our mild Oklahoma weather."

"I know. I was just thinking a good bath may be in order. I realize she is a dog, but I don't care to have her smell like one in the confines of the van."

Taking Katie's hand, Reno lifted her from her crouched position. "Your hands are like ice. Why didn't you have your gloves on?" He didn't wait for an answer. "Come on. We'll scrounge for something to eat and a coffee to warm you up. Unless I miss my guess, I have one starving woman on my hands. Right?"

"Always!" Katie laughed. They walked back to the cabin. Sam followed, choosing to flop down outside on the porch.

In the great room, they shrugged off their coats and Katie shivered in the chilliness. Reno, noticing, said, "You look for something to eat. I'll see about getting a fire going."

While he worked with the fire, Katie's search of the cabinets turned up several cans of soup, a jar of instant coffee, canned peaches and pears, and crackers kept fresh in a tin. Emptying a can of vegetable soup into an enamel pan, Katie lit the gas stove and put on the kettle for hot coffee.

Satisfied his fire was firmly ablaze, Reno rose up and stepped over behind Katie. "My job is done. How's yours coming along?"

Katie felt nervous with Reno standing so close, but at the same time she loved it, wanted him closer. She continued to stir the soup nonchalantly. "Soup's done, too. I must not be the only one hungry." She smiled at him over her shoulder.

Bending his dark head, Reno kissed her lips, placing his hands on each side of her hips. When he raised his head, Katie's eyes stayed locked on his. "No, you're not the only one who is hungry," Reno said hoarsely.

Slowly, Katie switched off the gas burners. She turned within his hands and pressed herself against his tight frame. Winding her arms around his neck, she pulled his head down to hers and kissed him hungrily.

Intense heat flowed up from deep between her legs, spreading throughout her body. Her senses registered the hissing of the kettle, the smell of wood smoke clinging to Reno's hair, mingling with his male body scent, and the warmth of his skin beneath her fingers.

Swinging her up into his strong arms, Reno carried her through to the bedroom. This had been in the back of Katie's mind since Reno had called her that morning. To be in his arms, feel his body against hers. In anticipation, she felt the moistness and heat gather between her legs and flow through her veins.

Suddenly shy, Katie buried her face in his neck. Gently, he laid her upon the bed, spreading the dark tresses of her hair away from her face.

"Katie. Oh, Katie," he murmured, stretching out beside her.

His lips played soft and feathery over her neck as his hands ran up and down the length of her back. Katie moaned softly, arching her back and pressing toward him. Their clothing became an unwanted barrier and she began tugging Reno's sweater up to feel the warmth of his bare skin. She was fast losing control, her pulse beating rapidly, the deep need rising within her. Cautioning whispers sounded at the back of her mind, but were overwhelmed by the need, the desire. It was a totally new experience, one which captured and held her.

Suddenly Reno pulled away, and Katie opened her eyes in bewilderment. A moan escaped as she reached for him. He smiled at her puzzled frown and tugged his sweater over his head. Katie smiled back, seeing he was moving away simply to remove his clothes. She sat up and began unbuttoning her own shirt, but Reno placed a restraining hand over hers.

"No. Wait," he said softly.

Pulling the covers back, he turned to Katie. He took a firm hold on the heel of one boot and slipped it from her foot. Then he removed the other, smoothly and gently. Taking her foot in his hands, he massaged first one, then the other. The sensations he induced were almost more than Katie could bear.

"Reno... please," she whispered.

But he would not be hurried. He removed each piece of Katie's clothing, slowly, gently, kissing her ivory skin repeatedly, sending shivers shooting through her nerve endings. Katie watched his hands, fascinated. They were rugged and workworn, in sharp contrast to her pale skin, but his every touch was exceedingly tender. His dark gaze roamed warmly over her body, repeatedly turning to light upon her face, taking in the growing passion reflected there.

Katie was in awe of how natural she felt with Reno. Surprisingly she found no embarrassment in his inspection of her. How could she, with his looks plainly speaking his admiration?

Pulling the covers around her shoulders, Reno tugged off his own boots. Katie allowed her eyes to roam over his bare torso. She watched his thigh muscles tighten and the muscles of his back ripple as he slipped from his jeans. Her gaze flowed upward until reaching his face, where she found his eyes twinkling with laughter. Her cheeks burning, Katie lowered her lids.

Slipping beside her beneath the covers, Reno teased in a husky voice, "Is this an independent, modern woman blushing?"

Then there was no more talk. Reno crushed her lips with his, forcing her mouth to part, kissing her deeply. Katie responded to his every touch, her nerve endings screaming with the sensations Reno was causing.

Their lovemaking was slow and languid, as if they had all the time in the world, as indeed they did. Katie pushed any thoughts of the outside world away and allowed herself to drift into one governed totally by feelings and sensations.

Reno caressed her body with his lips and his hands. Katie did likewise to his, enjoying, exploring, the smooth heat of his skin, the strength of his muscles. He discovered the sensitivity of her stomach and kneaded with his palm, over and over, while teasing her skin from her neck to the points of her breasts with his tongue. Moving against him, she delighted in every touch.

Gradually Reno's tightly controlled passion became unleashed. Katie matched his passion and lost herself to their lovemaking. She pressed toward him trying to become one with him, and their bodies flowed to the music which only they could hear.

"Reno..." she breathed. Was it her voice? Her mind whirled as he hungrily covered her mouth with his. His breath was hot upon her ear as he tenderly covered her body with is own, careful to keep his full weight from her, as if fearful of crushing her smaller frame. He slipped between her legs and she welcomed him into her moistness, a cry of both pain and release escaping her lips. Their two bodies moving in fluid rhythm, Katie gave herself totally to Reno with a wild abandon she had never before known she possessed.

Katie lay facing Reno in the circle of his arms, the quilt pulled up snugly to hold in their body heat. She smiled, contented as a warm kitten, and reached up to trace the strong line of his jaw, gazing at him with a look of wonder. Reno's velvet-brown eyes mirrored her own feelings. Their light flooded Katie with a heady warmth.

What had transpired between them Katie could not put into words. For the first time since her father's death, she felt totally comforted by the solid strength of the man who now held her. Gone was the pent-up sorrow, the hurt, the ache of hollowness that had seemed to follow her for the past year. All was replaced by the birth of something golden and new.

For long minutes, the two lay thus, gazing into each other's eyes, their looks speaking of their contentment, their pleasure of each other.

Sighing, Reno rolled to his back and shifted Katie's head to his shoulders, holding her in the curve of his arm. His hand absently stroked her skin and she nuzzled close to his warmth. Shadows deepened as the evening of winter closed in. Soon they would have to go, and Katie didn't want to. She didn't want to disturb the warm, intoxicating world in which she found herself enveloped.

They'd made no promises to each other. Reno had made himself very clear about his feelings. But Katie felt totally different, changed by fire that had burned between them. Somehow, in a way she couldn't explain, she had given herself to Reno, had absorbed a part of him, and together they had formed an unbreakable bond. Surely Reno felt the difference, too.

Pushing all speculative thoughts and reasoning aside, Katie chose for the moment simply to bask in the afterglow of feelings, marveling at the experience she and Reno shared. She sighed and stretched her legs, rubbing up against Reno's warm body. Reno shifted, bringing both arms around to encircle her and resting his cheek upon her hair. There was no need or desire for words. They dozed off into their golden world and the darkness of night closed in.

Reno stirred, kissed Katie's shoulder and shook her softly. "Hey, wake up, sleepyhead."

Grinning in the darkness, Katie said, "I'm awake. And why are we whispering?"

"Because it's expected in the dark. Are you hungry?"

"For what, sir?"

"Oh ho, let's not have any of that risqué talk," Reno murmured, nuzzling her ear, his hands roaming the silkiness of her skin.

Katie felt the thumping of his heart against her, and automatically her body responded to his caresses. His lips found her mouth, kissed her deeply, then reluctantly broke away.

"We have to think about going," he said heavily.

"I know."

Throwing back the covers, Reno sat up and switched on the bedside lamp. Sitting up, Katie turned her head from the lamp's bright glow and modestly covered herself with the quilt while searching for her clothes.

"Wait right there, Miss Katie," Reno said, slipping into his jeans.

"What?"

"I said wait right there." Hurriedly, Reno pulled on his sweater, then grabbed at the quilt and proceeded to wrap Katie up in it.

"What are you doing?"

"No need to get dressed yet," Reno explained. "I'll wrap you up and you can eat your soup in luxury in front of the fire."

"But—" Katie began.

"No buts about it." Reno lifted her mummy-wrapped frame and carried her, giggling, into the great room of the cabin. He lowered her into one of the big chairs before the fireplace, whose flickering flames now burned low. "We've got to get you fed. Can't have you fade away using what's left of your strength to put on all those clothes," he teased.

Brushing her hair back, Reno bent and kissed her softly. The low fire's glow lit his face as he slowly pulled away, and Katie looked into his dark brown eyes. *I love him,* she thought. *I am in love with the man.*

But she didn't speak of her thoughts. Instead she followed his teasing manner and said, "Now how am I supposed to eat, all wrapped up like this?"

"That, my dear, is your problem."

Katie stuck out her tongue and Reno gave a deep-throated chuckle. He added more wood to the fire, poking it to get a good flame, then stepped into the kitchen area to finish what Katie had started earlier, whistling a low tune while moving about.

Fumbling with the folds of the quilt, Katie pulled it from her shoulders and wrapped it under her arms high above her breasts. Resting her head against the chair back, she listened to Reno's whistling and movement and stared into the flames.

I've slept with a man I've barely known three days, she thought. *And I'm in love with that man.* Maybe she was just falling in love. Would she be able to pull herself out if she had to? Katie wasn't sure. It didn't matter. She didn't want to. He was what had been missing in her life. Someone to be a part of, to have be a part of her. He filled her up and made her feel whole, alive.

But Reno... A coldness swept across her heart. How did Reno feel?

Instinctively she knew Reno cared for her. There was an attraction between them. A feeling Katie couldn't put into words and could not concretely explain in any way, but sensed was true, vibrant and binding. And Reno's feelings were revealed by his every touch, by the look of his eyes—when he didn't bring that cold mask across them.

Was she wrong this time? Were her instincts betraying her? Was she simply projecting what she wanted everything to be? No. Katie gave an imperceptible shake of her head. She couldn't be wrong; she just couldn't be. The feeling, the hunch was too strong.

But would Reno allow himself to love her, to make a commitment on which they both could live and grow? Would he be so afraid of making another mistake that he would push her away, wouldn't even give them a chance?

Well, whether he would admit it or not, he was involved with her, Katie rationalized. He hadn't been able to stop himself from wanting her, or from bringing her to this cabin to do something about it. That in itself was a start. And if it was right, Reno would realize it, too. An old maxim, a favorite of her mother's, came to mind: "to everything there is a season."

It may take Reno a little time, she told herself, but their season would come.

"What are you smiling about, Miss Katie?" Reno's voice startled her. He stood by the chair holding a tray, a curious look on his face.

"Oh . . . just that it's so nice here by the fire." Katie lowered her eyes quickly, hoping Reno could not read what was written there.

They ate the small meal in comparative silence. It was difficult for Katie, not blurting out the turmoil of feelings going on within her. She wasn't one to play coy, flirtatious games with a man. If she cared, she said it straight out. But she knew Reno didn't want to hear any talk of love. It would only make him feel guilty, fearful perhaps that he could not return her feelings. He might feel trapped and even regret having brought Katie up to the cabin. Katie couldn't bear that. She had no regrets at all. And she never would; no matter what happened between them.

She would gamble. She would keep quiet and trust nature and the powers that be for Reno to be drawn to her, to realize the love they could share together.

Finding he wasn't hungry, Reno touched little besides a few slices of the peaches and several cups of coffee. He looked across to Katie and noticed she had cleaned her dishes completely. How such a small human being could eat so much was beyond him. Where did all of Katie's food go? A half-grin spread across his face as he remembered the last several hours. She had sure burned the energy then.

Katie looked up and caught his gaze. Reno was the one to look away, silently cursing himself. The look she gave him was so damned contented, so trusting, so caring. He wasn't about to use the word "love," even to himself.

Just then Sam barked several times from outside the door and rubbed her paw across the wood for emphasis. Reno stood, setting his tray aside. "I'll let her in. While you get dressed, I'm going to see to the horses."

He knew he sounded short, was acting gruff, though he tried not to. Slipping on his coat, Reno grabbed a lantern and got away from the cabin as quickly as he could, Sam brushing past as he stepped out into the darkness. It was six-thirty. He and Katie should have left long ago.

Reno tried to keep his mind totally on the job of loading the horses into the trailer, but there wasn't much to it and his thoughts kept straying back to the woman now dressing inside the cabin. The glow of the bedroom light shone out through the darkness. Gathering the length of rope in loops within his hand, Reno glanced up just in time to see Katie pulling her thermal shirt over her soft breasts.

"Damn," he swore aloud. How could he be so stupid as to think he could bring her up here, go to bed with her and have that be the end of it. He knew it couldn't be like that with Katie. Hell, it meant something to her when she slept with a man. If he wasn't sure before he'd lain with her, he was positive now. That woman had not been with too many men ever in her life. There was a freshness about her, like a north breeze blowing over the dew grass of morning. She had touched something in him long forgotten, long buried.

It didn't matter, Reno thought firmly. Yes, Miss Katie was special, no doubt about that, but things were ending right here and that was all there was to it.

The bedroom light went out, and slowly Reno stepped onto the porch, opening the cabin door. Katie stood at the sink washing the few dishes. She turned and shot him a quick smile. In spite of himself, Reno found the warmth of her smile generated to him and he smiled in return. *Damn, she's a beautiful woman,* he thought.

The ride back to Tyne was quiet, and Reno's mood darkened the closer they got to Katie's motel. The silence between them lengthened. Reno felt he owed it to Katie to explain his feelings. But the more he thought about it, the more uncertain he became of just what those feelings were.

Pulling into the motel parking lot, they noticed Katie's van parked in front of her motel room. "Goodness," she said, surprised. "I didn't expect Mr. Carter to bring it over here. I haven't even paid him yet."

"Ted won't worry. He'll just figure you'll catch him tomorrow."

Reno parked the pickup and trailer on the far side of the motel lot across from Katie's room. Switching off the ignition, he leaned back with a sigh. Katie looked down at her hands folded loosely in her lap. Sam moved about in the cramped quarters restlessly. Without a word, Reno reached across and opened the door. The big dog jumped out, heading for the neighboring field. Reno left his arm resting on the back of the seat, but not touching Katie.

Regarding her with his dark gaze, Reno mulled over what he needed to say. "Katie," he began. She looked at him then, and he was relieved to see her eyes were clear, with no traces of tears. Involuntarily he brought his hand to stroke the silk of her hair, which framed her face in mild disarray.

"Katie," Reno began again. "I want to find a way of thanking you for today and not sound like some kind of heel." He smiled wryly. "I don't think there is a way."

"There's no need for you to say anything," Katie said. "I had a wonderful day, too."

"I think there's a need," Reno said, then paused, raking a hand through his hair. "Look, I wanted to be with you today, Katie. I needed to be with you. And that's a whole lot more than I've said to a woman in a good number of years. But, like I said before, I'm not looking to get involved or go on for any more than one day."

Reno thought he saw Katie's face grow pale, but it was difficult to tell in the dimness of the motel lights. She simply nodded and turned away, saying, "I understood that when I agreed to go with you to the cabin. And the enjoyment of the day isn't all on your side, you know. I thank you, too, Mr. Martin."

She was cool and smooth, as if today was an everyday occurrence and Reno damn well knew it wasn't. She wasn't crying or regretting her passionate actions in guilty afterthoughts. So why didn't he feel better about everything than he did?

He walked her to the door of her room. When they passed the van, he saw a note lying on the dashboard. Opening the door, he retrieved the paper, read it and passed it to Katie. "Told you Ted wouldn't worry about the money." The note was a bill with the message that Katie's keys were in the motel office.

"It was thoughtful of him to bring the van over. Now I can just drop him a check."

Reno took the room key from her hand and unlocked the door. Pushing it wide, he turned and gave a two-fingered shrill whistle for Sam, who immediately came bounding out of the darkness. The dog slipped between them and on into the room. Reno pulled Katie into his arms for one last time, his senses taking in the slightness of her frame and the sweetness of her fragrance. Memories of the recent hours flooded his mind.

"Ah, Katie, I wish things were different. I wish I were different." Bending his head, he intended to brush her lips in a brief kiss, but Katie clung to him and he found himself answering the demands of her lips.

Dragging his mouth from hers, Reno set Katie firmly from him. "Good-bye," he said hoarsely and turned, leaving her standing in the doorframe, the ache within him almost unbearable. A few steps away, he stopped at her call.

"Reno," she said, waiting for him to face her. The motel lights bathed her in a dim yellow glow. Her face was flushed and her lips bore evidence of his kiss. "Reno, you won't be able to forget me. You won't be able to forget us."

Then in a quick, fluid movement she slipped into the room and shut the door behind her. Immediately a light went on within the room, its glow showing brightly around the edge of the curtain.

Something within Reno sensed the truth in her words.

Chapter Eight

Katie tried to hold those parting words in her mind all the long way home. They were something to cling to in the face of her overwhelming doubts. She had had no intention of saying such to Reno last night, but the words had just tumbled out. And they had seemed so true at the time. But perhaps they were only true for herself and not Reno. Katie would never be able to forget him, not ever. He had touched the very heart of her. The nagging feeling of leaving something behind persisted. As did the nagging feeling of something left unfinished, something more to come.

It was early evening when Katie pulled the van into her drive. She felt drugged with fatigue, as if the highway were still passing beneath her. Sam, freed from the confines of the van, bounded ahead, and they both mounted the creaking wooden steps to the apartment.

Normally cozy, the apartment didn't feel so at the moment. After turning up the heat, Katie went through all the rooms flipping on the lights, seeking to drive away the empty feeling of the long-vacated apartment.

Her apartment was the top floor of a converted older home. It was airy and open with a combined living-dining-kitchen area and a bedroom that had once been a sun porch. The basic color was off-white accented with deep browns. Katie had decorated with family pieces and finds from rummage sales. The whole place reflected rather a modern version of a twenties atmosphere.

With Sam haunting her hungrily, Katie filled the dog bowls, then thought of herself. Opening the refrigerator door, she smiled. On the top shelf sat a carton of fresh milk, a dozen eggs and a large homemade pie. Aunt Claire's doing, no doubt. Atop the pie was a folded paper in standing position. It said: Call me, Katie girl!

Katie sat at the table, rested her head in her arms and cried. It was wonderful to have family to care for you as Aunt Claire and Uncle Will did. But right now their love seemed to point up the lack in her life, what she had touched and left behind in Oklahoma.

Her tears flowed, wetting her arms and puddling on the table. Sam came over and rested her head on Katie's knee, whining in concern. Finally Katie was able to slow the flow of tears and gently stroked her loyal friend's head. "I'm okay, girl," she crooned.

In the bathroom she rinsed her face with cool water and, dabbing with the towel, confronted her reflection in the mirror. "For heaven's sake, Katie girl," she said aloud, using the endearment first given to her by her father. "Don't give up yet. You could very well be right about you and Reno. At least give it a chance. Give him some time." She forced a smile and stared at the stranger who looked back with dull eyes.

Knowing she had to, no matter how much she didn't want to, Katie dialed Aunt Claire's number. She felt a flash of guilt realizing she'd forgotten until that moment to call and advise her aunt and uncle of just when she would be returning home.

Aunt Claire answered, then said, "Wait a minute, Katie." Katie heard her aunt muffle the receiver and call to the others in the background to be quiet. Katie thought of the lively atmosphere at the family's home, then pictured Reno and the children. "Oh, now, Katie," Claire breathed. "Where are you? Are you home? And I do wish you'd call more when you're off gallivanting on these trips."

Katie smiled inwardly at the familiar term and answered, "Yes, I'm home. I didn't call before because there was no need. If I spent all my money calling home you wouldn't approve, either."

"Yes . . . well, I'm just glad you're home. You sound tired." Claire Garrett missed very little.

"I am," Katie said. "I drove all day today. Only got in a few minutes ago. Thanks so much for the pie and fresh groceries."

"You're welcome, dear. I'll let you go now. Have a hot bath and a good night's sleep. I'll be in to see you in the morning." Katie knew she was saved only by the lateness of the hour. Otherwise, her aunt would have driven over right then to make sure Katie was really home in the flesh.

After hanging up, she dawdled over another cup of coffee, then hauled from the van only what was absolutely necessary for the night. She would empty everything else and straighten up tomorrow. Following Aunt Claire's suggestion, she took a hot bath and then curled into bed with a big piece of the pie, which turned out to be peach, and a glass of warm milk. As she was reaching to turn out the bedside lamp, the telephone rang. Startled, Katie stared at its ivory smoothness set against the pastel linen of the table cover. Involuntarily she thought of Reno, and a chill shot up her spine. The ring sounded again.

"Hello," she answered, breathless and hesitant.

"Katie? Katie, is that you? This is Cel."

Katie's heart sank, and silence hung for seconds as she gathered herself together. Finally she managed, "Yes, Cel. It's me."

"You sound strange," Katie's boss said. "Are you all right?"

"Fine. Just tired."

"I've been calling all day," Celia said. "I need you in tomorrow. I need help on some editing and also your assistance on an editorial I'm writing. I'm down to the wire before deadline."

"Oh, Celia, I'm tired."

"I know, but I'm in a bind. Sleep late, and come in around ten. We can manage then. Please—I need you."

"Okay," Katie sighed. Celia was a friend in need. At least she had agreed to a few extra hours.

Katie's hand lingered on the telephone as she replaced the receiver. How could she have even thought it would be Reno? She was a fool to try to make more out of their affair than it had been, at least on Reno's part. That is what people called that sort of thing—an affair. The thought stabbed her heart. Punching at her pillow, Katie burrowed into the covers. Oh, she just didn't know. The hunch was so strong, it refused to go away. There was something real and binding between her and Reno Martin. Or was she simply imagining it?

Aunt Claire did indeed arrive bright and early. It was barely eight-thirty when she bustled in the door and gathered Katie in a hug. Holding Katie's face between her hands, she gave her niece a thorough inspection. Aunt Claire always did this, as if to make sure all of Katie had come home and that all was well.

Katie grinned, sincerely glad to see her aunt this morning, her spirits much improved from the night before. The sun was bright and the weatherman promised a warming trend. How could she be down or anything go against her?

"Hello, Aunt Claire," she said. "I've just made coffee."

"You need more than coffee. Go shower, and I'll fix you some breakfast," Claire ordered.

"I have showered, but I'll take you up on the breakfast deal while I dress," Katie said. "But not too much," she called over her shoulder from the bedroom. When she reappeared, Claire had coffee and toast and jam upon the table and was scrambling eggs.

"You need to shop today," the older woman said.

"I know, but it will have to be this evening. I have to get to the office later this morning."

"Katie, you need rest," Claire protested. "You look terrible."

"Thanks."

Claire set the eggs before Katie and joined her at the table. "If you're going to have to go, I'd best talk fast," she said. Katie smothered a grin. Aunt Claire always talked fast.

As they chatted, Claire relating local news of the past week, Katie was keenly aware of her aunt's close scrutiny. *Surely Aunt Claire will see a difference,* Katie thought. *I'm not the same person who left here.*

"Sarah Malloy is pregnant again," Claire was saying. "It's wonderful for her, I guess. I mean, Sarah is very happy. For so long she couldn't get pregnant. But perhaps it is time she stopped. She turns forty-five this year, and this will be her fourth child."

"But Aunt Claire, you had Beth at fifty and always said it was the most blessed experience of your whole life."

"Ah, but Will and I started our family when I was in my twenties, and the rest of our children were nearly grown when Beth was born. Sarah's are all under six. Besides, there is a world of difference between me and Sarah Malloy."

Katie smiled. It was so very true; no one was like Claire Garrett. Now fifty-five, she could easily pass for ten years younger. She was of average build, with a firm full figure, despite, or perhaps because of, the bearing and raising of seven children. She took great delight in her own life and everyone else's, though in a kind, loving way.

"So, how did the trip go?" Claire asked, changing the subject. "Is the van safe?"

"The van is fine and the trip was fine," Katie answered, choosing her words carefully and looking down into her coffee. Reno's face appeared before her, his velvety-brown eyes twinkling with laughter. Katie strove to sound natural. "I got an interesting piece on the woman with the pecan orchard—Annie Anderson. It will probably be slated for the May or June issue of the magazine. I think Ray will be pleased with it."

"What about this man...Mr. Martin did you say? What about him and his family?" Claire sipped her coffee and watched Katie across the top of the cup.

Katie, too, took a sip of coffee, then faced the older woman with what she hoped was a bland expression. "Yes. Reno Martin. Sam and I might still be sitting there if he hadn't come along. His family was very kind, and I may even get another article out of the whole thing." The image of Reno and his strong, sure hands as they pointed out the structure of the house appeared. Katie reached for the coffeepot. "Another cup, Aunt Claire?"

"Umm...please," Claire answered, pushing her cup forward.

Throughout the rest of the visit, Katie had the feeling her aunt waited to hear something, wanted to ask a question. But half an hour later the older woman rose to leave, the question left unasked. Katie was relieved. What could she say to Aunt Claire? "I'm in love and have slept with a man I've only known three days"? Heaven forbid!

At the office she was greeted as if she'd been gone for a month instead of barely two weeks. "I'm more important than I realized. Maybe I should ask for a raise," Katie joked.

"You'll get one, too, if you can help me get through this mountain of work by deadline," Celia called over her shoulder on her way to her office.

Katie rarely saw Celia when she wasn't a bundle of activity and in a rush for something. Following after her calmly, she said, "It can't be as bad as all that. Where's Ray?"

"Little Rock," Celia answered. "And that's why it is as bad as all that. Here, study this copy. See where you can cut. We don't have the room."

So it was back to work as usual, only more of it. The magazine was going into expansion, adding twenty pages and more color. Katie worked ten-hour days during the week, all day Saturday and part of Sunday. The world in which she moved was the same as ever; only Katie wasn't. And she felt she never would be again.

At times Katie found herself simply sitting before her desk, pen poised and daydreaming of herself and Reno together. As if by the very process of picturing him, she could draw Reno to her, will what she wanted to happen.

And she still jumped every time the telephone rang.

At the end of the week, she thought of Summer and her promise to write. A letter might be just the prod Reno needed.

Immediately guilt reared its protesting head. She couldn't use friendship with the child to reach the father. But she would have to write Summer or the girl would be hurt. Resolutely Katie pushed the false guilt aside. It wouldn't matter what happened between her and Reno. Summer was a friend, and Katie did not intend to let the child down.

She wrote to Summer, not mentioning Reno, only saying to tell all the family hello. It was surprisingly easy to think of a hundred things to say to the young girl. Sealing the flap, Katie sprayed the envelope lightly with fragrance and laughed at herself. So much for keeping Reno and Summer separate.

The weeks passed. Mother Nature blessed the whole country with a warm, early spring. Spring bulbs pushed up from the ground and the dormant buds edged out. The Midwest especially enjoyed higher than normal temperatures. By the middle of April, Katie had written Summer twice and received three enthusiastic letters in return. She was getting to know her new young friend.

Still, no communication came from Reno. And Katie was losing hope it ever would.

Her spirits faltered. She tried pushing Reno from her thoughts, but found it difficult, nearly impossible. His image was ingrained in her mind. She lay awake nights, his memory playing at the edge of her thoughts, demanding attention. How could one man have affected her so? And in only a few days of knowing him, a few hours which could be easily counted.

The instinctive tie Katie felt with Reno ebbed, but refused to completely fade. It persisted in tugging teasingly at her heart whenever she tried to deny it. She worked long hours, exhausting herself so sleep would come as soon as her head hit the pillow. Her appetite waned and she drank large quantities of tea and coffee, a fact which didn't help her nerves or sleep patterns. What remained of her normal cheerful disposition was an act.

One morning while riffling through papers strewn across her desk, she upset her coffee mug, sending it crashing to the floor and shattering to pieces. Katie stared at the wreckage for a long moment, her hands shaking, willing herself not to scream. The telephone rang and she ignored it.

I have to stop this, she thought. *I have to put Reno behind me.*

Bending to the floor, she gathered the broken pieces of mug and dabbed at the coffee with tissues. Blessedly the telephone stopped its incessant ringing. Hearing the click of heels approaching, Katie dumped the broken pottery into the trash and turned her back to whoever it was. She wasn't ready for anyone to see her face.

"Katie, there you are." Katie recognized the office receptionist's voice, but didn't turn around.

"Yes, what is it, Virginia?"

"I've been ringing your office," the young girl said reproachfully. "Jim Sheldon's on the phone. When you didn't answer, he insisted I check around for you. Do you want to talk to him?"

"Oh, yes.... Yes, I do," Katie said. "Put him through." She leaned back in her swivel chair and tried to compose herself while waiting for the call to come through.

"Hello, stranger." Jim's low southern drawl came across the wire. "Are you still beautiful and single?"

Katie grinned, picturing his constantly twinkling blue eyes and the shape of his mouth when he smiled, as he was no doubt doing at the moment. "No false modesty here. Yes on both counts. And I wouldn't be a stranger if you would keep in touch," Katie responded.

"You also have such a thing as a telephone," Jim bantered in return.

"I'm not a thoroughly modern woman. You know how old-fashioned my family is. We don't call men. Now, to what do I owe this honor?"

"I'm attending the workshop down in Memphis next weekend. Are you going?"

"I'd not planned on it, Jim. We're working like crazy here. The magazine is expanding."

"So I've heard. There's still an opening here for you should you change your mind," Jim said.

"I won't. I'm perfectly satisfied where I am."

"Okay. But I won't quit trying. And how about changing your mind and coming to the workshop. It's been a long time, Katie," Jim said huskily, and Katie warmed to his tone. No doubt about it; Jim was a very sexy man. Perhaps with his help, she could succeed in pushing Reno completely from memory.

"So, you've convinced me, Jim. I will see you in Memphis."

Katie found Celia at her desk, telephone cradled between neck and shoulder while she sorted through mounds of paper in wild disarray on her desk. Raising a finger in Katie's direction, she said into the phone, "I'll have to get back to you," and replaced the receiver none too gently. Turning to Katie, "I've been wanting to see you," she said, before Katie could even open her mouth. "I know something is up with you, and I've waited long enough. Okay, okay, I know you will say you can handle it. You always say that...about your father, selling the house, moving. Maybe you don't want to talk about it, but I can suggest you get away again for a few days."

"Cel, if you will just let me get a word in and not do both your own questions and my answers," Katie said with a smile.

Celia looked sheepish. "You're right, dear. Go ahead."

"I don't want to talk about it."

Celia let out a full laugh. "Ah, Katie. Well, you must have come in here for something."

"Yes. I concur with your suggestion of a few days off. I'd like to go to the Southern Magazine Writer's Workshop in Memphis next weekend. I'll need that Friday off."

"Umm." Celia sifted through some papers, then said, "Here it is. I can get you a room at the Lexington, where the workshop is to be held, for half price. Pack your bags."

Katie entered the lobby of the Lexington Inn with just under an hour to spare before the start of the first lecture. Thick tan carpet gave slightly beneath her Western boots as she made her way to the long, polished wood registration desk. There were several clerks on duty, busily running back and forth, serving numerous guests. Katie set her two small pieces of luggage down and waited her turn behind three other people.

The Lexington's lobby was large and followed the trend of modern motel-hotels in returning to the luxurious amenities. There were plush chairs and sofas in varying tans and maroons, burnished oak tables, an enormous fireplace and an array of tall potted ferns.

A large number of people milled around and an oversize colorful banner welcoming the members of the fifteenth annual Workshop hung high on the wall. A smaller sign directed people of the conference down a hall where Katie presumed the lecture rooms were located.

When it came Katie's turn for registration, the desk clerk looked up and raked her with his eyes, taking in her blue cotton T-shirt and her dusty faded jeans. An aura of haughty disdain swept his face as he raised an eyebrow and said, "May I help you?"

Katie's eyes met his. "Katherine Garrett—with the conference. I have a reservation."

He tapped his pencil on the desk and ran a finger down the reservation sheet. "I'm sorry, miss. I don't see your name listed. Are you sure you have the right hotel? The Lexington?"

Katie smothered a smile at the clerk's accent on "Lexington." He seemed a man who had stepped from another century. "Check the name of Whitney Publications. They made the reservation," she said patiently.

The clerk checked again. "Oh, yes. Here it is. I apologize, Miss Garrett." He didn't sound at all sorry. He had her sign the registration form, then reached behind him for a key and passed it across the counter with another of his scornful looks.

Lifting her chin and lilting her voice to match, Katie said, "Please have a club sandwich and a pot of tea sent to my room immediately!" Then slowly she winked one eye suggestively. Allowing herself the pleasure of seeing mild shock register on the clerk's face, she whirled from the desk before he could catch her own face break into silent laughter.

The next instant Katie collided with a firm shoulder. The first things to register were a man's blue denim shirt, tall lean frame and strong hands which grabbed her by both arms. She looked up with surprise into the smiling face of Jim Sheldon.

"Well, hello," he said. They both laughed at once.

"Did you just get in, too?" Katie asked, spying Jim's suitcase.

"Yes, and I caught you teasing that poor man," Jim answered, nodding in the direction of the registration desk. The clerk had now turned his back and his balding head waxed white in the fluorescent lighting from above.

"You did, huh?" Katie chuckled. "I couldn't help it. He's such a pompous ass. Besides, it livened up my day...and his."

"Well, wait here while I get my key from the pompous ass, and I'll help you get your bags to your room."

Katie glanced at her watch. "Can't. I've only forty minutes before the first lecture to shower and change. Anyway, this place has people to do that sort of thing if you wish. But these are light. See?" She easily lifted her cases, one in each hand, for proof. "Gotta run."

"Wait." Jim reached out and grabbed her arm, bent his lanky frame, and brushed his lips to hers. "See you later."

Katie grinned slowly and looked at him from beneath her long lashes. "Yes, later." She turned away, remembering the way Reno's kisses had made her lips tingle, burn. The way he had set her on fire. Would his memory always step unbidden into her thoughts?

Chapter Nine

The room was spacious, with the same plush carpeting and color theme as the lobby. Katie pulled the heavy drapes wide, allowing the bright western sun to shine through the large picture window.

Room service was prompt, bringing her tray only minutes later. Taking a bite out of the sandwich, Katie shook off her sandals, rummaged through her case for a robe and headed for the shower.

Emerging from the bathroom, her hair wrapped in a towel to keep it dry while showering, Katie heard a light tapping. It was coming from a side door she'd not noticed before. Apparently it led to an adjoining room. The door was double locked by the knob and a sliding bolt. The tapping sounded again, rhythmic and louder.

Cautiously, Katie unlocked the knob and slid back the bolt. Hesitant but curious, she opened the door. Jim Sheldon stood leaning against the doorframe, another door on his side wide open. He grinned down at her. "My, what becoming headgear."

"What in the world did you tell them to get this room number?" Katie asked, mystified.

"I didn't tell the old pompous ass anything," Jim said, indicating the clerk who had registered him. "He apparently saw our little kiss and decided all on his own. Handing me my key, he happened to mention my room was right next to 'my friend's,' Miss Garrett."

Katie eyed him skeptically.

Jim raised both hands in protest. "Honest—it's the truth."

"Well, I have to get ready." Before Jim could utter another word, Katie closed the door right in his face, but not hard. To tease Jim, she didn't bother to lock it. Then she wondered at her action. Did she really mean it in a teasing manner, or was she hoping for more? It didn't really matter. Jim wasn't a man to take advantage.

Many times, since they had first met two years ago, Jim had come on to Katie, but never forcefully. He had simply made it known to her he would like a more intimate relationship.

Though she'd been attracted to Jim and liked him immensely, Katie shied away from the bed scene he wanted. And that was strictly all he was offering. Jim Sheldon was wonderfully tempting, but not quite enough.

Katie still wanted what she could not have. Reno. To share with him a home, a family. She rubbed her eyes with the flat of her hands, as if by that motion she could brush him from memory.

At three o'clock Katie entered the lobby. Chuckling within, she thought of the pompous desk clerk and what he would think of her now. She was dressed in eggshell-white twill trouser pants and matching cotton crocheted sweater. Her full-bodied auburn hair was swept back on one side and secured with a white comb. Low-heeled sandals, also an eggshell white, enclosed her feet, and small gold loop earrings graced her ears. Suspended on a chain around her neck was a pendant of gold filigree set with tiny opals that had belonged to her mother.

Following the signs, Katie hurried down the hall from the main lobby. A friendly woman checked her name for the conference and gave her a name badge to wear. Allowing for late arrivals, the lecture had not started precisely at three o'clock and more people were still coming behind Katie.

She took a seat in the back row and opened a small pocket notepad. Five minutes later Jim Sheldon slipped quietly into the seat beside her.

"If old pompous ass had seen you looking like this, he really would have gotten ideas," Jim whispered.

"Seems like he got enough as it was. I still think you told him something to get that room."

Jim grinned. Then Katie's attention was called to the front of the room as the presiding speaker approached the podium and coughed into the microphone.

Katie recognized the speaker as Web Barinson, a noted nature researcher and writer, who also wrote some fiction, usually with country or rustic pioneer life as a background. She tried to pay close attention as Barinson introduced the other writers and editors who had lecture sessions scheduled, but her unruly thoughts kept straying to Reno. Absently she doodled on the notepad.

Her mind remembered everything as if she had just seen him yesterday. She saw the dark lock of hair that fell stubbornly across his forehead and the thickness of his mustache, tinged with gray. Mostly, she remembered how sad, but determined, he had looked the last time he faced her.

Why? Why now, of all times, did memory of him return in full force to haunt her? She had thought that by coming to the conference, seeing Jim Sheldon, she could push Reno's memory from her mind. Instead it seemed to have worked in reverse. She felt the tie to him ever stronger. Imperceptibly she shook her head, bringing her thoughts back to the moment at hand. Jim gave her a curious glance to which she did not respond.

At four-fifteen the introductory session broke for dinner, but a lecture was scheduled for seven-thirty that evening.

"You don't really want to go to the session tonight, do you?" Jim asked.

"What else do you have in mind?" she said as she walked with Jim to join others of the conference gathering in groups in the lobby.

"Dinner here and dancing at a country-and-western club called the Honky Tonk. Really." Jim laughed as Katie raised an eyebrow at the corny-sounding name. "It's down the street about a mile. New. Just opened about six months ago—large wooden floor, live band—supposed to be the 'in' place."

"How do you know so much?"

"I get around," Jim countered, grinning mysteriously.

"Katie. Katie and Jim!" At the sound of their names, both looked around to see a pretty, blond, rather plump young woman hurrying their way.

"Well, hey, Rhonda!" Katie cried and opened her arms wide to give her old friend a hug. Rhonda Birdwell had been on the magazine staff with Katie, but upon publishing a novel had quit to write fiction full-time.

"I'm so thrilled to see you both," Rhonda said, including Jim in a friendly greeting by taking his hand.

"So, how's books?" Jim asked.

"I've got a new one coming out next month," Rhonda said proudly. "With the moderate success of my first book and selling short stories, I've been able to eat—but just barely." She laughed. "I'm hoping this workshop helps."

Seconds later the three of them were joined by two other workshop participants, Joe Thomas and Belle Meeker. Jim knew them well, but to Katie they were only acquaintances. They free-lanced, having written many pieces for Jim's magazine. Their expert talents were relatively expensive and Whitney Publications couldn't afford them.

Jim began coordinating the evening for everyone, turning it into a party affair.

Katie's attention to all Jim's plans wavered as she sensed someone's eyes upon her. Searching the lobby quickly, her gaze was caught and held by piercing dark brown eyes she knew so well. Katie sucked in a sharp breath. *Reno.* He stared at her from across the room. The bustle and activity of those around her faded into the background as she saw only him. He looked every inch the grand ranch owner in an expertly styled, tan Western suit that he wore easily. Slowly he reached up and tipped the brim of his Stetson to Katie.

A smile of undisguised pleasure broke across her face. "Excuse me a moment," she said, absently touching Rhonda's arm and never taking her eyes from Reno's.

They met each other in the middle of the lobby.

"Hello, Miss Katie," Reno said, taking her hand and drawing her from the flow of traffic to the side of the lobby containing floor-to-ceiling windows. The late-afternoon sun shone brightly through the glass, allowing Katie to clearly see Reno's face, every feature she remembered and had focused on in her dreams.

He was very tanned, the hand holding hers rough and callused. He was thinnner, lighter.

"Hello, Reno," she said, her heart pounding wildly. "This is a surprise."

"For me, too. You here for the Workshop?" He nodded in the direction of the large poster.

"Yes. And you?"

"Horse auction."

"All the way from Oklahoma?" Katie said.

Reno smiled gently. "It's not uncommon. Tennessee is known to have some fine racing stock."

"I didn't think." They paused a moment, Katie searching his eyes, his expression, and realizing Reno was doing the same to her. Then Katie said, "How are the children? Maggie?"

"Good. Summer writes you, doesn't she?"

"Yes, quite often," Katie said.

"Then you know all there is to know," Reno said. "Summer and Tobias, her new boyfriend. The first of many, I guess. It's pretty hard on ol' dad."

Katie grinned. "Yes, she's mentioned him, but only a bit."

"You should hear it at our house."

The two fell silent, Katie wishing she *could* hear it at their house. She watched him carefully, trying to keep her emotions in check. Reno seemed so calm and controlled, as if their meeting was a casual, pleasant happenstance and no more. But to Katie it was more. So much more. There was no real way to hide her pleasure, and she didn't try.

"I've missed you," she said quietly.

"I've missed you, too." His velvet eyes burned into hers and then a coldness fell across his face, closing his expression to all emotion. Katie felt a cool draft touch her shoulders. Reno glanced at his watch. "I've got to run—business dinner." He inclined his head toward the front doors, and for the first time Katie noticed two men watching them curiously.

Bitterly disappointed, she'd be damned if she would say more. She had practically thrown herself at him as it was. "I'm glad we ran into each other. Maybe I'll see you again sometime," she said coolly. Reno's jaw tightened, but before he could respond she turned and walked crisply to where Jim and Rhonda stood waiting.

Holding back tears, she clenched her fists, trying desperately to paste a smile to her lips as she rejoined her friends.

"Who in the world is that hunk of a man, Katie?" Rhonda breathed, curiosity fairly oozing from her pores.

"Oh, just someone I used to know," Katie said shortly. "Are we ready for dinner?"

By Katie's manner, Rhonda and Jim sensed better than to say more, but the two exchanged concerned glances.

"Yes. I'm starved," Jim said, taking Katie's arm. "Let's eat. The food here is fantastic."

"Well, how often do you come to a swank place like this, Jim?" Rhonda asked, stepping to his other side.

"Several times a year," Jim teased. "Don't you know—I'm a man of the world."

Jim was seeking to lighten the mood, and Katie obliged by grinning to please him, though she felt more like she was gritting her teeth.

"Yes, Rhonda, Jim is a man of many worlds. Not all of them here with us," Katie bantered.

"Stick with me, girls. I'll show you a wild time." With Jim guiding, the three linked arms and regally entered the formal dining room.

After placing their order, while waiting for cocktails to arrive, Katie excused herself and went to the ladies' room. Two women sat before a long vanity in the richly carpeted lounge, so Katie walked on through to the smaller mirrors in the rest room. Placing her purse on the metal shelf, she pulled out a tissue and dabbed at imaginary smudges of mascara.

Reno. Who could believe she would run into him here like this? Memphis was a large city. What cruel chance had brought them together in the same hotel at the same time? Was it chance? And had some instinct within her picked up on his presence even before she saw him? Was that why memories of him had been incessantly plaguing her thoughts the last few hours?

It didn't matter. He obviously didn't want anything to do with her. If she hadn't seen him, he probably would have left without saying a word.

Dreams, dreams, Katie thought, tears clouding her eyes. Foolish, childish dreams, and that's all they were. Now she must separate the dreams from the reality and accept it.

Seconds ticked by as Katie observed herself in the mirror. She could say she was ill and beg off for the rest of the night. The thought of the empty hotel room changed her mind. Oh, she didn't know what she wanted. Damn, Reno. Just when she was getting everything together again he had turned her world upside down once more.

With hard, swift strokes, Katie took a brush to her hair and forced herself under control to face Jim and Rhonda. Replacing the brush in her purse and closing the purse with a strong snap, she squared her shoulders and strode resolutely back into the restaurant.

Surprisingly, as the evening wore on Katie did enjoy herself. The food was excellent and Jim's and Rhonda's light warm humor was a balm to her soul. Jim teased her seductively with his hand beneath the table, tickling her knee and stroking upward until she grabbed his hand. All the while the two of them kept straight faces and listened attentively as Rhonda talked. Katie knew Jim was teasing but at the same time trying her out.

She wished she could respond as he wanted her to, wished she could fall into his waiting arms and take comfort. At least he wanted her. But she couldn't. She had no real passion to give. She would only be pretending at something which wasn't love and never would be.

Sensing Katie's reluctance, Jim gave her hand a gentle squeeze. His eyes spoke a silent acceptance. Momentarily, a surge of affection for him swelled within her. She wanted to change her mind, to allow herself the comfort he was willing to give. But Reno's image intruded and refused to be banished from her mind.

As they walked through the lobby to Jim's rented car, Katie involuntarily scanned faces. Even during the short ride to the club she was tensed, her eyes checking for Reno's truck. *This is crazy,* she thought. *I've got to stop.*

Jim pulled into the blacktopped parking area of a large building, the front of which was fashioned as an Old West saloon and made of rustic pine boards. The name Honky Tonk blazed across the top in gaudy flickering lights.

The club proved to be a lively place even early in the evening. Now barely past seven o'clock, it was rapidly filling with people. Jim led a meandering path through tables and people to where Joe and Belle had already laid claim to a table big enough for the group. Politely sliding out a chair for Rhonda, he took Katie's hand and whirled her out onto the polished wood dance floor.

"Jim," Katie said loudly enough to be heard over the music. He either didn't hear or ignored her. "Jim. Jim!" she said, pulling his hand but not wishing to make a scene.

Still he ignored her, leading in a lively two-step around the other couples on the floor and stopping in front of the band. He leaned over to say something to the bass player. The music was much too loud for Katie to catch a word of what he said.

When his attention was back on her, she managed, "Jim, I really don't want to dance."

Pulling her in a close embrace, he said, "Oh, sure you do. It'll be good for you."

Anger at the whole male species rose in Katie. "How do you know what will be good for me? And you are not dancing to the music."

At that moment the music changed to a slow number, and Jim gave Katie an I-told-you-so look. Gathering her even closer, he rested his cheek against her hair and moved his body against hers.

"Look, Jim, I tried to tell you. I'm just not ready for—" Katie began, trying to push away from his warm thighs, but Jim cut her off.

"Shuush," he said, still holding her firmly. "The guy you've been watching for all evening is here." Jim spoke low, his breath brushing her ear.

"What?" Katie sucked in her breath. "How in the world . . ."

"I'm a journalist, a magazine reporter, remember? I'm trained to notice little things like a woman's preoccupation and wandering eyes. I added two and two and came up with you and him. And he is now standing over at the bar."

"Oh," Katie said in a small voice, laying her cheek against Jim's chest.

"Do you want to leave?"

"No. I just want to have a good time and forget him."

"Okay, my lady." Holding her close, Jim waltzed her around the floor.

Katie could not resist glancing toward the bar and seeing Reno. His back was to her as he leaned against the bar with one elbow and talked to the two men Katie had seen earlier at the Lexington.

Back at the table, Jim pulled his chair closer to Katie's and draped an arm loosely around its back. Except for a few dances with Rhonda, he stayed by Katie all evening. Striving to be heard over the music, the talk was lively and loud. With a great effort, Katie managed to keep her eyes from straying any farther than to the others at the table.

She and Jim danced quite a bit, but every moment Katie was self-conscious, extremely aware Reno was in the club. Once, while on the dance floor, she caught sight of him dancing with a shapely blonde. Envy swept through her. Or was it jealousy? Perhaps the two were the same.

Two other men attending the Workshop at the Lexington, friends of Belle Meeker, joined their party, adding to the already rowdy antics at the table. Katie sat back, her mind trying to close out the loud talking and even louder music that was beginning to wear on her nerves.

A shadow appeared at her side and a warm hand pressed her shoulder. Katie looked up quickly to see Reno bending near.

"May I have this dance, Miss Katie?"

Jim put a restraining hand on her arm, then rose to face Reno. Jim was the taller man, but Reno's presence seemed to dominate the space.

"That is with your permission, of course," Reno said, addressing Jim.

Jim shot Katie a questioning look. Unable to speak, she put her hand in Reno's and walked out to the now packed dance floor.

The number was a slow one, and Reno held Katie in his arms, pressing her against his full length. His breath was hot and smelled of whiskey as it fanned her cheek. She moved with him to the beat of the music, her body rigid. Her emotions tumbled over one another: anger, uncertainty, longing. She didn't know how to act, but her body decided for her and she relaxed as Reno pressed harder and moved seductively against her. A throbbing began deep in the pit of her stomach and spread upward. Her muscles melted against Reno's stronger frame.

Slanting his head back to see her face, Reno asked, "Who's the guy you're with?"

The tone of his voice startled her, and Katie faced him squarely. A grin touched his lips, and she knew instinctively Reno was well aware of what was happening within her. "Jim Sheldon—an old friend," Katie said, her voice unsteady. Could he actually be jealous?

"It seems there's a lot more to your conference than just notes and lectures."

"Umm . . . to your horse-buying business, too."

She sensed rather than saw Reno's smile as once more he drew her close and she pressed her face to his neck, blanking out for a few precious moments all else but being in his strong arms. He glided her slowly across the polished wood floor and Katie felt again the magic kinship of her spirit with his. When the music stopped she stepped back and looked at him blankly, trying to bring herself back to the moment. He didn't let go of her hand; instead he led her to the lively beat of a two-step as the band started up once more. The two whirled around the crowded floor, their eyes intent on each other, oblivious to the occasional brush against other dancers.

This time when the tune ended, Reno led the way back to her table. Gallantly, he held her chair and nodded a polite thanks to Jim, as if casually returning something he'd borrowed.

"Thank you," he said to Katie, his jaw tight and eyes unreadable.

Katie said nothing, only watched him turn and walk back to join his friends at the bar. Remaining silent under Jim's questioning gaze, she stared into the amber liquid of her drink and thoughtfully swished the melting ice cubes. Making no attempt to join in the boisterousness at the table, Katie tried to chase the lump from her throat with the burning liquid. She felt as if she were choking. Several minutes later she turned to Jim.

"I'm going back to the hotel. I'll catch a cab," she said, leaning close to be heard above the racket.

"Wait." Jim followed after her and took her arm. "I'll take you back. Rhonda is having a fine time with Joe anyway. She can ride with him."

"Oh, Jim. There's no need. You stay and have fun."

"I'm taking you back," he said firmly.

The ride back to the Lexington was quiet. Jim tried once. "What's going on with you and this guy?"

Katie sighed and said only, "I wish I knew."

In the lobby she turned to Jim. "Thank you, Jim . . ."

"I'll see you to your room," he cut in, resolutely taking her elbow and entering the empty elevator.

Their steps made no sound on the thick carpeting as they walked along the hall to Katie's room. Katie unlocked the door and Jim placed both hands on her shoulders, turning her to face him.

"Katie, every time we've been together I've tried to get closer to you. Maybe I've put the cart before the horse, but no guy in his right mind would *not* want to go to bed with you." Jim paused, and his blue eyes searched hers. "When I saw you this afternoon, I knew how I felt. I care, Katie. And I'd like to be more than just a friend. If it's not too late."

Katie's eyes widened, startled by his admission. "Oh, Jim, I'm so confused right now." She groped for words, needing to be honest with him. "I care for you, too; I have for a long time. But I've fallen in love . . . one of those one-side love affairs, I'm afraid. Before I'm capable of giving to anyone else, I have to get myself straightened away." Her brows knitted together in concern, she looked at him questioningly. "Can you understand?"

"Yes." He leaned down and lightly kissed her forehead. "If it doesn't work out for you, Katie, I'd like to give us a try. Now, get some rest. I'll see you in the morning," Jim said, turning toward his own room.

Stepping into the darkened room, Katie closed the door and leaned back against it, hot unshed tears burning her eyes.

Chapter Ten

Lifting his glass of whiskey from the bar, Reno turned just in time to see Katie and Jim Sheldon walking toward the front doors. An unfamiliar ache rose within and he turned back to the two friends he was with, Louis Strait and Web Connors, and tried to follow along with their conversation. It was hard to keep up, though. He kept seeing Katie's red lips and her haunting green eyes. The young blonde he'd danced some with before came up boldly and asked him for another dance. Reno went along with her for a few dances and when they returned to the bar another blonde, a friend of the one Reno was with, was hanging on to Louis. The two women gave their names, but Reno didn't bother to remember them as he ordered another round of drinks for them all.

Web Connors begged off, saying he had a wife waiting for him at home. Reno knew he did, too; a real pretty woman with hair much the same color as Katie's. At the thought of

Katie—and Katie and Jim together—the ache started afresh. Involuntarily seeking comfort, he ran a hand up and down the blonde's back, smiling at her. Coyly she smiled back. It wasn't any good. No woman had been any good for him since that day with Katie. When he'd tried starting up again with Diane Holt, she'd gotten riled enough over his lack of attention, she'd thrown a beer at him and said she never wanted to see him again.

Reno stayed with Louis and the blondes, drinking and trying to enjoy himself, but when the young woman hinted at returning to her place, Reno politely excused himself. He felt revulsion: at the woman, at himself, at the whole noisy club.

Outside he took in a good clean breath, allowing his fogged brain to clear somewhat, and hailed a cab, leaving the rented car for Louis. When the cab pulled under the covered entry of the Lexington, Reno carelessly peeled a ten from his money clip and handed it across to the driver, who thanked him profusely.

Stopping a moment, he carefully placed his Stetson upon his head and straightened his coat and tie, then pushed purposefully through the wide glass doors. Katie and a rising ache within him seemed to propel him toward the registration desk.

It was past one o'clock, and the lobby was quiet, just one clerk on duty.

"Can I help you, sir?" the clerk asked.

"What is Katie—Katherine Garrett's room number?" Reno said.

The clerk hesitated. "I'm sorry, sir. We're not allowed to give out that information." He eyed Reno skeptically. "I...I could ring her room for you, sir, but it is late."

But Reno was already turning away, inwardly cursing himself. "No...forget it," he growled. What had gotten into him anyway? Katie wasn't about to see him... And the last thing he needed was Katie Garrett. He'd broken from her once, hated doing it. He didn't intend to get involved with her again.

He headed for the bar and ordered another whiskey. He took a drink, then stared into the amber liquid. *The same color as her hair.* With a hard smack of the glass to the bar, Reno again headed for the registration desk.

He looked at the clerk for a moment, contemplating grabbing him by the throat, but reason prevailed.

The clerk looked back. "Sir?"

"Hand me a piece of paper. I'd like to leave a note for Miss Garrett," Reno said.

"Yes, sir." The clerk passed over a sheet of paper and pen.

Reno scribbled on it, then folded it in half and handed it back. He watched the clerk turn and search the cubbyholes lining the end of the wall, the room numbers marked beneath small, but clearly visible. The clerk slipped the paper into the one marked 326. Reno turned and strode toward the elevators.

On the way up, he argued with himself. He wasn't stone sober, but then he wasn't so drunk that the ache would go away. Only Katie could remove the ache. Dominating all other thought at the moment was the overriding desire to see and hold this woman who kept popping unbidden into his mind. Coming to Katie's door, he leaned a hand against the doorframe and checked the room number once more. Then he pounded. "Katie!" He pounded again. "Katie!" he said even louder, his voice just below a shout.

The door flew open and there she stood, her auburn hair tumbling down across her shoulders, billowing out soft and wild. Light shining from behind illuminated the shadow of her body through the thin pink fabric of her robe. Her green eyes flashed up at him from a pale face, cheeks flushed from sleep.

"What are you doing?" she demanded. "Do you want to wake the whole floor?"

His eyes watching those inviting red lips closely, Reno pushed her inside, kicked the door shut with one foot and pinned Katie up against a closet door, his arms on either side of her shoulders. Slowly he removed one arm to tilt back his Stetson.

Katie glared up at him, her green eyes flashing, the fine cords of her neck tight in anger. "What do you want?" she said, her voice a hoarse whisper.

"I want to do this." Reno caught the sweet fragrance of perfume and woman mixed as he bent his head to kiss her.

Reno had been drinking. Catching the nauseating smell of alcohol, Katie twisted her head to escape his lips. At the same time she longed to give herself to his strong frame now pushing up against her. Her pulse pounded in her ears as she felt the heat of his hard thighs rubbing against her. But how dare he think he could just waltz in whenever it suited him and take her to bed!

"Reno. Reno. No!" She gasped and pushed at him with all her might. At that moment the door connecting Katie's room with Jim's opened.

"Katie? Katie, you all right?" Jim called, slowly pushing the door open.

Hearing the male voice, Reno whirled and stared in surprise at Jim Sheldon standing in the connecting door dressed only in jeans. He turned back to Katie, his eyes brittle with anger, jaw muscle tensed. Addressing Jim, but looking at Katie, he said, "I'd like to speak to the lady—alone."

"I'm okay, Jim," Katie agitatedly smoothed her hair. "Really. It's all right."

Jim hesitated, clenching and unclenching both fists. Then he nodded. "If you need me..." He didn't bother to finish, only stepped back through the door, closing it softly.

Reno's dark eyes bore into Katie. "Pretty convenient for 'old friends.' No wonder you didn't want any kissing. You were worn out."

The crude remark stabbed deeply, but Katie's pride came to the forefront. Let him believe what he wished, Katie thought as she raised her chin and looked at him defiantly, saying nothing. She would not honor such a comment with even a denial. The two glared hotly at each other.

"Oh, hell," Reno said huskily, and before Katie realized his intentions, he'd reached out and caught her to him.

Katie attempted to resist, but Reno's strong arms held her tightly. Placing a restraining hand behind her head, he brought his lips down to hers, pressing roughly, forcing her lips to part.

Katie could not hold herself immune. His lips were warm, sweet. She caught the familiar scent of his skin, mixed with the odor of whiskey. Relaxing toward his hard frame, a low groan formed deep in her throat.

Sensing her response, Reno gentled. Massaging her silken lips with his own, he pulled away, then tenderly pressed down again. Instinctively Katie parted her lips wider to allow his probing tongue greater access. She caught her breath as somehow his hands found a way beneath her robe, caressed her skin and pressed the small of her back, igniting a fire which flared swiftly up from her stomach. Her hands wound around his neck and curled into the thickness of his hair as she pressed her body even harder against him. All thought, all reasoning, evaporated into a mist of euphoria, and Katie lost herself in total longing for fulfillment of the moment.

Then Reno pulled away, dragging his mouth from hers. Dazed, Katie attempted to cling to him, struggling to focus and bring herself back to reality. Gently he slipped her hands from around his neck. She swayed toward him and he steadied her, holding her shoulders.

"No, Katie," he said, his voice a graveled whisper. Firmly he placed her from him. As she watched him in total confusion, he said, "That's all I came for." Straightening his Stetson, he walked to the door.

"Reno." At her call he stopped and turned, his hand resting upon the doorknob. Katie looked at him in the dim lamplight. The brim of the Stetson shadowed his eyes, making them unreadable. "It's not what you think . . . between Jim and me."

"I know. You just answered that question."

She looked at him evenly. It had to be said. She couldn't let him walk out of her life and not be sure he knew. "I love you." Katie held her breath as the words seemed to float in the air.

"Katie . . ." Reno paused, staring down at his boot. Then he turned toward her once again. "Katie, I think I'm in love with you, too. But sometimes that isn't enough. I'd like to take you to bed right now . . . I want you . . ." He drew in a ragged breath. "But that's not fair to you. It isn't your way . . . and, hell, I don't think it can be my way with you. Give me some time, Katie. I've got to be sure. I can't make any mistakes."

A wealth of love rose within Katie. Seeing Reno's fear, she longed to hold him, comfort him as she would a small boy. But Reno wasn't a boy; he was a man. And he didn't want her comfort, was beyond comfort in a situation in which only he could decide what was best for himself.

"There are no guarantees in life, Reno. You can't let yourself be so afraid of making mistakes that you miss the living. And what's between us can't be denied. We have a beginning. It is up to us what we make of it." Her voice was soft, but not pleading. Relief washed over her from at last being able to express her feelings. She looked at him steadily, the undisguised love she felt written plainly on her face.

"You're the man I've waited half my life for, Reno Martin. Are you going to throw away what I'm offering you?"

In the stillness of the moment, Reno regarded her. Katie's pulse hammered in her temples as she held her breath—waiting.

Reno released the doorknob. Slowly his hand went up, caught his hat by the brim and tossed it to the desk. A half-grin lit his face. "That's all I need . . . a woman with common sense."

He gathered her to him, rubbing his cheek roughly against hers. The stubble of his unshaven face burned Katie's more tender skin, but the feeling went unnoticed as the sensations of desire burned even hotter.

"I love you, Katie." Reno breathed the words softly in her ear. Katie moaned aloud, melting against him.

"Reno . . ." Her breath caught in the back of her throat. Again his hands made their way beneath the thin robe, exploring the smoothness of her skin, then pressing tightly at the back of her waist. Raising up on tiptoes, Katie nuzzled at his neck, luxuriating in his warm smell, the saltiness of his skin.

Joy flooded her whole being. *I love him. I love him.* The words sang within, her heart full to bursting.

Reno's lips moved to her throat, burning a trail down across one shoulder. His hands fumbled with the tie of her robe and then the fabric slipped free to the floor. Katie gasped as Reno's hands explored her heated skin, flitting everywhere at once. She had to have him, to become a part of him. To that end, she pressed even closer, pulling at the purl snaps enclosing the top of his Western shirt. A low growl vibrated from Reno's throat, and he pressed his mouth over hers, claiming her fiercely.

Easily Reno lifted Katie into his arms, carrying her the few steps to the bed. His dark gaze fastened on hers as he laid her upon the cool sheets. All the passion, longing and love that she herself was experiencing reflected from the depths of his brown-black eyes. Drawing in a ragged breath Reno allowed his eyes to caress her body. Parting his shirt, Katie raked her fingers down the smooth skin of his chest, hooking into the waist of his jeans. Reno bent his head and lightly brushed her breasts with his lips, teasing fleetingly at their pink nipples with his tongue.

Arching toward him, Katie tugged at his shirt impatiently. "Reno...Reno..." she moaned, needing to feel his body next to her.

Straightening, Reno switched off the bedside lamp, plunging the room into total darkness. Katie waited impatiently, hearing the rustle of movement as Reno shed his clothes. Then all was still. She sensed Reno standing there but could see nothing in the pitch blackness of the room, the heavy drapes pulled tightly and blocking out all light. "Reno?" she whispered. He moved upon the carpet, and there came a slight click. Katie smiled; he had locked the connecting door.

"I don't intend to have any interruptions," he said with a low chuckle as he stretched out beside her.

Immediately Katie melted into the strength of his arms, relief washing over her. He had stayed. She didn't worry about tomorrow. He was here now.

Reno pulled her halfway across on top of him and caught her mouth to his, his kiss probing and demanding. Clinging to him, Katie massaged his chest with her breasts, savoring the delicious closeness and warmth of him. His body was so hot it made the surrounding air seem cold. There was no thought in her world now, only feelings.

In a fluid movement, Reno rolled her to her back. Dragging his lips from hers, he nibbled at her ear, then with his lips seared a trail down her skin to the ivory softness of her breasts. She caught her breath in shallow gasps as he probed and massaged, seemingly aware of her every response.

Gently he kneaded and stroked low on her stomach. He remembered, Katie realized as she, too, sought the sensitive places of Reno's body, remembered from that day so long ago.

Sensation after sensation flowed over Katie as the tide upon a beach. Desire welled within her, so strong she felt she was drowning. Tears sprang to her eyes. Embarrassed at feelings she had never known before, Katie sought control.

Reno shifted his weight against her side and covered her legs with his. His motions slowed as he smoothed his hands tenderly over her body. Katie knew he was responding to her sudden tenseness by gently easing her body into relaxation. Wonder at his care broke over her.

His hands were powerful. Hands that could easily wield an ax, toss fifty-pound feed sacks, bridle a horse, now touched her as he would a rare gem, gently, almost reverently. And with every touch he spoke his love.

Emotion flowed again and Katie rose high on its wave. Her heart overflowed with love, and a longing so intense she thought she would burst filled her completely. She sought physically to give this love to Reno. She moaned aloud, not caring how she sounded, only knowing that she wanted Reno to wash away the ache.

Reno covered her with his body, nuzzling her neck as he slipped between her legs. For a brief second, relief rushed over her. Then he was moving against her, and Katie lost all reasoning. She was alternately drowning and floating high in a blue sky. A muffled cry sounded, but it seemed far away and unrelated to her. She matched his rhythm, giving herself to him, taking him into her.

Then she was coming back. She became aware of the pulse beating loud within her ears and of gasping for breath. Reno lifted his heavy chest from hers, resting his weight on his arms, and she felt him shudder. He was so warm. He kissed and nuzzled her ear, her hair at the temples. She was part of him and she loved him. Tears trickled from the outer corners of her closed eyes and fell down the side of her face. Reno felt their wetness on his own cheek and lightly kissed at the salty streaks.

"Aw, Katie, don't..."

"It's not...it's that it's all so beautiful."

"Shush...I know, I know." He kissed her lips softly, then her neck and shoulder. At the same time he moved again within her. And again the fire burned and her breath came in gasps. A flame of desire shot through her and she pulled at Reno's muscled back, arching against him as he strained against her. It was gentler this time, but even more magical. The sensation ebbed from them both, and Reno tenderly eased away, lying beside her, kissing her shoulder and stroking her silken skin with his work-roughened hand.

He rolled to his back, and Katie molded herself against his rock-hard body, resting her head in the crook of his arm. They lay thus, touching body and soul, complete in their own world. Allowing her hand to play across his expanse of chest, feeling a sparse hair here and there, Katie savored the wonder of the moment. She wanted to impress into memory the smell of his skin, the feel of it, and just how he breathed and felt against her. She wanted to remember forever their sharing of this golden glow and what it felt like to be a part of this man she had given her love to.

Katie stirred and smiled, half in a dream, half in real memories of the night before. Chilled, she reached out for Reno's warmth, but her hands contacted only bare, cool sheets. Rising up on one elbow, she listened, realizing she was alone. The room was no longer in pitch blackness; daylight filtered in around the edges of the heavy drapes. Though she knew he had gone, her eyes involuntarily scanned the room, her mind rebelling. *No! No! He couldn't be gone.* She slipped from the bed and ran to the bathroom. The door was open, the small tiled room hollow. *Reno was gone.*

Slowly Katie struggled to bring her mind back to working order. Surely Reno wouldn't have just left, with no word, nothing. Naked and suddenly terribly cold, Katie reached for her robe thrown carelessly upon the floor. Her eyes caught a white sheet of paper jutting from beneath the edge of the telephone. Eagerly she reached for it, clutched the robe around her, and read.

"Dear Katie," Reno had written. "Last night"—this he had crossed out, but Katie could still make out the words. Then, "I have to get away and think. Please give me time. Reno."

Katie stared, almost not comprehending, at the white sheet of lined notebook paper. She wanted him, needed him. Was last night even real? She scanned the written words again. There was no "I love you." But he'd said it—last night.

The paper had been taken from her small notebook, and this reminded Katie of the present and the conference. Sweeping her hair back from her face, she glanced at the clock. It was after eight, and the first session started at nine. Suddenly she was very tired. She just couldn't rush through getting ready and then have to face a bunch of strangers. Or Jim Sheldon.

Picking up the phone, she dialed room service and ordered breakfast—with a pot of coffee, not just one cup. She made sure they would not arrive for twenty-five minutes. She shrugged from her robe and stepped into the shower. The extra-warm water pulsing down upon her skin felt delicious, and for a good five minutes Katie allowed the water to flow over her hair, down her face and tingle her back. Rubbing her skin vigorously with the lathered washcloth, she was unable to keep remembrance of the night before from her mind . . . the way Reno stroked and massaged her skin.

Time. Reno wanted time. What else could she do? He was a part of her; there could be no other man. *What if he didn't come back?* The thought stabbed like a knife through her very being. *What if she could never again feel Reno's strong arms around her?* Resolutely Katie pushed these dark thoughts aside. The only thing she could do was wait. And believe. She had to believe he felt the same as she and would come back to her.

Was she being a fool? No, she loved him. And in this instance both she and Reno and any future they may have together depended on all the love she had to give. She had to love him enough to give him room, room to be himself. Yes, she had to believe.

Chapter Eleven

Midmorning, just as Katie was about to leave the room, a clerk called to say she had several messages downstairs at the front desk. Reno, she thought, running from the room and down the stairs, too impatient to wait for an elevator.

There were two: a message from Celia to call the magazine and a plain sheet of hotel stationery with scribbling on it. Katie looked at the paper, puzzled, her heart sinking to her toes. It made no sense.

"Do you know anything about this?" she asked the clerk, showing her the paper.

"No, ma'am." The young woman shrugged. "It must have been put in your box by mistake."

"Thank you..." Katie said. Then, "If I get any other messages, please notify me immediately."

Reno. Will I ever see you again? The thought came unbidden and unwanted.

Jim met her in the lobby. Taking a good long look into her face, he put an arm around her shoulders and kissed her forehead softly. He never asked any questions.

Skipping the lecture session, they went for coffee and talked of inconsequential things. With every word, in every gesture, Jim kept his distance, at the same time conveying to Katie his unequivocal friendship. If she needed him, he was there.

Katie was grateful. But only one man could help her now, and he had left.

She stayed for the rest of the conference weekend. For all the good it did. Her concentration wandered as her mind returned repeatedly to Reno. Though she knew she wouldn't see him, her eyes involuntarily searched, scanning faces, rooms, looking for his dark hair, the slope of his shoulders.

Driving back to Porterville, Katie pressed the gas pedal harder and harder, anxious to be home, thinking being there would help remove the lonely ache inside. But it wasn't so. Sam greeted her enthusiastically, and Katie was glad to see her special friend, but she could summon no real joy. Sam, the apartment, her lush jungle of plants, even the old neighborhood, all the things that used to give such pleasure, held no appeal. There was no one to share these things with, to share her life with.

Katie remained quiet and reticent. If her aunt and uncle noticed anything wrong, and Katie was sure they did, they kept their questions to themselves. Even Celia for once kept quiet, though Katie noticed her inquisitive looks now and again. For all this respect of privacy, Katie was grateful. She didn't want to talk about it. It was taking all her strength just to keep above the drowning waves of uncertainty.

She tried to hold to the positive thought that Reno would come to her, but as the days wore on her confidence lagged.

Why did he not call? Was it going to be the same all over again?

She reread Reno's note again and again. He'd asked for time. What it came down to was believing in Reno. He wasn't a man to leave things as they were, without so much as an explanation, even if that explanation would have to be a painful one. She had to wait.

The weekend following the conference, the Garrett farm hosted a large picnic, a family reunion and neighborhood gathering held every June. Katie had nearly forgotten it this year. She was tempted to beg off, but her moods were causing Aunt Claire and Uncle Will enough worry, without adding to it.

Sunday morning dawned clear and summer warm. Katie awoke hot and sticky from Sam's hulking body lying too close, the dog having crawled onto the bed in the night as usual. She ran her hands over the dog's sleek fur, listening to the quiet, realizing the others in the house—Aunt Caire, Uncle Will and little Beth—were all still asleep. All day Saturday had been spent in preparation for the picnic, and Katie had stayed, helping Aunt Claire with bed linens, towels and food until eleven o'clock. Now her aunt, usually up with the chickens, was sleeping late. Katie was glad. It would do her no good to be so worn out she couldn't enjoy what she'd worked so hard for.

Relishing the few precious silent moments alone, Katie quietly slipped downstairs with her clothes and small toiletry bag. Sam, like a black shadow, followed just as quietly behind, stopping at the back door to be let out.

After washing up in the kitchen sink, Katie dressed in a cotton India-gauze sundress of dark enough blue that all she needed to wear underneath were panties. Using an old cracked mirror hung on the inside of a cabinet door, she brushed her hair up into a loose bun and applied a sparing bit of makeup.

She set the coffeemaker going, knowing the aroma was sure to wake the others. Still moving quietly, she found a plastic bowl and slipped out the back door, doing her best to arrest the door's squeak. Aunt Claire had mentioned needing strawberries yesterday. Little Beth had been given the job of picking them, but she did more playing than picking, and ate half of what she did manage to pick.

A bluejay perched nearby scolded loudly. Katie watched it for a moment as it turned its head this way and that, squawking at her approach. She wished she could show him to Reno.

A slow, boiling anger was forming inside her. Last night had been the worst yet. She hadn't slept more than three hours, and that fitfully. Her mind had played back every feeling, every sensation remembered from the wonderful night she and Reno had spent together, somehow intertwining it all with their day alone at the cabin. She felt again the warm sun upon her hair, how close she had felt to him, their communication even without words. She recalled his musky male scent, the silky thickness of his hair about the nape of his neck, and the way his hands stroked her body. Sometimes those hands had scratched her lightly, so callused they were from hard outdoor work. She remembered, felt and grew heated.

She'd hesitated staying the night at the farm, thinking perhaps Reno would call the apartment. Well, waiting for Reno Martin was one thing, but she couldn't just stop her life. She couldn't just sit around waiting for him, always waiting, waiting.

How dare he treat her like this! Why was he doing this? What was wrong with a phone call just to say "Hey, I'm thinking about you—and I haven't died or dropped off the earth"? Why was Reno leaving her in this limbo state?

Perhaps he never intended to call. Never. It was time for her to face that fact. Her chest felt as if a vise were clamped around it and was squeezing hard.

She would not allow Reno's actions to control her. It was going to be a beautiful day spent with family and friends. She would think about Reno tomorrow and perhaps come to some sort of decision. One thing was certain: she had run out of patience.

Homemade sausage sizzled and dollar pancakes were browning upon a large iron griddle when Katie returned to the house. Aunt Claire, spatula in hand, looked up with a quick smile.

"Good morning, Katie. Day's going to be just perfect as always. Oh my, you've been berry picking already! Here, set them in the sink." Claire spoke all this in a rush, turned the pancakes, then glanced at her niece sharply. Katie said nothing, only smiled vaguely and began rinsing the strawberries.

Claire lowered her voice. "Katie, let me help. At least talk to me."

"There isn't anything you can do, Aunt Claire," Katie said, her voice punctuated by a sigh. She longed to tell her aunt, release her feelings, only suddenly it all seemed too much to try and explain. The strawberries were thoroughly rinsed, but Katie continued running water upon them anyway.

"Perhaps not, but I can listen," Claire said.

"Have you ever had to wait for a man, Aunt Claire?"

Claire took a deep breath. "Yes, dear, I have."

"Then you know," Katie said.

"Umm..." The older woman stirred at the sausage, uncertain what to say, listening.

"A person can't wait forever," Katie said.

"No, one can't."

Uncle Will came in then, Beth riding piggyback on him. Ten minutes later two Garrett sons, who now shared an apartment in Porterville, arrived. Thirty minutes later the house was bursting at the seams. The annual reunion picnic had begun. From breakfast that morning to the afternoon barbecue people would be streaming in and out, feasting constantly on food piled high on the kitchen table as well as tables set up outside.

Katie managed to consume a pretty good breakfast along with helping Aunt Claire serve anyone else who showed up and wanted to eat. At ten-thirty the breakfast kitchen was closed, however, and everyone shooed outside. Katie's favorite cousin, Karen, arrived with her husband and newborn baby. Katie stayed to admire the infant, trying to catch up on some news, then was dragged away by Beth to push the little ones on the swing.

Inevitably a guitar and banjo were brought out, and Katie was enlisted to play. Uncle Will refused to accompany her, saying that because he was Renfrow's brother people would be comparing him, and he just couldn't match up. Dal Carpenter had no such compunction and took up the guitar alongside Katie. After Uncle Will had had several loosening beers, he brought his guitar and joined in. Katie was having a marvelous time, forgetting Reno—almost.

Katie knew most everyone, had since a child, but Aunt Claire made a point of introducing Katie to several men she had not met before. To this procedure, Katie submitted good-naturedly, trying to smile and act interested for Claire's sake. But about one o'clock it began to get aggravating because one man, younger than Katie by several years, had apparently taken a shine to her. This knowledge made Katie extremely uncomfortable, so finally she excused herself and entered the house from the back. She was pouring a glass of iced tea when Uncle Will appeared from the hallway.

"Oh, Katie. I've been looking for you. That Martin feller from over in Oklahoma called asking after you. I told him how to get here and to come on out." Uncle Will looked pretty pleased with himself, happily inviting more of the family's friends to join in, making his favorite niece happy also, he hoped.

Katie swallowed hard, her eyes wide. "When...just now?"

"A few minutes ago." Will's eyes narrowed as he watched her. "It that okay, Katie?"

"Yes...fine, Uncle Will. Did he say where he was?"

"Just on this side of town. Ought to be here any minute now." Will eyed her speculatively. Katie smiled slightly, wanting to reassure him. The older man nodded, hesitating about saying more, but apparently changed his mind and stepped through the screen door.

Several emotions converged on Katie at once: anger, elation, anticipation and fear. Yes, definitely fear. Was he going to tell her he never wanted to see her again? Oh, God, don't let it be that. Quickly she jerked open the cabinet door with the cracked mirror and brushed at her hair with her fingers, then absently smoothed her dress. Minutes later, through the front kitchen window, she saw a shiny blue pickup coming up the dirt drive. Small clouds of dust billowed out behind the wheels. Katie could make out the driver's dark, thick hair—Reno's hair. As he pulled the truck to a stop beneath a giant elm, Katie went to meet him.

She had to step around two teenage couples clogging the front steps and past a group of elderly ladies sitting in lawn chairs who watched her with undisguised curiosity. Alighting from the truck, Reno balanced against the door's open window, waiting for her. The laughter, children's cries and general hubbub of conversation from the gathering faded into the background as Katie slowed the last few steps, searching Reno's face for some clue as to what was to come.

The two looked at each other for a long moment. Katie was uncertain what to say, confused as to just how she felt. Reno smiled hesitantly.

"Hello, Katie."

"Hello." While their words hung in the air, Katie was aware of the branches of the giant elm above swaying in the breeze. The sun glinted on Reno's dark hair and the brightness caused him to squint slightly.

"You're angry," he said.

"You write a nice note. I don't suppose you know how to use a telephone?"

Reno's jaw muscles tightened. "Are we going to stand here in front of all these people and fight? I called half the Garretts in Porterville looking for you today. Good thing I started at the bottom of the list. I came here to ask you to marry me."

Katie's eyes widened. She didn't know how to respond or even how she felt. For a week she had been keeping her emotions on hold, trying not to fly to pieces, as longing and ache for Reno battered at her, as fear that she would never see him again persecuted her every moment. Clenching her fists, she stared at him.

"Do you know what I've been through this last week?" She fairly hissed the words, striving to keep her voice low so no one could overhear. "I woke up alone, Reno. I didn't know if I'd ever see you again, and now you show up asking me to marry you. Do you expect me to just be able to fall into your arms? I can't regulate my emotions like a water faucet, you know."

"I left you a note explaining," Reno said.

"What? Four words?" Katie quipped.

"Look, I..." Reno began and then his attention was drawn to a point beyond Katie. Following his glance, she saw Aunt Claire and Uncle Will, hand in hand, approaching.

Katie turned her face away momentarily to compose herself. Facing the pair, she spoke as normally as possible. "Uncle Will, Aunt Claire, I'd like you to meet a close friend, Reno Martin." She stumbled over the term "friend," but only Reno seemed to notice as he shot her a sharp glance.

Uncle Will extended a hand to Reno, saying, "Welcome, Mr. Martin. We spoke on the telephone."

"Glad to meet you," Reno said, accepting Will's offered hand in a firm shake. The two men sized each other frankly. "Please—name's Reno."

Katie felt Claire's scrutiny as the older woman said, "So glad to have you here, Reno. Did Katie explain about our gathering? It's a special reunion, an event we hold every June."

"No," Reno drawled slowly. "We hadn't gotten that far yet. We were just saying hello." His brown eyes caught Katie's and held them, questioning.

"Well, Reno, glad to have you join us," Will said. "Can I offer you a beer?"

"Actually, Mr. Garrett, I have something to discuss with your niece." Reno looked to Katie as he spoke. She didn't know what to say, staring into the dark velvet of his eyes.

"I see." Will paused, studying them both. "Well, young man, see that roof peeking up over the rise down yonder? That's an old barn, a good place to have an uninterrupted conversation. And I suggest you have Katie lead you through the house and down the back way." With that, Uncle Will took his wife by the elbow, steering her away.

Katie picked up Claire's whispered protest: "But Will, maybe..."

Reno took her hand. "Okay, Katie?"

She simply nodded and led the way to the front door, feeling curious eyes upon them. They walked through the

house and out the back, though even here they weren't
without witnesses.

The small old barn, cool and dim inside, had many side
planks broken or completely gone, allowing the breeze and
sunlight to filter through. The dirt-packed floor was strewn
with hay, several bales piled in one corner. On one side, a
ladder led up to a loft that was partially filled with neatly
stacked bales. Reno glanced quickly at Katie, smiled, and
pulled her toward the ladder. She followed him willingly,
knowing exactly what he was going to do. She'd done the
same thing many times in her teens.

They climbed to the loft, and Reno pulled the ladder up
behind them. Katie moved back on soft strewn hay, behind
the bales to the corner of the rafters. She wasn't angry any
longer, only confused. She wanted Reno to take her in his
arms, but foolish pride formed a barrier, forcing her to act
aloof.

Reno followed her back on the hay and took her hand in
his, rubbing her fingers with his thumb. "Why did you think
you'd never hear from me again?" he asked, his voice low.
"Especially after that night? What in the hell kind of man
do you think I am, Katie?"

"But you just left. I woke and you were gone, Reno."

Reno sighed, "I know. Not the best thing I could have
done, but I knew if I saw your green eyes looking at me
again, I'd never leave you, and I had to think rationally. I
had to think through my feelings." Katie saw the pain written on his face as he talked. It was not easy for him to re-
veal himself so completely. "And, Katie, I left the note. I
asked only for time. Surely you understood I would contact you again."

"Yes, I did—then. But the days passed and still no word.
I thought... Oh, I don't know what I thought," Katie said.
Tears filled her eyes and trickled slowly down her cheeks.

Reno gathered her in his arms. "Don't, Katie. I'm sorry."

"There's nothing to be sorry for. You were being you. And you are right. I should have known I'd hear from you again. Only..." She couldn't finish. Reno was kissing her eyes, cheeks, trailing down her neck, taking her breath away.

"Don't, Reno." Katie pushed at him. "We have to talk."

Ignoring her mild protest, Reno breathed into her ear, "We can talk later."

He kissed her then, a demanding, probing kiss. Katie melted against him, her strength ebbing away, into him. Gently Reno shifted, laying her back upon the straw. Resting his weight upon one arm, he stroked her silken cheek, and they gazed at each other.

Katie reached up and touched the frown lines of his forehead, the plain of his temple and strong cheekbones. *I love you*, she thought, her full lips parting unknowingly. The fire of a deep, growing hunger reflected from Reno's dark eyes, and Katie moaned, digging her fingers into the thickness of his hair, pulling his lips to hers. They were warm and sweet, as she had remembered them. Catching the musky male scent of him, she breathed deeply.

Dragging his mouth away, Reno nibbled her lower lip, then seared a trail of kisses down her neck. "Oh, Katie, Katie..." he said, his voice a ragged whisper, his hands stroking her hair. "I tried to get away... but I couldn't. I kept remembering the smell of you, the feel of you... Oh, how I've wanted you."

And Katie wanted him, too. Impatiently she tugged at the cotton fabric of Reno's shirt. He moved slightly and the top snap gave, then the others followed easily. Touching his heated skin with her fingertips, she sighed with pleasure. Reno's hand slipped beneath the hem of her dress and stroked upward along the ivory smoothness of her thigh.

Katie gasped and clung to him. His voice came to her as if from far away. "This is crazy—I'm crazy." His breath

came hot and fast, brushing her ear. "It'll never work....
Ah, but Katie, I love you."

"Reno." Her breath caught as his hand moved to the
vulnerable area of her stomach. "Reno...I love you, too."

Emitting a low moan, Reno covered her face and her neck
with burning kisses. His fingers found and released the front
tie of her dress, also slipping the straps from her shoulders.
As he moved to the soft skin of her breasts, Katie arched
against him, floating away into the golden world governed
only by feeling as sensation after sensation flowed over her
being. He was here, Reno was here, and she never wanted to
let him go again.

Suddenly voices penetrated Katie's consciousness, bringing her back to reality with chilling clarity. She fought it,
wanting to stay in that delicious world of feeling, but the
sounds came again, closer: a feminine giggle and a male
tone, low and cajoling. Reno, hearing too, stiffened beside
her.

"Please, Mary Ann. We're alone now." Katie recognized the voice as belonging to the youngest male Garrett.
"Mary Ann..." The words were muffled and were followed by a faint feminine voice.

Realizing fully her state, Katie blushed furiously while
Reno smiled broadly. Trying to pull her clothes back in
place, Katie scooted cautiously to the edge of the loft, but
not close enough to be seen.

"Oh, no, you're not alone, Bobby Lee," Katie called. The
stillness which followed could have been cut with a knife.
Katie sensed Reno behind her stifling a chuckle.

"Aw, Katie, is that you?" Bobby Lee finally answered.

"Yes it is, and we were here first."

"Well, how about letting us have a turn now," Bobby Lee
said brightly.

"Nothing doing," Katie said, then added, "My van's
parked beside the garage—the shady side."

"Gee, thanks, Katie."

"Just remember how you were raised, Bobby Lee," Katie cautioned. A strong male arm clamped around her waist, and Reno pulled her back again into the corner of the loft. Hearing the movement as they left, the younger couple below laughed aloud.

"Reno, no!" Katie pushed at him as he nuzzled the back of her neck. He moved away, leaning up against a bale of hay.

"You're right," he said, trying to straighten his face from a chuckle. "Aren't you afraid you might be giving those two kids an excellent opportunity for trouble?"

"Bobby Lee's eighteen. I guess he knows what trouble is without my judging for him." Her hair in wild disarray, Katie removed the pins that held it, allowing it to fall around her shoulders.

Reno's shirt lay open, and Katie's eyes fell to his darkly tanned chest. Her face grew hot and she glanced at Reno. He was smiling, watching her closely. "How do you do it to me, Reno?" she asked in wonder. "I've never felt this way before. I mean, you touch me and I..." She blushed even more and looked away.

"I know," he said huskily. "Me too." She felt his eyes upon her, watching as she smoothed her fingers through her hair and tied the front strings of her dress. "Well...are you going to marry me?"

Why she had not even considered he would ask her to marry him she didn't know. She had fantasized about being with him and the children, even one of their own. Yes, she had thought about marriage in a roundabout way, but never dreamed he would suddenly ask her like this. She looked at him, wide-eyed, remembering his words of moments ago: "It'll never work." She knew even now as he was asking her that he didn't believe they had a chance. What kind of chance did they have if Reno was so unsure?

"But you don't believe it will work," she said.

Regarding her steadily, he said, "I don't know. I know only I don't want to return home without you."

"Reno, if you're not sure—" Katie said, but Reno cut her short.

"No, I'm not sure, but as you said, Katie, tomorrow holds no guarantees." His eyes were hot upon her, demanding an answer. "Is it you now insisting on guarantees?"

Yes she was. Suddenly she was terrified; terrified of loving and losing Reno. And love him she would. She knew she would grow to love him with all her being. There would be no going back for her if she married him. She would be like the massive banyan tree, putting down thousands of deep roots. But would he? Would he always balance on that edge of uncertainty, never commit to giving himself fully because of it?

For a brief second, the dream from that morning months ago flashed before her thoughts. Could the promise it held be true? She looked into Reno's eyes.

"Yes, I'll marry you," she heard herself say.

They lay in the loft, talking, hardly daring to touch, knowing what would result, until the sun sat low to the west. They planned and discussed. Reno was adamant about marrying right away. He would not return home without her. And he'd been absent long enough. The shipment of horses he'd bought in Memphis was due to arrive at the ranch the coming week.

The children would be delighted, Reno assured Katie, even if they weren't present at the wedding. "You see, we have to get married now." He chuckled. "We can't very well live in sin around the kids."

Evidently, Reno had given the matter much consideration in the last week, because he had an answer for every problem Katie brought up.

"With your van and my pickup we can carry an awful lot of your things back now." Reno said. "We'll find time this winter to come back for anything else you may want."

"Where did you get the pickup anyway?" Katie asked.

Reno grinned sheepishly. "I bought it in Memphis. I had to have some way of getting to you."

Finally Reno took Katie's hand and lifted her to her feet. Kissing her deeply, he was careful to keep his hands in one place around her waist. When he pulled away, Katie stood looking at him, dazed, longing after his lips. "We'd better go tell your family the news," he said. "We can do it up right tomorrow night when you're my wife."

Chapter Twelve

Reno, dressed only in jeans, chest and feet bare, poured a cup of coffee and listened to the water splashing in the bathroom—Katie bathing. He thought of her red lips, the way they had looked yesterday after he'd been kissing her in the barn. He warmed slightly thinking of her smooth skin and how she moved to his touch. With these thoughts, he got up and riffled through some papers looking for a map. Not that he needed to check their route home; he knew the best way but he needed the activity to take his mind off Katie and the uncomfortable ache that rose within him at the moment.

He picked up the map, and a large white sheet of paper slipped from beneath it—their marriage certificate. Reno retrieved the certificate and stood looking at it for a long moment. The wedding had been short, performed by a preacher Katie had known all her life. In the space of two hours, they'd had blood tests, gotten the license and become husband and wife. The thought still shook him. The preacher had said, "Kiss the bride," and Reno had bent to see Katie looking up at him with such love written on her face. Guilt and uncertainty had almost overwhelmed him. He wanted life to always be this beautiful for her, for her to always look at him that way, but he knew only too well what could happen to a man's and woman's love.

Reno and Katie had not been alone since yesterday in the barn. They'd spent Sunday night in separate bedrooms at the Garrett house, still full to overflowing with relatives. It seemed rather hypocritical to Reno, but Katie cast him a pleading glance and he remained quiet. Katie's family welcomed him immediately like one of their own. It was rather a new experience for him, never having had a real family of his own as a child, and Lynn's parents against him from the start.

They telephoned the children after dinner. Katie paced behind him the whole time he was breaking the news, worried as to what their reaction would be. She needn't be, Reno tried to tell her. But Summer had a calming effect when she talked to Katie. And when Katie hung up, she was beaming. Joey had said, "Hi, my new mom."

Reno grinned, thinking what a miracle his two children were. He was anxious to get home to see them, to walk in his own house, see the horses. And now it would be Katie's home, too.

He poured himself another cup of coffee, sat at the table, stretched out his legs and wondered what in the world a woman could find to keep her splashing in the bath so long. It wasn't as though they had been out branding cattle. Mentally he made a checklist of what still needed to be done. All day long they had packed things Katie just couldn't leave behind. What furniture Katie couldn't take now would be hauled to Will and Claire's house tomorrow.

Miraculously, they'd found someone who wanted the apartment, so Katie was out of her lease.

Actually, she wasn't bringing that much: her typewriter and files, an antique rocker made by her grandfather, some of her mother's dishes, a television. And, of course, she kept coming up with just one more thing. Supposedly the one-more-things were all done and the van and pickup finally packed. Reno hated to have Katie more than an arm's length away from him, but she refused to leave the van, so they would both have to drive. Reno knew she was giving up enough for him already.

He turned off the kitchen and living-room lights, walked to the bedroom and almost stumbled over Sam sprawled at the foot of the bed. "Sorry, Sam," he said, reaching down to pet the dog. "But let me warn you, there won't be room for both you and me in this bed tonight." Sam's answering look seemed to imply, "Wanna bet?" Pulling back the bedcovers, Reno realized he'd not heard anything from the bathroom for a few minutes.

"Katie?" He tapped the door lightly, then peeked in. She was reclining in the old tub, her eyes closed, wet tendrils of hair framing her face. Reno thought she was fully asleep, but as he moved to grab the large towel from the towel rack, she opened her eyes and blinked.

"Oh, I must have drifted off." Slowly she smiled up at him. Her lips, red and moist, parted slightly.

Reno ran his gaze over her body, the skin turned pink by the warm water, and felt again the heat begin low within him. He held up the towel. "Come on. Get out before you get waterlogged, if you're not already."

Showing no hint of embarrassment, Katie stepped from the tub. Reno wrapped the towel around her, rubbing her back. For some reason he couldn't figure out, he kept his face averted from hers. He caught the scent of fragrant soap fresh upon her skin; her warm breath fanned his face. He looked at her then, taking her face between both hands, her soft cheeks in sharp contrast to his work-roughened tanned hands. Her green eyes, flecked with gold, searching his own.

"You're beautiful," he said. The words sounded odd to him. It was hard for him to compliment a woman. At times he felt things, beautiful feelings, but he just didn't know how to put them into words. For Katie he wanted to try. Gently he lowered his lips to hers and felt her catch her breath, shuddering. The towel slipped to the floor, and Reno moved his hands to the satiny smoothness of her back, gathering her to him.

The heat that ripped through him as he felt her bare skin threatened to engulf him, body and soul. He fought for control, wanting to give Katie pleasure, to receive pleasure from her. Lifting her light frame into his arms, he carried her to the bed. Hurriedly he shed his jeans, a bit self-consciously, as Katie's eyes frankly watched his movements.

Stretching out beside her, he pulled her close, molding her against him. They looked at each other, smiling. Gently Reno brushed wisps of hair from Katie's temples, threading his fingers through her hair, flowing out dark against the cool pillow sheet.

He reached up, switched off the bedside lamp and took her to him in the darkness. She moaned, and he buried his face in her neck, kissing her scented skin down to the peak of her breasts. Passion rose, demanding fulfillment, and Reno strained, tempering it with tenderness. Then he lost himself in her, in the wonder of loving.

Later he lay listening to Katie's rhythmic breathing as she slept curled against him. Before drifting off she had mumbled, "I love you, Reno." Her words echoed within him.

"I love you, too, Katie," he murmured now, tightening his arm possessively around her. But would it last, he wondered, or would what they had get lost in the daily routine of living? He'd tried marriage once and failed. What would happen this time? It wasn't Katie he was doubting. He stroked her hip and she moved against him, responding even in her sleep. No, no doubt about Katie. She was a strong woman, full to overflowing with love.

It was himself. Could he give what it took to love day in and day out, through the good times and the bad? So many times lately, memories of his marriage to Lynn kept popping up, memories he thought he'd dealt with and put behind him. There were so many times with her when if he'd just done things differently, reacted differently, their marriage could have been different.

He sighed, rubbing his cheek against the softness of Katie's hair, a comforting movement. Regrets never changed things, only added more strain. He couldn't waste energy now on regrets.

Katie, ah, Katie, he thought, who is this man you've married, who you think is so strong and invincible, who you're betting your life on? A wry grin swept his lips in the darkness. When it came to work, the horses, building, even raising the children, he was those things, but the union of marriage was a different matter altogether. Always Reno had been a loner; he had been born that way, and the circumstances of his life had contributed to it. But marriage called for sharing, giving yourself to another person, and Reno just didn't know how. Katie, in her giving, had become a part of him. He had to have her with him now, regardless of what happened later. Could he learn to give himself to her? Was he learning even now? He desperately hoped so.

They pulled beneath the Martin Ranch sign late the following afternoon. As the van topped the rise and pulled into the yard, Katie gasped. In her mind's eye she had seen the ranch as it looked in the starkness of winter. Now everything was in bloom, bursting with life. Stepping from the van and stretching, she caught the fragrant sweetness of honeysuckle, her eyes taking in two enormous green oaks framing the house. A crimson-budded climbing rosebush threaded its way along the porch rails. Maggie and the children came running from the house, and Sam pushed Katie out of the way, leaping from the van and barking an eager greeting to old friends.

"Think you're ready for this, Miss Katie?" Reno said, draping an arm around her shoulders.

"Yes," she said simply, smiling up at him.

The greeting she received from Maggie and the children couldn't have been warmer, dispelling any bit of apprehension still lurking in the back of her mind: they wanted her. Summer and Joey each took one of her hands, and they walked to the house. Behind them, Maggie and Reno followed.

"You made the right choice, Reno," Katie heard Maggie say. No doubt he had consulted the older woman before asking Katie to marry him. Foolish jealousy tugged at her. Quickly Katie smothered the emotion. She must allow Reno the freedom to be himself, to come to her in his own time. Maggie was a good and wonderful friend—to them both.

A man coming around the corner of the house shouted a greeting and took Reno's hands in a strong clasp. "Hey, Reno. Congratulations, ol' buddy." From Reno's past descriptions, Katie recognized the man as Sonny Norman, Reno's friend and sometime partner. He was rakishly handsome, with light brown hair, darker mustache and blue eyes, eyes which now bestowed upon Katie the look a man has when he beholds a beautiful woman. "Should have known you'd pick a thoroughbred, Reno. Do I get to kiss the bride?"

Before Reno could answer, Sonny stepped over and brushed Katie's lips with his. She blushed furiously, stammering a hello. Sonny grinned and shot Reno an incomprehensible look. Reno shrugged, grinning in return.

"Well, come on, everybody," Maggie said. "I have a hot meal prepared. Let's sit and relax and enjoy it."

"Yes, no doubt my wife is starving," Reno said, laughing. "We only ate two hours ago."

"That was a light snack," Katie protested. "And yes, I'm starving!"

Reno put his hand to the back of her neck, stroking lightly with his thumb, grinning down at her. A quiver shot through her. Reno noticed and grinned even wider. Joey danced ahead of them, chanting the mixed-up words of a song, happily pulling at Sam. Summer walked quietly beside them, seemingly content.

My new home, Katie thought as she stepped across the front entry. Somehow the comforting thought held a hint of challenge.

Katie lay in Reno's bed that night—their bed, she corrected herself, and waited for him to come from the shower. A soft, cooling breeze stirred through the open windows, but still the house was warm. Katie lay covered by only a sheet and listened to the crickets and cicadas making a riotous racket. Far away she heard an owl calling.

"That's it, turn the lights out on me," Reno said, coming in the room.

"I did." Katie laughed. "There's enough moonlight in here anyway."

"Maybe for you."

Katie heard a thud, and Reno let out a curse. "Reno? You all right?"

"Yeah, I just stubbed my toe. I don't see too well in the dark."

"But it's not all that dark."

"It is to me." He was chuckling as he slipped into bed, drawing Katie to him.

Reno's bare skin was cool and smooth from his shower, his hair still damp. "Umm, you smell good," Katie murmured as she snuggled close. His hands caressed her stomach and moved upward to claim her breasts. Katie sighed, enjoying the feeling.

"You're tired," Reno whispered, softly kissing her temple.

"I was just trying to decide about that. Your hands feel awfully good." Katie snuggled closer, savoring the nearness of his strong frame.

"Go to sleep," Reno said, muffling a chuckle, which Katie detected anyway. "I'm beat. I'm not a twenty-one-year-old stud, you know."

Katie giggled. "Thank heaven for that. I'm in the hands of a master."

"Go to sleep," Reno commanded.

Katie settled contentedly on her side with Reno curved around her back, his arm draped across her stomach. Again she savored the feeling of sleeping next to him, realizing that again it would be all night and she would wake up beside this man she so loved.

"Reno?"

"Umm?"

"This is so wonderful." The words didn't quite suit, but Katie could think of nothing else. "Lying here like this and knowing we'll do it most every night for the rest of our lives. I'll never tire of it."

For a moment Reno's breathing stopped, and Katie, puzzled, sensed him stiffen. "Yes, it's great...for me, too," he said, his voice betraying the uncertainty he felt about their future. Katie fell to sleep wondering about their future, too, her bright and beautiful dreams edged with something indefinably threatening in the background.

Sometime in the night, Katie grew cool and slipped on her gown. That was fortunate because, upon awaking, she found Joey curled in bed beside her, a stuffed monkey clutched in his small arms. She smiled at the way his young face looked so cherubic in sleep. The little guy hadn't even awakened them; he had simply crawled into bed where he found room.

Reno was already up and gone. Katie had expected this; a rancher's day started even before the sun. And the sun was just peeking above the horizon, the birds beginning a riotous squawking. Sensing Katie was awake, Sam came around the bed and laid her head upon the mattress, wagging her tail slowly.

"I'm coming," Katie whispered, slipping quietly from the bed. Pulling on a light robe, she padded to the kitchen and opened the back door for Sam, leaving it open, allowing the morning breeze to blow through the screen. Katie relished the morning air, cool and new. Later the day would become baking hot.

Reno had coffee made, and Katie poured a cup, then rummaged through the refrigerator for breakfast makings. She was a new wife and mother; time to start her work, she thought. The bacon was just beginning to sizzle nicely when she heard Reno's steps upon the porch. Flipping his hat to the nearby coatrack, he stood there a moment looking at her.

"I was right, that night months ago. You seem to belong here," he said, his voice husky. He held his arms wide, and Katie went to him gladly, her heart singing. It would take time, but slowly, surely, his uncertainty would fade, Katie thought, and she would do all she could to assure him.

"All right, you two, watch that in front of the children." Summer's teasing voice sounded from the hallway. Her eyes looked barely open, her hair pulling out of the braid she'd worn in the night.

Reno bent to give his daughter a kiss. "Yes, my child, but you might as well get used to it," he said, stepping to the sink to wash his hands.

"Good morning, Summer," Katie said brightly, stabbing at the bacon with a fork.

There was a pause, and then Summer said, "Good morning, Katie." Something in her voice drew Katie's attention. The young girl stood in the archway to the hall staring at Katie, a dull look in her eyes. The breakfast. Of course. Summer always rose to get her family breakfast, even when school was out and she could sleep late.

"Oh, Summer," Katie said hurriedly. "I found this bacon in the refrigerator and thought I could be a help to you by starting breakfast." Her side vision caught Reno pause in washing his hands, but he said nothing. "I didn't know what else you may have planned."

Nervously she stepped back to wipe her hands on a dishtowel, then passed the towel to Reno, who stood with his hands dripping wet, watching both Katie and Summer. Summer cast Katie a questioning look and bent to pull eggs, juice and jelly from the refrigerator. Katie sipped her coffee in silence. It was such a stupid little thing. She was not about to take away from Summer something the child loved doing. She hadn't come here to take Summer's place, but to join in.

"Pour your father a cup of that hot coffee, babe," Reno said nonchalantly, but Katie could feel him studying the situation. She reached to cover his hand with hers, her eyes speaking their understanding.

Without a word Summer placed the cup of coffee on the table, then returned to the counter, measuring out into a bowl the flour, baking powder and other ingredients for biscuit dough.

Reno talked of the horses he'd purchased in Memphis, the new paddocks they were building for them. Katie listened intently, wanting to learn more about his work and his life.

Suddenly Summer said, "Katie, I'm mixing biscuits, but they may not be how you like to make them. And maybe you'd rather have something else. Or scrambled eggs instead of fried . . . we could scramble them if you want." The words came out in a rush.

Startled, both Katie and Reno stared at Summer. She stood in the middle of the kitchen, flour covering her outstretched hands, a stricken look upon her face.

Katie smiled gently. "Biscuits are fine, Summer, and I'm sure you know how your father and Joey like them more than I. You can teach me."

"Well, I just meant, now you and Daddy are married, it's the right thing if you do most of the cooking...the way you want."

"I think the best thing would be for you and me to cook together," Katie said, stepping to the stove. "Right now let's not let this bacon burn." She grinned at the young girl and saw Reno hiding a smile in his coffee cup. Summer looked sheepish.

From the hallway came a little voice. "I don't care who cooks, 'cause I'm hungry." Beholding Joey standing in the archway, rubbing his eyes and clutching the stuffed monkey by the ear, they all broke into laughter, Reno choking on his sip of coffee. Katie jumped to help him, patting his back, and Summer quickly took charge of the bacon.

"What's so funny?" Joey asked in all innocence, sending the three into more chuckles.

"Too hard to explain, son," Reno said, taking Joey upon his lap. "We'll eat in a few minutes."

"Get that bacon in the warmer, Summer, and that dough in the oven. I'll fry the eggs," Katie commanded. "I make pretty good gravy if you'd like me to give it a try."

"Sounds great!" Summer said, smiling broadly. Then after a few minutes, "Katie, could you clear the dishes this morning? Tobias may come over, and I want to be sure and have a bath and my hair washed."

"Katie's not even been here a whole day, and already you're giving up your jobs, Summer," Reno said.

Both females turned to Reno, a teasing light in his dark eyes, his lips twitching into a smile. They nodded to each other and bombarded him, Katie with a hot pad, Summer a dishtowel. Joey, on his father's lap, caught the brunt of the weapons and burst into giggles.

"Do you see what it's going to be like around here now, Joey? You and I will have two women to contend with." Reno looked pointedly at Katie, his dark gaze filled with warmth and a trace of gratitude. Tingling joy shot through her as she returned his look, both of them still, locking out the world for a split second.

In the early evening, the sun near to setting but still warm, Katie, Joey and Sam emerged from the house and headed up the hill to where Reno could be seen in a far paddock. Joey's small hand in Katie's felt warm and friendly. He smiled up at her and swung her arm. "Let's run, Katie."

She grinned back. "Okay." And off they went, still holding hands, Sam bounding ahead. Running with her young playmate, Katie felt like a child again, her legs soaring over the packed ground, hair blowing in the wind. But several yards from Reno, she gave out, puffing loudly. "You'll have to go on, Joey. I'm not use to this."

When she reached Reno, she had finally regained her breath, but just barely. "What's wrong, Miss Katie? Getting old?" Reno teased, handing her a hammer, nails and wire cutters.

"No... just better," she shot back. He brushed her lips with his, and a quiver of delight shot through her at the contact. He smiled, his knowing eyes holding a promise.

"Daddy, Daddy." Joey pulled at Reno's hand.

"Okay, son. Up you go." Reno lifted Joey to his shoulders, and together they walked back to the barn. Joey ran off to play with Sam while Reno replaced the tools in a small shed. Throwing an arm around Katie's shoulders, he led her to the same fence where they had stood talking that cold early morning months before.

"I'm sorry I left you alone most of the day," Reno said, his eyes dark and brooding. "There's just so much work to catch up on. Sonny's good, but he can't do everything alone."

"And you've missed it all... all this," Katie amended for him, encompassing their surroundings with a wave of her arm.

"Yes, I've missed it," Reno agreed softly.

"It is beautiful," Katie breathed. Her eyes gazed at the paddocks neatly laid out against the darkening blue sky to the east. A gusty breeze rippled the leaves of the tall cottonwood tree at the corner of the fence and waved prairie grasses far up the hill. Horses trotted the confines of their fences and a bob white's call sounded from far off.

Reno's breath came hot upon her skin as he softly kissed the side of her neck. Her hands touched his damp shirt, and she smelled the sweat of his skin mixed with his own scent. Not an offensive odor, but sweet and strangely inviting. As he moved his feather-light lips up to caress her mouth, a familiar stirring of pleasure began deep within.

He pulled away and smiled down at her. "Later, after a shower." A brown filly pranced to the fence and nuzzled Reno's shoulder. He turned to stroke the horse's forehead and neck, saying, "This is Sugar, Katie. That isn't her full name, of course. She has a registered name long enough to choke a horse." He grinned at the pun. "But we prefer Sugar. She's a fine quarter horse I intend to breed well."

Katie reached up to stroke the sleek copper-brown horse, too, and Reno went on to explain about Sugar's lineage and the different males who would be good mates. Patiently he answered Katie's questions, going over for a second time things she didn't understand. Katie felt a sense of unity envelope them as Reno drew her into his world.

"It must give you a great deal of pride to see every day what you've built with your own hands," she said.

"Yes . . . yes, it does," Reno said, his eyes surveying the ranch. Then he turned his dark eyes to Katie, questioning. "And what about your work? Do you think you'll get as much satisfaction out of free-lancing an occasional article for the magazines as you did on permanent staff?"

"I find satisfaction already in the job of being your wife," Katie said, hugging him around the middle. "As for my articles, my first one is going to be on your house and the methods you employed to build it.

"*Our* house," he corrected. "Will we be famous? Do I get paid?"

"No." Katie laughed. "But we will get your name and house's picture in the magazine. How's that for fame?"

"Can't complain, I guess." He took her hand. "Come on. I need a shower, a cup of coffee and you—in that order."

Katie laughed, a light, joyful laugh, content in their closeness as she had not been at any time in the past two years, practically any time since she could remember. As they walked toward the house, Maggie hailed them from the side porch. Katie was glad to see the older woman, had been wondering all day when she would see her. But she had been too busy with the chore of settling in to walk up the hill to the Latimer cottage.

"Well, Katie, I can see you're happy. Did you get all settled in?" Maggie said.

"Pretty much, with a lot of help from Summer."

"That child's one in a million." Maggie started down the steps. "Come up and see me anytime."

"You're not leaving?" Katie said, wide-eyed. "Why, we've hardly seen you."

"Just wanted to get a look at the both of you, child. Now I've seen, I'm going home," Maggie quipped, she and Reno grinning at each other. "I'll see you a lot more, don't you worry—uh-oh."

Katie and Reno followed Maggie's gaze to a white Cadillac pulling in the drive and around to them at the side. Reno's expression became unreadable. Removing his hat, he ran an arm over his damp hair, then replaced the hat low across his forehead. All three watched as Millicent Stephens elegantly alighted from the car and took a few steps toward them.

Chapter Thirteen

Millicent Stephens regarded the three of them for a long moment. She looked the same as Katie remembered her. She was beautiful for a woman of her age. Her silver hair, white suit, matching white heels, even her white car all blended together to present a sophisticated picture.

"Evening, Millicent," Reno said.

"It's a fine thing, Reno Martin, when I have to hear second-hand that my grandchildren have a new mother. Or perhaps to put it more accurately, you have a new wife." Millicent's eyes flashed with anger, but her voice remained cool. Her attention was directed toward Reno, as if by ignoring Katie's and Maggie's presence she deemed them of no importance.

"I've only been home one day, Millicent, and I had pressing work to attend to at the ranch." Reno's voice held no apology, only explanation. He drew Katie into the circle of his arm. "This is Katie, my wife. I believe you met her

once before." He inclined his head toward Maggie. "An
Maggie Latimer you know."

Maggie, hand on hip, gave a slight snort. Millicent's eye
flicked over Katie, touched on Maggie, then went back t
Reno. With ill-concealed contempt, she said, "Yes, Maggi
Latimer I know. And this is the woman you've chosen t
bring into the same house with my grandchildren? Th
woman you picked up on the roadside."

Katie drew in a sharp breath. "Go inside, Katie," Ren
said quietly.

"No," she said in a hushed whisper, shaking her head an
slipping her hand in his. She couldn't imagine what Mill
cent Stephens had against her, but she needed to face th
thing with Reno.

His expression dark and his jaw muscle taut, Reno sai
"Millicent, I think you'd better leave."

"I want my grandchildren, Reno. I don't want ther
brought up by another woman. The way you father them
bad enough." Though Millicent retained a cool facade, K₂
tie could see that facade slipping, betraying the hysteria be
neath.

"Millicent, you know that's impossible," Reno, sensin
the older woman's slipping control, spoke patiently.

"Reno, I'll make trouble for you." Millicent clenched h₁
polished nails into her palms.

Reno's eyes narrowed, watching her closely. "Yes?"

"The loan at the bank . . . I'll see it canceled." Millicent
gray eyes revealed pure cold hatred, and Katie shivered ₂
the madness she saw.

"Suit yourself," Reno said quietly, never moving his ey₁
from her face. Katie felt her hand being crushed within hi

Millicent grabbed at the Cadillac's door handle. Her lor
fingers slipped and reached again, opening it with a jer
"I'll do it, Reno. Don't you bet I won't." Gravel and du

lew as Millicent backed the Cadillac, turned and headed
lown the drive, her foot heavy on the accelerator.

Katie stood transfixed, looking in the direction of the now
lisappearing car and wondering at the cause of such ha-
red. She turned to find Reno gazing down at her, his eyes
o dark no pupil could be seen. And she could read nothing
rom them; he'd drawn the concealing blanket once more
across his features. From behind them Maggie spoke.

"Let's go inside and have some coffee."

As the three of them mounted the steps to the kitchen
orch, they saw Summer and Joey peering wide-eyed
hrough the screen.

"You two go upstairs and get washed for bed," Reno said
ruffly. Summer nodded without a word and took Joey's
land.

"But Daddy, why was Grandma so mad?" Joey asked.
"Why doesn't she like Katie? Huh, Daddy?"

"I said go upstairs and get washed!" Reno thundered.

The children, unaccustomed to their father using such a
one, turned and scampered up the stairs. Reno's face
agged. "I'm going for a shower."

Katie watched him, incredulous, as he left the kitchen
vithout even a glance. She turned to Maggie, who was put-
ering with the coffeemaker. "Is anyone going to explain to
ne what is going on around here?"

Maggie sighed. "Millicent hates Reno. Has since he took
ynn away from her power and all her plans for her daugh-
er. Oh, and what plans she had for Lynn! She wanted her
o marry a rich lawyer from Muskogee, fellow who ended up
ecoming a state senator." Maggie looked far out the win-
ow, remembering. "Actually, I think Lynn married Reno
1 a power play against Millicent, wanting to kick the traces,
o to speak. I've known Millicent almost all my life. She was
nce dirt-poor. Set her sights on Adam Stephens and his

money, married him, then decided he wasn't good enoug
for her, and harped him to death.''

''The woman is . . . well, she's verging on madness, Mag
gie. I could see it in her eyes.''

''Yes, I believe her bitterness, greed and hate is finall
threatening to push her over the brink,'' Maggie sai
pouring them each a cup of coffee. She raised the suga
bowl to Katie, and Katie shook her head.

''The children deserve an explanation as to what has ju
gone on here,'' Katie said.

''Yes, they do,'' Maggie agreed, then continued though
fully. ''For all her faults, Millicent does love the childre
deeply, in her own way. She'd never hurt them knowingl
That's what all the ruckus is about, has been since Lynn
death. She wants the children in her power, to do with the
what she feels is the right thing. And what she failed wi
Lynn.'' The older woman looked at Katie. ''I think for
while she had accepted things as they were, with Reno le
ting the children visit her often. Now she sees you, the chi
dren's fondness of you, as a terrible threat and will d
everything within her power to bend, or break, Reno to g
what she wants.''

''Can she do it, Maggie?'' Katie asked.

''Millicent has a lot of power, Katie,'' Maggie answere
''Just how much damage she can do, you'll have to discu
with Reno yourself. He'll try to close you off, determine
as is his way, to handle everything alone.'' The older wom
knotted her veined hand into a ball and shook it at Kati
''You're going to have to fight, girl, to help him.''

In the silence that followed, Katie sipped her coffe
pondering. Then she said, ''You must love Reno ve
much.''

''Yes,'' Maggie answered. ''We've become good friends

''Why does Millicent hate you, Maggie?''

"Umm...perhaps because I know who she was before she became the high-and-mighty Mrs. Stephens. Perhaps because we once were in love with the same man and I won." Maggie's eyes twinkled. "But more, I think, because I'm Reno's and the children's friend."

The house was quiet, the rooms now quite dim as the sun set. "I'm going to talk to Reno," Katie said, rising and turning on the kitchen light.

"You do just that, my girl," Maggie said, patting Katie's arm. "I'm getting these old bones home."

Passing through the hallway, Katie heard Joey playing in his room above and saw Summer hesitate on the middle stair. Smiling encouragingly at the young girl, she said, "We'll talk in just a bit, okay?" Calmed by Katie's manner, Summer gave a half-smile and hopped back up the stairs.

Reno was in the bedroom, dressed in clean, though faded, jeans and pulling on a shirt. Katie went to him, arrested his hands from buttoning the shirt, and slipped her arms around his bare waist. Reno's arms closed around her, and she smoothed a cheek against his skin, cool and fragrant from his shower. He felt so good against her, so strong and comforting.

"Reno," she said softly. "Reno, we must talk."

He tensed and pushed away, finishing the buttoning of his shirt. "I'm sorry about what Millicent said, Katie. She was angry with *me*, though, not you. We've never gotten along."

"Reno, she threatened you. What is it that she can do?"

"Don't worry about it. She was just mouthing off." His voice was clipped as he turned from her, adjusting his belt through the loops of his jeans. Katie sat on the bed, her shoulders sagging.

"Don't do this to me, Reno. Don't do this to us," she said. "I'm your wife now. Please let me share your life. Don't shut me out." Stillness enveloped the room. Katie heard Reno's breathing, the cicadas start up and a moth knock against the screen.

"I have a loan application in at the Tyne National Bank. The usual, for feed and stuff until fall. Only this time the amount I've asked for is much more—the rest of the payment for the horses I bought in Memphis. Millicent is the main stockholder in the bank, but more than that, she wields a lot of power over many businessmen in town. To put it bluntly, she knows a lot of secrets people would rather stayed secret."

"And she can see this loan canceled?" Katie asked.

"After what she said, I'm considering it already canceled." Reno let out a dry laugh.

"Reno, what about the ranch?" Katie asked hesitantly. "Does the bank hold the mortgage to it, too? Can she do anything?"

Bending close, he took her by the shoulders. "No, Katie," he said gently. "The deal for the ranch land was between me and Maggie. Really, Millicent can do very little to me. She is living in a fantasy world where she thinks she can control everything and everyone around her. I'm sorry if the way I was acting upset you. It's disappointment more than worry. Without the money, I won't be able to pay for those horses which are due to arrive tomorrow."

"I have a little money saved, Reno. It's not a whole lot, but maybe . . ."

Reno stood up. "No, Katie. I won't take your money."

"But, Reno, it's not my money. It's *our* money."

"Look, I don't want to talk about it. I'm beat, and right now I have to go up there and make some sort of explanation to my kids about what went on. Let's just drop it, okay?" He left the room, and Katie sat there forlornly. The term Reno had just used, "my kids," echoed in her ears.

A moment later Reno appeared at the doorway and held out his hand to her. "Come with me, please?"

Katie gave a slow smile. He looked like a little boy trying to make up for a wrong. She put her hand in his and together they went up the stairs.

Katie remained quiet while Reno did his best to explain to the children about their grandmother's attitude, not leaving out the fact that she loved them very much. The disagreement was between Reno and Millicent, not them. By the look on their faces, Katie sensed security return once more to their world.

After tucking the children into bed, Katie and Reno returned to the kitchen. Katie sensed Reno pulling away from her, brooding. While she poured them each a cup of coffee, he opened the screen door and stepped out onto the porch.

"We may get rain tomorrow," he commented when Katie stepped out behind him and placed the steaming cup in his hand. Katie waited, sensing Reno needed the quiet. A cooling breeze blew from the southeast, and she lifted her hair, enjoying the night air on her skin.

Reno bent and brushed his lips on her neck. Taking her cup from her hand, he set it alongside his on the porch rail. Knowing what he had in mind, Katie protested, "Reno, we have to talk."

"Later," he mumbled just before his lips crushed down on hers.

Heat rose in Katie at Reno's demanding touch. Now was their time, just for them. A time when worries could be forgotten, the world pushed aside. He lifted her into his strong arms, and as he fumbled with the screen door, carrying her inside, she giggled. "Aren't you going to lock up? What about burglars?"

"We have Sam—somewhere."

He laid her on the bed, stretching out beside her, and kissed her deeply. She bit her lip, stifling a moan, as his hand slipped beneath her cotton knit shirt and up to her bare breast. "Don't you ever wear a bra?" he murmured into her ear.

"Why..." Katie caught her breath. "Don't you like it, sir?"

A low chuckle sounded from Reno's throat. "You know I do."

Katie's head began to whirl. She was rapidly being brought higher and higher as Reno's hands smoothed her shirt upward, freeing her breasts, and pressing his lips to her heated skin. Moonlight shone through the open window, falling across the bed and illuminating the paleness of Katie's body. Reno pulled away and looked down at her, his gaze moving up from her breasts to lock onto her green eyes. She looked back at him, unable to turn from the longing she saw reflected in the blackness of his eyes.

"Reno..." she whispered. Then all recognizable thought faded as she lifted her body to meet his. She moaned aloud as his hands moved low, roughly loosing her jeans and pressing her stomach. She pulled his shirt free at his waist and raked her hands underneath on his smooth back. Urgently, she pulled repeatedly at the shirt, needing the feel of his skin upon hers. Moments later they both lay bare, Katie nuzzling Reno's neck, relishing the closeness. This was where she wanted to be, needed to be.

Fire shot through her as Reno tenderly touched the inside of her thigh, then stroked upward to the softness between her legs. He drew her to him, into that magic world where only their love existed.

Later Katie lay dozing against Reno's chest, unwilling to leave her blissful world. Gently he lifted her from him and slipped from the bed. "Reno?"

"Shush..."

Katie heard the floorboards creak as Reno padded through the hall. She heard a bump and Reno's "damn," then the closing of the back door. Seconds later, the bed gave as he lay back down.

"What did you trip over this time?" Katie whispered.

"Sam. I needn't have worried about the door. She was right in front of it."

Katie giggled, and Reno wrapped a strong arm around her waist, drawing her close. "Come here, honey," he said in a voice gruff and low.

Honey, Katie thought. It was the first time he had ever called her that. Sensing his need for her, Katie pressed herself against him. If Reno was reluctant to allow her help in other ways, at least she could give him the comfort he sought now.

It was after eight the next morning when Reno finished the morning chores and entered the kitchen. Summer was beginning breakfast, Joey watching cartoons in the living room.

In the bedroom he found Katie still asleep, curled into the sheet. He looked down at her sleeping form and smiled, remembering the previous night. Both their jeans lay together in a heap on the floor, his shirt across the headboard, Katie's on the nightstand. Gathering their clothes, he threw them across the arm of Katie's rocker, then bent to give her a light kiss.

In the kitchen once more, he grabbed a hot biscuit from the pan fresh from the oven, tossing it lightly in his fingers.

"I'm going over to Sonny's and then into town," Reno said. "Don't wake Katie."

"Oh, Daddy, you're not even going to sit down to breakfast?" Summer moaned.

"No time this morning." Reno kissed her cheek, then added, "Look after your brother."

Rolling her eyes skyward, Summer said, "Of course…wait." Quickly she grabbed another biscuit, halved it and spread it thick with jelly. Tossing it to her father, she said, "Here, you'll need two."

Walking to the truck, Reno passed the climbing rosebush, catching its sweet scent in the early-morning air. Last night Katie had smelled of roses. He felt much better this morning after last night's loving with Katie. Being with her had eased his frustration and disappointment. And this morning as he worked, he'd sized the situation with Millicent. Now he knew what to do.

Millicent couldn't really do him any lasting harm, but would definitely be a thorn in his side. Just what he didn't need now, Reno thought, when he wanted things to go right for him and Katie. If they were to have any chance of making this marriage work, they needed some peace.

He cursed his stupidity—biting Katie's head off yesterday when she'd so generously offered him her savings. But how could he explain to her, even when he didn't fully understand himself? It was his job to provide for his family, his wife. It sounded stupid to his own ears, so he tossed the thought aside.

Sonny waited on the front porch for him. "Hey, Reno. You didn't bring that beautiful wife along," he said as Reno stepped from the truck. Reno didn't smile, but shot him a searching look. Sonny held up his hands. "Just joking, just joking. Can't help a guy from noticing beauty when he sees it, but I know she's yours. Still can't believe it," Sonny continued, shaking his head. "The great loner, Reno Martin, marrying again. I thought once was enough."

Reno smiled wryly. "Yeah, well..."

Sonny laughed again. "Can't say as I blame you. That Katie would tempt anyone. Now, what's up, partner?"

Reno sketched in the problem and Sonny let out a whistle. "So old Milly is on her high horse again. What do you want me to do?"

"Those horses should be arriving this morning. I talked to Louis Strait over in Memphis earlier. He says he'd like to give me more time to get another loan, but he just can't. He needs the money now, has another buyer up in Chandler."

"I just bet he needs the money," Sonny broke in. "He could probably lend to Fort Knox."

"It doesn't matter," Reno said. "His terms are money now, or no horses. And I want two of those paints for sure. I think they are more than Strait realizes. If he did, he'd never sell them. Or else he just doesn't care... Anyway, I want you to stall them until I get back from town with the money. Now, they'll probably be in a hurry, because I think part of Strait's hesitation is that his new buyer is willing to pay more."

"Okay," Sonny said mischievously. "Can I use any method?"

"Well, don't kill or maim them, Sonny," Reno said, climbing back into fhe pickup. "Be subtle."

"Hey, where are you going to get the money? I got a bit..." Sonny called after him.

Reno only waved. He knew Sonny couldn't have much, but he was touched at the offer.

Millicent had been true to her word, Reno discovered at the bank. "I'm awfully sorry," Paul Sanders, the head loan officer, said, embarrassment preventing him from looking Reno in the eye. Reno knew it wasn't Sanders's fault, but smoldering anger kept him from shaking the man's offered hand as he turned and left the office.

He drew all the money from his savings and checking, closing the accounts. It seemed almost a childish move, and would prove inconvenient. He'd now have to go all the way to Muskogee to do his banking. But he couldn't see doing business with a bank that wouldn't even give him a loan. And he'd need nearly every bit of the savings to get those horses.

Next he visited the only car dealer in town and sold the truck he'd purchased less than two weeks before in Memphis, losing several thousand on the deal. But, wanting a quick sale, he didn't quibble on the price. With the truck money, the savings and what he'd already paid as down payment, Reno had enough to purchase the two horses he was gambling on to build the future of the ranch. Things would be slim around there, maybe for several years, but he'd hang on and make the ranch one of the biggest in eastern Oklahoma.

If only Katie stayed by him. He experienced a pang of regret about the savings account. He'd planned to use that bit of money for a small honeymoon. A surprise for her, down on the Gulf, Padre Island, just the two of them for a week after he'd gotten things straightened at the ranch. They needed that time together; and a woman needed a honeymoon.

Then, turning his thoughts back to the horses, he hurried to Ted Carter's garage to borrow some sort of vehicle and head back to the ranch. He had to be quick. No telling how long, or even if, Sonny could hold those truck drivers there.

The sun was high when Katie awoke, the room growing warm. Gradually the sounds of people moving in the house, the television, came to her. Then the memory of last night's confrontation with Millicent flooded in. *Reno.* She had to talk to Reno. The horses were due today. *And he wants them,* she thought. *He wants them so much.* Quickly she slipped into a cotton robe and padded barefoot to the kitchen.

"Katie!" Joey threw his small body at her and wrapped his arms around her legs. Holding him to her, she rubbed his back.

"Good morning, Katie," Summer said brightly, looking up from a book. "I saved you some breakfast."

"Good morning, kids. Where's Reno?" Katie said, involuntarily casting a gaze out the window, looking for him.

"He went into town about twenty minutes ago. Said not to wake you," Summer answered as she pulled a plate from the warmer loaded with eggs, sausage and biscuits.

Katie's heart sank. He'd left without her. Whatever he was going to do, he was going to do without her. Suddenly she couldn't bear the thought of the large breakfast set before her, and she moved Joey from her knee. "I need a cup of coffee first."

Summer glanced up from her reading. "Do you feel all right, Katie?"

"Fine, honey." Katie managed to smile. "I'm just not real hungry and would love a cup of coffee." She poured a cup from the coffeemaker and listened with half an ear to Joey's chatter. The other half of her thoughts brooded over Reno, the problems, real or imaginary, Millicent could cause, and the way Reno shut her out.

Several minutes later Joey came again to wiggle onto her lap and lay his tousled hair upon her chest. The unexpected loving gesture drew Katie from her thoughts, and she slipped her arms around the boy, holding him close. Oddly enough, the position was a comforting one, more so for herself than Joey, she thought. Summer and Joey were such loving children, to have taken her so immediately into their hearts. If only Reno could do the same, love her completely, trust her completely.

"You sure are quiet this morning, Katie," Joey said.

"That's because you do enough talking for all of us," Summer said wryly.

Joey laughed and stuck his tongue out at his sister.

Katie heard the scrape of boots on the back porch and looked anxiously toward the screen door, expecting Reno. But it was Sonny Norman who stepped through the door. Stopping on the threshold, he stood staring at the three of them sitting at the kitchen table, and slowly a grin spread across his face.

"What are you staring at?" Summer asked. "Have we suddenly grown horns?"

"I think I just got me an idea how to keep that truckload of horses here until Reno gets back."

"What?" Summer said. Katie watched Sonny closely, also wondering what was going on.

"Your daddy went to town for the money for those horses, and we have to keep them here until he gets back. And Katie may be the key." A grand look of self-satisfaction settled upon Sonny's face as he poured a cup of coffee. "I'm thinking we'll need both of you kids, too."

"What are you talking about, Sonny?" Katie asked.

"You didn't talk to Reno this morning?" When Katie shook her head, Sonny went on to explain. "Seems as if Lou Strait may just have another buyer for those horses. More money, so he's in a hurry and isn't willing to wait for Reno to get another loan. Reno thinks he can get enough money for two of those horses, and he sent me over to keep those drivers here until he gets back. Now if we're in luck, those drivers haven't talked to Strait yet this morning and will want to use our phone, which could be out of order. Or, if they have spoken to the boss and he's told them not to fool around, maybe one look at Katie and they'll take time for coffee, maybe a piece of pie, and maybe a tire on their trailer could turn up flat. Katie, why don't you go slip into something that shows off your tan real nice?"

Katie stared at Sonny, and Summer looked from one to the other. "You mean Grandma cut off the money Daddy needs from the bank?"

Katie closed her eyes a second and sighed. "Yes, but I'm not sure your father wanted you to know that fact. As he 'd, the disagreement is between himself and Millicent, not hildren."

"Seems like anything Grandma does affecting the ranch affects us, too," Summer said. "She must be really mad this time."

"While we're sitting here jawing, the truckload of horses could be arriving any minute," Sonny pointed out.

"I think you'd look super in that white pair of shorts and peasant top I helped unpack the other day, Katie," Summer said blandly.

"Oh, you do, huh?" A slow smile escaped Katie's lips. After several moments with everyone staring at her, she said, "Okay, I'm game. Let's see if we can keep those men occupied."

While Katie hurriedly dressed, Summer dispatched Joey to Maggie's to borrow something fresh-baked and began brewing fresh coffee.

Katie, not at all sure of what she was doing, peered at her reflection in the mirror and applied makeup. What will Reno say of her acting this way? Well, if it got him those horses, she'd stand on her head for those men. Pulling the elasticized neckline of the blouse off her shoulders, she stared at the strange femme fatale image reflecting back at her and made a face. Hearing the roar of the truck engine, Katie hurried to the front window to see a large truck towing a horse trailer pull into the yard.

Chapter Fourteen

As the men pulled the truck around to the side nearer the barn, Katie and Summer watched from the kitchen window, keeping well back to remain unseen. The men sounded the truck horn several times, waited, then slowly alighted from the cab, looking around expectantly. Still, there was no sign of Sonny. Katie and Summer looked at each other, neither sure what to do.

At last, when Katie was sure she could stand it no more, Sonny and Joey ambled around from the back of the house, Sonny shaking hands in an easy greeting. All the time Sonny took in coming, joking, gabbing, every precious minute was that much more for Reno to return. Katie chuckled inwardly at her dramatic thoughts, but they just had to get those horses. It was important to the future of the ranch, to Reno, and what was important to Reno was important to

She couldn't keep her eyes from sliding to the clock, ~ticed Summer doing the same thing. So far, ten minutes had been eaten up since the men had driven into the yard.

Several minutes later, Sonny and the men entered the kitchen, Joey tagging behind. Introductions were made all around. Katie's eyes strayed again to the clock; five minutes since the last time.

Sweetly, while handing each man a cup of coffee, Katie explained about Reno's being in town and returning any moment.

"Oh, no problem," the taller of the two said, eyeing Katie appreciatively. Apparently they had not spoken to their boss as yet. Katie smiled in return. Summer opened the oven door where the pie sat warming, and its enticing fragrance filled the air.

"Would you men like a piece of fresh-baked pie?" Katie asked, exaggerating her Southern drawl.

"Believe we would," the bigger man said with a wide grin. "Thank you."

While Summer reached for plates, Sonny started converstion rolling again and Katie marveled at the way he could talk so much and really say nothing. Time was ticking away.

Then the shorter, stockier man broke in. "All right if I use your phone to call the boss, ma'am? I'll reverse the charges."

Katie jumped at the question, smiled to cover her nervousness and nodded to the slimline telephone sitting at the end of the counter. Holding her breath, wondering if it would work, she pretended to listen to Sonny's conversation while her whole being was in tune to the man at the telephone. The call went through. The man spoke into the receiver to "Boss," then his face tightened as he listened. He called to the tall man.

"I thought you were going to take care of the telephone," Katie whispered.

"Too drastic," Sonny replied. "We'll make it. All we have to do is stall." And stall they did.

Informed of the change of plans by their boss, Louis Strait, the two men prepared to leave. "Boss says, Martin's not here with the cash, we're to head on out."

"Oh, he'll be here any minute," Sonny drawled. Katie offered them more pie and coffee, trying to act coquettish, but it simply wasn't her thing, so she gave up. Still, the minutes ticked away.

"Sorry. Strait's the boss," the tall man said.

Sonny, keeping up a stream of words, followed the men to the door. Maggie was just stepping up on the porch and Sonny greeted her affably, needlessly making introductions again. Every bit of it ate up time, if only seconds. Chewing her bottom lip, Katie glanced at the clock and thought, *Surely Reno will get here soon.*

While Sonny followed the men on out to the truck, Maggie asked Katie, "What's going on here?"

"It's a long story, Maggie." Katie sighed. "We're trying to keep this truck here until Reno gets back from town, but unless he gets here soon, we're not going to make it." The screen door creaked and Summer stepped out and put an arm around Katie's waist, leaning close. Joey followed, climbing up on the porch rail, turning a radiant face toward Katie and Maggie.

Katie eyed the children quizzically. Then a shout came from the far side of the horse trailer. "Flat tire. Damn it all!"

Katie looked again to the children. Grins tugged at their mouths. "You two go on in the house with Maggie. One look at your faces and those men will know for sure, if they don't already, and they probably are making some pretty close guesses." Wiping the grin from her own face, she went to join Sonny. He was shaking his head, doing his best to look consoling.

The men weren't buying it, of course, but what could they do? The tire was definitely flat and had to be fixed. Good-naturedly, Sonny set about helping to unload the horses and fix the flat. Also good-naturedly, he did his best to procrastinate and get in the way. A good tire replaced the punctured one, and the tall man was just tightening the lug nuts when an ancient gray truck appeared up the drive. Katie gasped, half in surprise and half in relief, when she recognized Reno at the wheel.

She ran to greet him. "What happened? Where's your truck?"

"I sold it." Reno's dark eyes raked over her, then passed to the three men at the trailer. Feeling his displeasure, Katie realized what he saw: her added makeup, the skimpy outfit.

"Reno..."

"Hey, partner," Sonny broke in, grinning broadly. "Pay the men. They're anxious to be on their way."

"You got the cash, Martin?" the short, stocky man said, wiping his hands on a rag.

Reno nodded and pulled out a wad of bills, counting out the amount. "This plus what I've already paid Strait for those two..." Reno pointed out the two horses he favored. "Strait agreed."

Sonny cut the two horses from the others and the remaining three were loaded back into the trailer. Watching the trailer drive out of sight, Sonny slapped Reno on the back. "We did it, ol' buddy. You got those horses. This calls for a celebration. I'm getting a beer." And he headed toward the house.

Slowly Reno folded the yellow receipt, pocketed it, then walked to the corral to view the new horses, now prancing around its perimeter. Katie followed, slipping her hand into his. "We did it," she said, her face shining up at Reno's. "I didn't know Sonny could talk so much or so fast."

Reno's jaw muscle tightened, but he didn't look at her. "Sonny has the gift of gab. Uses it on women mostly."

"Reno, look at me," Katie demanded. He did, and Katie gazed up into the smoldering depths of his dark eyes. "What are you so mad about? These clothes? It doesn't mean anything."

"I didn't mean for my wife to be used in getting these horses."

"I wanted to help, we all did, and Sonny thought...well, we thought me looking nice couldn't hurt."

Reno gave a short laugh. "I'm sure of that. You look cheap."

Reno's words stung. "Well, I guess if I'd dressed this way for you, you wouldn't think that. And all I wanted to do was help. You left this morning without me, not including me in any plans, or letting me be a part of things. I just wanted to be of some help," she repeated. "And how did you expect Sonny to keep that trailer here alone? I'm presuming gunpoint was out. We stalled, did everything we could think of to buy time." Her voice grew louder as her temper rose. She waved her arms to the horses. "And there they are. We all got them. I think instead of criticizing, the least you could do is say thank you." But she didn't give him a chance to say anything. Whirling from the fence, she ran for the house, past the astonished faces in the kitchen, and into the bedroom, slamming the door behind her.

Reno turned back to the corral fence and rubbed a hand roughly through his hair. He'd wanted to stop Katie, but she'd run too fast and pride had kept him from calling out. Foolish pride. Getting these horses meant a lot to him, improving the ranch meant a lot. And the trouble Millicent had set herself to cause was bugging him. But none of it was more important than Katie.

He was a grown man—and scared to death. It was crazy, unreasonable, but the feeling had such a hold on him, he couldn't shake it. He was scared of losing this woman he loved. As he had lost Lynn...only he'd never loved Lynn this way. She'd never given him a chance; she was always leaving.

He needed Katie now like he'd never needed anyone before. He wanted her there when he got up in the morning, as she was this morning, curled in the sheets. He wanted to come up to the house and find her there, waiting for him, and they could have something cold to drink. They could talk, or just sit.

If he lost her...the fear was paralyzing him and he knew it.

He hadn't looked at it the way Katie had...this morning. He did as he usually did, thought it out and figured what to do. He hadn't wanted to worry Katie. He just wanted to take care of her. Somehow he felt responsible for putting her in the position of suffering Millicent's insults. But he could see it now as she saw it. Slowly he turned, and with long strides walked toward the house, conscious that he would have to face inquiring faces inside. But he had to close this distance that had sprung between himself and Katie.

The murmur of voices from the kitchen stopped when Reno entered the house. He didn't pause or even look in their direction, but walked straight to the bedroom door, his boots echoing on the wood floor. He half expected the door to be locked; it had been his experience in the past. But the knob turned easily at his touch and the door swung open. Katie sat in her rocker, legs pulled up and clutched around the knees. The eyes she turned to him were red, the thick mascara smudged, but the tears were gone. She looked away, but not before he read the embarrassment. Thank heavens he saw no more anger.

Closing the door behind him, Reno came and sat on the bed. He rested his arms on his thighs and looked down at the floor, wishing desperately he knew how to put his feelings into words.

He tried. "I didn't look at it the same as you this morning. I just did what I normally do. I didn't mean to shut you out. I'm sorry. But when I saw you dressed and made-up and realized what the idea had been...well, no man likes to think of his wife as buying something for him in that way." He waited.

"It didn't really work, you know," Katie said finally, her voice almost timid. "I'm not adept at wooing men in a sexy way to get what I want. But it wasn't like you used me. It was my doing. Forgive me if I embarrassed you. I'm still pleased that we did manage to hold them up." About the morning, and his leaving her out of the decisions, she said nothing.

They both sat still, awkwardly. Reno was not sure what to do, wanting to hold her, but pride still whispering in his ear. Slowly Katie unwound her legs and came to him. He pulled her down and laid her back on the bed, holding her close. She felt so good to him. The remains of strain lingered, but it would pass. He hoped it would pass.

From that morning, Katie realized there was a lot she had to learn about the man she had married. They shared a strong tie, something from within bound them both, but it was a tie which needed nurturing and understanding if they were to grow together. For the first time Katie saw what a true loner Reno really was. She had thought it was just his bad experience with his marriage to Lynn that had made Reno shy away from entanglements; but it was more. He was a man used to running through life alone. Since childhood he had taken care of himself, alone, never leaning on anyone else. Now it was hard for him to allow Katie to become a part of his life, a part of him.

Though Katie tried to push the doubts, the uneasiness, from her mind, a thread lingered always beneath the surface. Reno, too, seemed on edge at times. Whether it was the problems Millicent was causing, or that he was picking up signals from herself, or she from him, she wasn't sure.

Only at night, when the bedroom door closed and they were alone, did Katie feel all barriers lift and she and Reno become a part of each other. They would make love, constantly learning more about each other's bodies, ways to please and enjoy each other. This was their golden time, when the magic that had shown itself from the very first was reborn. These times Katie never doubted. She could feel the love from Reno, sometimes tender, sometimes heated and demanding, but always strong.

And she marveled at him. Surely no other man in the world had hands like Reno. Strong and rough, but with the ability to touch her tender skin so gently and generate heat within her. Sometimes his hands played upon her body, knowing expertly where to massage and press, teasing her. She would catch a low chuckle from his throat as she strained against him to push him away, then pull him back, pressing herself against his hard-rock frame in her need of him.

Some nights they didn't make love, but simply lay together, content just to be with each other. They didn't talk much, but Katie learned to ask a well-placed question here and there, and Reno would open up, talking to her of a problem with a horse or something he'd seen that day that had interested him.

Katie always showered first, after the children were tucked in bed and while Reno busied himself with paperwork or a cup of coffee on the porch. Then she would lie beneath the cool sheets and wait while he showered. Oklahoma evenings generally cooled off quite a bit, and the windows were left wide open. They rarely used the air conditioning; Reno had designed the house for natural cooling and used an attic fan to draw the fresh night air inside whenever a breeze was absent.

One night, a week after the episode with Millicent, Reno, dressed only in jeans and his hair still damp from the shower, entered the darkened bedroom. He had adapted somewhat to Katie's habit of turning out the lights and generally didn't stub a toe. Tossing his boots to the floor in front of the closet door, he threw himself down into Katie's rocker. Katie came and sat upon his lap, the wooden chair giving several protesting groans.

"Think this chair will hold us?" Reno said.

"It held my mother and father," Katie replied. The moon bathed them in its light, and Katie traced Reno's jaw with her finger, taking in the fatigue around his eyes. From sunup to sundown, Reno and Sonny had been working, building new corrals, as Reno was expecting more clients than ever this year, more horses to breed, train and care for. Yesterday they had hired a man to help, but several regulars who were expected had not yet shown up.

Reno laid his head back upon the chair, closing his eyes, stroking Katie's back up and down. "What's the idea of clothes tonight?" It was the first time she had been wearing a gown when he'd come into bed.

Katie nibbled his ear. "No lovin' for us for a few days," she said.

"Ah . . ." Reno said knowingly. He pulled her head to his shoulder and moved a hand to her stomach, gently massaging. "Better?"

"Umm," Katie replied as she felt her muscles relaxing to Reno's manipulations. He was such a contradiction, this husband of hers. He knew so much about the workings of a female body, but so little about a female mind.

Katie was beginning to understand that Reno expected her to act, or react, much like Lynn or the other women he had known. Katie wanted to tell him, "I'm different," or, "It's different when you make a commitment," but she wasn't all that sure that Reno really was committed. He seemed to be holding back, waiting for something to happen. At least during the day. But not at night. Katie sighed. No, not at night—he gave himself to her then.

"Get what you needed in town today?" Katie asked. It was a small question, but any little thing he told her of his day let her that much more into his world.

"No," Reno said shortly. Katie waited, feeling the tenseness from his body. "I went for grain, to open a charge account at the feed store since the loan fell through. They wouldn't do it."

"There's another store, isn't there?" Katie said hesitantly.

"I tried them both."

"Could Millicent do this?" Katie asked, not believing such a thing could happen in this day and age.

"I think she did," Reno said. "This is a small town, people and business closely connected."

"So, what's to be done?"

Reno sighed. "It's no big deal, just another nuisance. I'll go to Muskogee tomorrow for what I need. There shouldn't be any trouble about a loan at Reemer's store there. I need to take care of some banking anyway."

"Does Millicent really think she can force you to give her the children?" Katie asked.

"I guess she does." Reno sighed and rubbed at his forehead. "She's a twisted woman, Katie, and trying to make sense with her doesn't always work. Hasn't for a long time." Lifting her from his lap, he said, "Let's go to bed, Miss Katie."

Curving her body into his, Katie welcomed his closeness. "Reno?"

"Umm?"

"Can I go with you tomorrow . . . to Muskogee? I need to take care of some banking. You know, get my money here from back home. And I need to do some shopping." It was stupid. Why would he say no? But just the same, Katie waited anxiously.

"Fine," he said groggily.

Relaxing again against him, Katie thought how wrong it was, this barrier that repeatedly forced its way between them. Why was it they were both so unsure of the other? Why did she feel she had to select her words so carefully? *We are meant to be together,* Katie thought fiercely. *I know we are.* Then what was the problem? Oh, she didn't know. Somehow Reno always seemed to be waiting for something. Something to happen. Could it be there was more trouble with Millicent than he had let on?

Katie snuggled closer to Reno and pushed all thoughts aside. She was very tired. After all, what was there to worry about in the middle of the night? The children were sleeping contentedly upstairs and she was lying so comfortably in Reno's arms. She and Reno were together. It had been her dream, and now it was reality. This, not the doubts, was what she must dwell on.

Katie felt a shimmer of excitement as they started for Muskogee the following morning. Summer and Joey had elected to spend the time with friends on a neighboring ranch rather than suffer through what they deemed a boring time in the city. Katie suspected Summer had put Joey up to the idea, because at first he definitely wanted to go along with his father. Katie was grateful. It would be the first time since coming to live on the ranch that she and Reno had a chance to be totally alone. She chuckled silently at referring to time spent shopping in a city of people as "alone."

She smiled up at Reno, anticipation written brightly on her face. He grinned knowingly in return and slipped his free arm around her shoulders. Summer glanced at them both, and a Madonnalike smile of smug satisfaction flitted across her lips. Joey, rarely still, now jumped up and down on the seat, pointing to the ranch house they were approaching. A small boy, perhaps a little bigger than Joey, waved a greeting from the front yard. A woman about thirty-five, Katie guessed, appeared from the front door, and she, too, waved in greeting.

"Hi, new neighbor. I'm Suzy Forester. It's about time Reno introduced us to his bride." The small blond woman was vivacious and friendly, and Katie liked her immediately. Grabbing Summer and Joey both in a big bear hug, Suzy waved them toward the house. "You all go on up and play. Kerri's in washing her hair, Summer." Turning back to Reno, she laughed. "So you finally went and took the plunge. The whole town is talking about it, you know."

Reno simply grinned at her remark and pulled Katie by the hand. "Say hello to your old man for me, Suzy. We'll visit when we pick up the kids."

"You'd better," Suzy hollered after them. "I want to get a word with your wife."

Katie was delighted at the way Reno seemed to want to be alone with her as much as she did him. She grinned at him as he pulled from the drive, the truck tires spinning as he pushed unnecessarily hard on the gas pedal. "A bit rude, weren't you, Mr. Martin? I didn't even get in a proper hello to the first friend you have introduced me to. Didn't even get to meet the children."

"Suzy Forester would have kept us all morning. When she gets to yakking it's easier to stop a raging river than to stop her from talking. She and her husband, Dal, have three children: a fifteen-year-old boy, Bobby, by Dal's first marriage, Kerri, twelve I think and little Roy, who was waving in the yard. There. Does that fill you in, Miss Katie? It would have taken Suzy two hours to tell you that."

Katie laughed aloud. "Yes, that fills me in."

"I didn't mean to sound like I don't like Suzy. Just that she really is a talker and I'm not in the mood right now," Reno explained. "I've known her and Dal since before they married. Dal and I worked the rigs together." He looked at Katie. "We'll visit on the way back. I don't mean to keep you isolated on the ranch. Guess it would be nice to talk to another woman."

"We've only been back just short of two weeks, Reno," Katie said. "That's hardly isolation. And there's Maggie." Quietly within she added, *And all I really need is you—for you to be my best friend*. She couldn't say the words aloud and didn't know why.

Chapter Fifteen

On the outskirts of Muskogee Reno pulled into the parking area of a fashionably rustic rock bank building. After opening a checking and savings account jointly for both him and Katie, he said to the woman handling the new accounts, "My wife needs to transfer money from Arkansas and set up an account."

"This is to be a separate account, then, Mrs. Martin?" the young woman asked.

"No, please just transfer the money to this account," Katie said, handing over her current bankbook containing the needed information.

"A separate account," Reno broke in.

"But Reno," Katie began, looking at him questioningly. "We don't need a second account."

The young clerk hesitantly looked from Katie to Reno. "A separate account," he repeated firmly.

Katie clenched her jaw, willing herself to bite back a heated remark, and nodded in assent to the woman, who immediately bent her head to the paperwork at hand.

Outside once more, Katie turned to Reno. "Why do we have to have separate accounts, Reno? We're married. Aren't we going to share all? And it would be so much easier."

"I'll provide for us," Reno said stubbornly, taking Katie by the elbow. "That is your money, and I want it kept that way. You may need it someday." Extracting several twenties from his wallet, Reno passed them to Katie. "That plus your checkbook ought to be enough."

"May need it someday." The remark echoed in Katie's thoughts and, wondering, she remained quiet. *Not today,* she thought. *I don't want to spoil today.*

From the bank, Reno drove to a small, but modern, shopping mall. Walking hand in hand, window-shopping past the various stores, strain from the earlier disagreement faded. They laughed, kissed and generally acted like young lovers on holiday.

Reno bought two hot jumbo pretzels and soft drinks. "Can't have my wife fading away from hunger," he teased. "After all, you only had a heaping plate of eggs, sausage and biscuits for breakfast. What, three hours ago? You must be starving."

Katie laughed and playfully slapped at him.

Finding an empty bench, they sat enjoying their snack and watching people go by. For a weekday morning, the mall was fairly busy, people cashing in on the pre-Fourth of July sales. Katie, an avid people-watcher, marveled at the many different types of people parading before her. Two willowy blondes passed, looking so much alike they could have almost been twins. Katie, having always wished to be taller, watched them a bit wistfully. One of the blondes looked toward the bench—and Reno—appreciatively. Katie glanced jealously to Reno, sure he had seen them, too, and was surprised to find his eyes, warm with love, resting on her.

A tiny toddler ran past on wobbly legs, his harried mother in hot pursuit. Reaching out an arm, Reno caught the little one around the waist. "Hey, cowboy, Mom's calling."

The little one giggled up into Reno's face, and the mother, breathless, thanked him for the capture. Whisking her small son away, she kissed and scolded him at the same time.

"You know, Reno," Katie said. "We haven't discussed children. Having any more, I mean."

The eyes he turned to her were dark, unreadable. "I think I'd like to have another child or two," he said slowly. "There's plenty of time." The words sounded hesitant, and Katie didn't press. If he didn't really want any more children, she could understand. She would love to have Reno's child, but not more than she wanted Reno.

Pitching the remains of their snack in the trash, they went to finish their shopping. Katie found a shorts set, perfect for Summer, and several T-shirts for Joey. Knowing funds were limited, she wouldn't have spent the money, but the things were on sale and the children were growing so fast they were in need of new clothes. Reno agreed and held out a nightgown for Katie's inspection. It was of the softest, thinflowing cotton knit, white speckled with blue flowers and lace trim. Katie's eyes lit up; it was beautiful.

"No, Reno. I don't need a new gown," she said with a shake of her head.

"Who said anything about need. It looks like you."

"No," Katie said firmly. He was trying to make up for his stand on the money issue. It would all be so much easier if he would allow her to contribute her money, but since he wouldn't, she would have to stay within a budget. At least until her money arrived from the account back home. Or checks from articles she intended to write. She would spend *that* how and when she chose.

Reno held the gown higher and waved it enticingly. "Aw, come on, Miss Katie. It's on sale." His eyes sparkled.

Hiding a grin at his teasing, Katie pivoted away and went to pay for the children's clothes. Reno came up behind her and stood very close, adding the nightgown to the other things on the counter. "We'll take this, too," he told the salesclerk. Katie felt his hard thighs pressing her from behind and reddened. He bent low, his breath brushing her ear. "You can wear it for me tonight," he whispered seductively. Glancing at them, the salesclerk smiled broadly, and Katie's blush deepened.

With various toiletries still on Katie's list, Reno drove to a large discount store, leaving Katie to her shopping while he picked up a few things from the automotive department. They lunched at a secluded corner table in a quiet restaurant.

"Think you have everything you came after, Miss Katie?" Reno said.

"Yes." Katie checked the list she'd hurriedly jotted down before leaving the house. "Wonder of wonders, I even remembered what Maggie wanted. Does she drive, Reno?"

"Some, when she feels like it. She's pretty much of a recluse, actually, but happily so." Reno paused while the waitress brought their drinks, beer for him, iced tea for Katie. "I guess we'll get the feed after lunch, and be off for home. Unless there's something else you need."

"No, I've taken care of everything," Katie said, her eyes roaming lovingly over his face. His hair curled slightly against his forehead, his dark eyes meeting hers. Lifting his beer, he took a long drink, but his gaze remained on her.

"Do you know what you do to me, woman?" he said with a grin, shifting in his chair.

Katie chuckled. "I have an idea. Me too."

At the feed store, Reno arranged for credit with no problem and the sacks of grain were loaded into the pickup. Katie rested against his shoulder on the drive home, extremely content. It had been a wonderful day, just the two of them. She wished she could see the money situation Reno's way, and wondered again at what he meant by "you may need it someday." If she couldn't understand it, she would just have to accept it; but it was going down hard. His not wanting her money made her feel an outsider, as if he couldn't fully accept her and the role she wanted to play in his life.

Suddenly Reno pulled from the road onto a wide, grassy shoulder. Katie, brows brought together, looked at him quizzically. "What..."

Reno's arms went around her and he cut off her questions by crushing his mouth down on hers in a long demanding kiss. Her head whirled dizzily, and all Katie could focus on was the sweetness of Reno's lips pressing hers, forcing her lips to part, wanting more. When at last Reno released her, Katie's breath came fast and uneven, her heart thudding loudly in her ears. The hot summer sun bore down, heating the truck cab, causing Katie to squint as she looked to Reno.

He smiled gently, stroked the hair from her temples. "I've been wanting to do that since this morning, but with the kids..." He shrugged. "And then we got so damn busy." Without further words, he shifted the still-running engine into gear and pulled out onto the road.

Katie snuggled again into his shoulder, thinking, *You want acceptance, Katie girl? You fool. You can't get much more accepted than that.*

"Hey, anyone home?" Reno called out as he and Katie stepped through the side door into the kitchen of the Forester home.

"Well, hello there." Suzy came from an adjoining hall. "Have a good time in town? Summer!" She called over her shoulder. "Your father and Katie are here." Then, turning back to Katie, "Kerri can't wait to get a look at you. Sonny has spread it all over town how beautiful you are, and Summer has been confirming it to Kerri."

Katie reddened, and when the two young girls entered she felt their close examination as they giggled together. Reno asked about Dal and the boys, and Suzy directed him to the garage, then shooed the girls out. "Let Katie and I have tea and talk."

Mostly it was Suzy doing the talking, and Katie suppressed a smile thinking of what Reno had said earlier. Still, Katie enjoyed her. She was so very alive and friendly, putting Katie at ease. Suzy spoke of the long-standing friendship between her and Dal and Reno. Reno had helped Dal build the Forester house and also the barn. In return, Dal had helped him.

"We were just bowled over when Sonny came with the news about Reno and you marrying. Couldn't wait to gossip it all over." Suzy shook her blond hair, naturally curly, Katie was willing to bet. "Why, Reno never said a word to Dal about even knowing you. But then Reno was always pretty closemouthed. Dal used to say, 'Reno will never marry again. Not after Lynn.' Now there was a mixed-up woman—like her mother, I suppose. Reno was a catch, I tell you. A real catch. Only Lynn couldn't stay put long enough to find out. She was always leaving him. Something didn't suit her, she'd take off. Must have left Reno a half a dozen times...."

Suzy's words brought Katie up sharply. Reno had mentioned he and Lynn had separated, with mutual consent, not that Lynn *left* him. She listened more closely as Suzy rambled on.

"Oh, she always thought she could get Reno to do what she wanted just by saying she was leaving. She knew he loved her, but she really didn't know him at all." Suzy chuckled. "Reno can't be wheedled into doing anything he doesn't want to. But I don't guess I need to tell you that. You'd have thought no one needed to tell Lynn after her little tantrums failed time after time, but give her credit, she kept trying it. Well, enough on Lynn. I'm sure I'm boring you with stuff you already know. Come on and I'll show you my roses, my pride and joy. Other than my children, that is."

But she didn't already know, Katie thought. Reno had said separation. That was totally different than Lynn's leaving him. Repeatedly. Was that what he was waiting for from her? Temper tantrums and leaving. Did he expect her to act, or react, in the same fashion as Lynn? The questions, the suppositions, whirled in her mind until she pushed them to the background. For now she must comment on Suzy's lovely rose garden, pay attention to her new friend.

They stayed for dinner with the Foresters, and Katie found Dal as equally friendly as Suzy, though as quiet as she was talkative. He was also head and shoulders above his short wife, but the two fit neatly together in personality. Reno and Dal shared an easy camaradarie, without the bother of a lot of words.

It was nearly ten o'clock when Reno pulled the truck into their own drive. A pole light set to come on at dusk lit their way in the darkness. Joey, nestled into the crook of Katie's arm, slept soundly. She shifted gently to aid Reno in picking up the small boy and carrying him to his own bed. Summer trudged sleepily behind.

Reno laid Joey on his bed and began to undress him. "I'll do it, Reno," Katie said. Reno nodded and went to kiss Summer good night.

Katie looked at the sleeping form of Joey and hoped someday he would really be her son. So far he still went to Reno for everything, even to tie his shoes. Give it time, Katie admonished herself. Joey never woke while she slipped his little body into pajamas and underneath the sheet. Summer was already asleep when Katie looked in. The young girl's clothes, a neatly folded dark lump, lay on the dresser. She was so tidy.

Katie turned and leaned against the doorframe, the semidarkness lit only from the glow of the pole lamp outside and a small hall night-light. These two children were a miracle, so accepting of her joining their lives, eager to have her even. But then they didn't remember their mother. At least Summer didn't seem to and Joey wouldn't, of course, as he was so small when she died. They didn't have any preconceived ideas about Katie herself or expect her to act in a certain way.

Her heart ached. She wanted Reno to accept her in this way. As Katie, not another Lynn. She didn't want to be blamed for Lynn's crimes. Was that why he insisted she keep her money? So she would have something if she left? Did he blame himself for Lynn's constant leaving? Surely not; he was a rational man. But then, sometimes where relationships were involved, people didn't think exactly rationally. Look at how confused she had been, how her emotions had run away with her since first meeting Reno.

She came downstairs, saw Reno relaxing on the porch with his feet propped on the porch railing, and went to take a shower. The water felt cool against her heated skin. Katie allowed the spray to beat down upon her head and face and run in refreshing rivulets down her body. She was afraid to speak to Reno about the fears running around in her head, afraid that if she did, he would pull even farther away from her. If and when he chose to speak of Lynn, it would be in his own time. Again, Katie felt she had to let time work on her side. It would take time for them to get to know each other and for Reno to lower the barriers and permit her to become a full and lasting part of his life.

Reaching for the knobs, Katie shut off the water and pulled back the shower door. Reno stood before her holding a large towel. He wrapped it around her dripping frame, rubbed her back, then took her into his arms. Resting her head against his chest, she said, "I'm getting your shirt all wet."

"No matter."

They stood thus for several minutes, content. Then Reno let her go and motioned to the hook on the back of the door. The flowered gown hung there. "See you in a few minutes," he said with a grin.

Later, curled against him in the darkness, Katie felt the throbbing sweet pain of desire. She could hardly wait for their time of love-making again; the time of sharing the glorious wonder of being a part of him.

Taking a breather, Reno leaned against the top rail of the corral, the August sun hot upon his back even at eight forty-five in the morning. Hearing a holler, he looked down the drive to see Katie coming up from the house. She waved, and he waved back. He watched her body, so familiar to him now, as she walked slowly toward him, a cup of coffee in her hand.

"Hope you haven't forgotten breakfast," she said.

"No, my stomach keeps reminding me. Thanks," he said, reaching for the mug.

"A man just phoned. A Jack Cooper. He'd like you to call back."

Reno nodded. "He's the owner of the stud I'm to breed Sugar with next week. I'll call him after breakfast." He thought of Sugar with excitement. She and the two new horses he'd gotten from Strait were the basis of his growing ranch. In spite of Millicent, the ranch was doing well, though her vindictive wrangling had cut into the profits. He'd lost two clients due to her nuisances. Two good clients. The fact irritated him, but there was nothing he could do about it.

Putting an arm around Katie, he said, "Come on, Miss Katie. I'm hungry."

While washing up in the bathroom, Reno noticed Katie's flowered gown hanging on the back of the door. He smiled, remembering when they'd bought it in town. She hadn't worn it lately, hadn't needed to. Catching the scent of her perfume he thought of the way her body reacted to his touch. Damn, she felt good. At night, when she lay with him, he forgot everything. But during the day, his fear returned to haunt him.

He felt as if he were waiting for their wondrous bubble to burst, was short-tempered with everyone for no reason. Surely the magic, what they were sharing . . . Reno couldn't put it into words . . . but surely it wouldn't last.

Summer poked her head around the door. "Daddy, two or three eggs?" Her round face looked hesitant, half expecting him to growl. Guilt welled up in Reno. Why was he so edgy lately?

"Three this morning, babe. I'm starving." He grinned to see her smile in return.

Sonny shared breakfast with them, and the table was extra lively with his talkative manner. Sometimes Reno felt jealous at the obviously appreciative looks Sonny directed to Katie, but he knew his friend well enough to know there was nothing to it. And Katie was beautiful. He looked at her now, and she looked back. For a moment the others at the table faded and they saw only each other.

After breakfast, Reno put in the call to Jack Cooper. A maid answered, and he had to wait almost five minutes for

Jack. "Yeah, Jack, this is Martin. Are we still all set for next week?"

"No...something has come up, Reno."

Instantly Reno became wary. A tone in Cooper's voice alerted him to trouble. "What's the problem, Jack?" he asked smoothly.

"I can't breed Timber with your Sugar." Cooper paused. Reno waited. "Aw, hell, Reno, I might as well tell you. Millicent was out here. What can I do? I have a big place here, fancy the way the wife likes it. But all this stuff takes money, and I'm in over my ears. The bank owns most of it. Millicent can make real trouble for me."

"You're losing out as well on this deal," Reno said, his voice clipped.

"I know that, but I'm caught in a bind. Come on, Reno. There are other horses."

"You got that right. But I'm telling you, Jack, you let Millicent do this and she'll never stop."

"I'm sorry, buddy, real sorry," Cooper said.

"Yeah, sure."

Reno hung up and stared moodily at the telephone, feeling all eyes in the kitchen resting on him. No one said a word. Not even the two jabberers, Joey and Sonny. Tension fairly crackled, and he could feel the curiosity. Getting so quickly to his feet that he upset his chair, he gave it an angry kick and strode from the kitchen.

Joey called after him, but he didn't look around, only strode at a good pace up the sloping hill behind the barn. Finally at the last corral, he stopped and rested his forearms on the top rail. His breath came ragged and his sweat-dampened shirt stuck to his back.

How he hated it. To have his emotions on view, to have anyone see his disappointment or his hurt. It was sitting there and having all his family looking at him that made him near as mad as losing the deal with Cooper. He was raw and hurt inside, and they had to see it. *Damn!*

Sugar pranced now in the corral below him, her copper color shiny in the sunlight. He watched, as always, with a sense of wonder. All his horses struck him in that way; he marveled at their strong muscles knitted perfectly together, the sleekness of their stride. Sugar and Timber together could produce an unbeatable line. Damn Millicent! What a waste.

Katie walked up the hill toward him, slowly. He didn't want to see her, talk to her, or have her see him at the moment. When she stopped beside him, Reno didn't turn around.

"The deal with Sugar. Did it fall through?" Katie asked.

"Yeah."

"Is it because of Millicent?"

"Yeah."

Katie put a soft hand to his shoulder, but still Reno couldn't bring himself to yield. "Reno, you should go and talk with her. Because of this thing between you both, the children won't go and see her. It's making them, Millicent, and us unhappy."

"I told you, a person can't reason with her. Especially me. It would do no good."

"I could go with you. Maybe together we could . . ."

Reno clenched his teeth, but still did not look in Katie's direction. "I said no. She's an old woman, set in her crazy ways. She has a heart condition that doesn't need upsetting, either."

"Well, maybe people have been sidestepping this crazy old woman with a heart condition for way too long." Katie's voice rose.

"Maybe so, but you stay out of it!" Whirling angrily, Reno saw Katie's face pale at his words. She looked as if he had slapped her.

"You want me out of it? Fine. I'll stay out of it. And you can just stay up here and suffer alone!" Pivoting, Katie ran from him back to the house. He watched her go, and his heart constricted tightly. *Was it now? Was it all ending now?*

He worked hard the rest of the morning, trying physically to rid himself of his frustrations. Sonny came out to work alongside of him a good deal, and after saying, "Reno, you're a damn fool," he never said another word—a miracle for Sonny.

For some reason Reno found himself glance repeatedly toward the front yard and the garage. At the sound of a car engine, he jerked up quickly. It was only Tobias, his older brother driving, coming to fetch Summer to go skating. Joey played in the backyard with Sam. When Reno saw Katie come out to hang clothes, the tightness in his chest abated some. Later he heard the strains of her banjo, not happy, stepping music like she usually played, but long, slow ballads.

At noon Sonny said, "I'm knocking off the rest of the day. Think I'll head over to Tyne and get a few beers. Wanna come along?"

Reno looked in the direction of the house and shook his head, saying absently, "Not today. Thanks, though." He needed to see Katie. Slowly, not knowing what to expect from her, he walked toward the house.

He found Katie in the kitchen, her typewriter, books and papers strewn across the table. She glanced up quickly, but then lowered her eyes, and Reno wasn't able to read anything. He stepped to the sink to wash his hands and noticed two plates covered with a linen cloth sitting on the counter.

"Is this our lunch?" Reno asked, nodding toward the plates.

"Yes."

Reno shifted uncomfortably. It wasn't his nature to apologize, even when he knew himself to be at fault. Couldn't she just see he needed her? He opened the refrigerator door and rummaged around for a soft drink. Uncapping the bottle, he leaned against the counter and fixed his gaze on Katie. She appeared to be absorbed in her papers, but Reno could tell by the twitching of her eyelids she was very aware of him. He began to grin in spite of himself.

Suddenly, she wadded up the piece of paper and threw it at him, laughing. He held out his arms and she came to him, pressing close. She was soft and warm and her hair smelled of roses.

"Reno..." she said, and he felt her tense within his arms. Then, "Nothing."

"What is it?"

"Nothing." She smiled up at him, and Reno noticed her eyes glistening. "Let's have lunch on the porch. Joey already ate."

Chapter Sixteen

The early November morning dawned as gloomy as Katie felt. A foggy mist hung over the ground, shadowing the trees, the clammy moisture penetrating the house as well. Katie dragged herself from bed, a heavy feeling of foreboding settling on her shoulders. It was the same sort of feeling she'd had the morning the van broke down, the day her father died, and the time Picolo, a favored cat, got run over. She didn't care for the feeling and tried to push it away, blaming the weather.

The weather seemed to affect everyone. Katie had to continually nag the children to hurry or they'd be late, and the breakfast table, even with Sonny's presence, was unusually quiet.

Reno was preoccupied, drawn into himself. He barely looked at her. Angered, Katie slammed his plate down on the table. He did look up then, but with the cold curtain drawn across his face. *What's happening to us?* Katie thought bleakly.

Finished packing Summer's lunch, Katie stepped to the bottom of the stairs. "Hurry up, kids. You'll miss the bus," she called. Reaching up with her hand, she massaged the back of her neck and moved her shoulders against a gathering tension.

Stepping up behind her, Reno kissed the sensitive spot under her ear, removing her hand and massaging with his own. "Got a crick this morning, Miss Katie?"

"Umm. I feel stiff all over. Guess it's the weather."

"Maybe you're getting old," Reno teased.

Katie playfully hit at him, then his gaze caught and held hers. His brown eyes looked so sad, so questioning. Between them lay a barrier Katie just didn't know how to breach, didn't even fully understand. But it was there, invisible though it was, stretching between them, keeping them apart. Lately, even at night in bed, Reno seemed to be holding back, no longer able to fully commit himself to their love.

Joey and Summer clambered down the stairs. "Ready, Katie?" Joey said. "Will you walk with us?"

"Sure." Katie smiled at the young boy. He asked her every morning, and every morning she said yes.

Saying good-bye to Reno, Joey slipped his hand in Katie's and, with Summer, they walked the dirt drive to where the school bus stopped on the state highway below.

"I had the neatest show-and-tell yesterday. Better than everyone else's," Joey stated.

"We've heard all about it thirty times since last night, Joey," Summer said.

"Well it was neat. Wasn't it, Katie?" Joey looked to her for confirmation, and Katie smiled at him and nodded. "Teacher said not too many mothers would help a kid put a dead snake in a bag and let them keep it in the refrigerator until class. That was a smart way to preserve it, she said. She's looking forward to meeting you, Katie." Joey tugged at her hand and beamed.

"Katie?" Summer said, then hesitated.

"What is it, Summer?" Katie prompted, watching the young girl's frown.

"Well, would you talk to Daddy about Grandma? My birthday is coming up, and I've never had a birthday without Grandma."

"Yeah," Joey inserted. "She always gives the best presents."

"Oh, Joey." Summer pulled a face, then once more turned to Katie, imploring, "I know she can be a real pain, but I miss Grandma.... And I'm worried about her, Katie. We're all she has."

Katie regarded Summer's concerned expression for a moment and sighed. "I can't promise anything, but I'll speak to him. But you know, Summer, there may not be anything he can do. Millicent has set herself against him. It wasn't anything he did."

Katie waited with the children for the bus and waved as it pulled away. Then, shoving her hands deep into the pockets of her thick wool sweater, Katie slowly walked back to the house. The foggy mist had lifted some, but the day remained gray. Except for an occasional teasing breeze, the air was still. The trunks of trees shone dark against the varying fall colors of gold, red and orange. In another week, two at most, the branches would be bare.

Katie was deep in thought when she heard Maggie call out.

"Morning, Katie. Mind if I walk with you, or would you rather be alone?"

"Hello, Maggie. I'd love to have your company." Katie looked at the older woman closely, detecting a slight favoring of her left leg. "You feeling all right, Maggie?"

"Fine. It's the wetness—gets to my old bones sometimes. You know, I'm not as young as I used to be," Maggie said, not as a complaint, but with a twinkle in her eye. "How are things going with you and Reno, Katie?"

Katie hesitated, knowing she couldn't get away with a casual "fine," or even a hearty "great." "Sometimes, I wonder myself, Maggie. After my trip to Davis, Reno seems more withdrawn than ever. I told him I wouldn't do the article if he didn't want me to. He assured me it was fine to make the trip, but I know he didn't like it. What's bothering him, Maggie? Is he waiting for me to act like Lynn? To run off? He's erecting a barrier between us, and I don't know what to do about it."

"Reno's experience with Lynn left its mark, to be sure, but that's not the whole problem, honey," Maggie said. "You have a maverick on your hands. He's a loner, a man who's never had anyone wanting to share his life, no one he truly wanted to share a life with. Oh sure, there are the children, but that's not the same as a wife, Katie. Just give it all time. It will work out."

Katie only nodded. She hoped and prayed it would all work out as Maggie said. But so far, with the passage of time, things only seemed to be getting worse.

As if reading Katie's thoughts, Maggie said gently, "Perhaps you should look at yourself, Katie. Sometimes a person must wait out the storm and allow the happiness they seek to find them. Maybe you're straining after what you want so hard, you're keeping it at bay."

The vision of the dream, the tornado, flashed through Katie's mind, and she looked at the older woman sharply.

But Maggie stepped away in the direction of her cottage, waving, indicating the conversation was at an end.

Katie returned to the house, thinking, "Gray days, they make everyone blue." A heavy dread settled upon her. This time she didn't shrug it away. Something was going to happen, today or tomorrow; all she could do was wait.

After making a fresh pot of coffee, she opened several windows, then sat at the table and spread the newest article she was working on before her. But she couldn't concentrate.

When Reno joined her for coffee, Katie decided she might as well tackle the subject of Millicent and get it over with.

"Reno, Summer's birthday is coming up," Katie said.

"I know. I had my eye on a new saddle over at Heath's, but I'm not sure the budget can stand it."

Katie took a deep breath and forced herself to face him. "Reno, Summer would like Millicent at her birthday. She's worried about her."

Reno stared into his coffee cup, his expression unchanged. When he didn't say anything, Katie covered his hand with hers. "Reno, we really should at least try to make peace. Together, we could go to her, try to reason with her. I'm sure she misses the children." Still Reno said nothing. "Maybe if I went to her...extended a friendly hand, so to speak. After all, it's because of me she's so mad."

Sighing, Reno passed a hand over his forehead. "No. I'll go see her. This mess has gone on long enough."

"Let me go with you."

"I said, I'll see her," Reno said, then gulped the rest of his coffee. "I'm going over to the side section to cut firewood. I won't be far; you'll hear the chain saw. I'll take a break around noon or so for lunch. If you need anything, Sonny's working with some horses in the corrals." Without even a kiss on the cheek, he rose and left, the screen door coldly banging shut.

"Damn you, Reno Martin," Katie hissed aloud, clenching her hands into tight balls. Closing her eyes against tears, she fought to clear the lump from her throat. Why did he keep shutting her out? He loved her, she knew he did. Why did he keep closing himself off?

For the next half-hour, Katie tried to work on her magazine article, but finally gave up. She'd read the same page three times without comprehending one word. Wandering around the house, she tried to clean. Then giving this up, too, she took a cold soft drink and stepped outside to the porch swing. The deep gray sky had paled, and here and there, patches of blue struggled to peek through. Sonny's whistling sounded from the barn, and Katie caught the distant roar of Reno's chain saw. Sam sauntered under the giant elm, disturbing two banty hens, who told her about in no uncertain terms. Ignoring the hens, the dog sprawled her massive body in their midst.

Katie idly watched the ranch activity and listened to its sounds, moving her boot against the porch floor to gently sway the swing.

The buzzing of the chain saw stopped. There was nothing unusual about the saw stopping. It could be one of a hundred reasons: Reno resting, oiling the chain, refueling, moving to another tree. But suddenly Katie knew it wasn't any of these. *Something was wrong.* She froze, straining to hear the saw start up again. Sam, sensing, raised her head. Seconds ticked by, Katie's heart pounding loudly in her ears.

Then she was running. Down the stairs and past the elm. Sam already on her feet and running before Katie.

"Sonny! Sonny!" Katie screamed. Sonny appeared behind the back of the barn. "It's Reno. The saw," Katie yelled and kept on running, her eyes searching the woods, looking for traces of where Reno had been working.

Ducking under a fence, she raced through the corral and under the fence on the other side. Sam's black hulk dipped into the trees, then darted out again, still running east. Katie's heart pounded, her breath rasping against her throat. She ran on. Reno had said not far, and she was almost at the end of this section now, maybe a quarter mile from the house. "Reno!" she called. "Reno!"

Sam ducked into the wood and Katie lost her. Entering the trees, Katie slowed, her eyes looking for signs of where Reno had been working. She heard the low idle sound of the chain saw and, following that sound, spied Reno's jean jacket hanging on some brush. Coming closer, Katie saw his water jug on the ground close by.

She took in everything else at a glance; a felled tree, splintered off from its trunk; Reno lying on the ground; the chain saw thrown clear several feet away, its engine still running.

"Reno?" Katie breathed, but her voice stuck in her throat as her blood ran ice cold.

Pushing aside branches of the downed tree, she reached him and knelt down. He was sprawled faceup on a thin carpet of leaves. Sam had beat her there and was licking Reno's hand and whining. Fear clawed at Katie's stomach as she gazed down and saw the sticky crimson stain spreading across Reno's shirtfront.

Her head whirled and she froze. *Blood. There was so much blood.* Dazed, she looked from Reno to the tree and knew it had fallen before he was ready. It had broken from the trunk, hit the ground and kicked back into his chest. The splintered wood jutted out obscenely like a spear.

Her mind rebelled. *No . . . no, it couldn't be true. It was only a bad dream.*

Katie forced herself to think, to act.

"Reno, Reno can you hear me?" She touched his cheek. It felt cold.

He was so very pale, his eyes were closed, and a gash above his left temple slowly oozed blood, matting in his hair. "God, oh God," Katie breathed as she pressed her fingertips to his neck. Gratefully, she acknowledged a strong pulse and shallow breathing.

Katie whirled at the sound of Sonny breaking through the brush.

"What in the hell . . ." Sonny knelt beside Katie. Taking one good look, he grabbed her shoulder. "I'm going for the truck. Just hold on, Katie."

Katie held to Reno's hand, fighting hysteria. She had to stay calm. Reno's life could depend on it. *Think,* she told herself. *Think.* Instinctively she began to talk to him.

"Reno, honey, I love you. Please don't leave me, don't leave us," she said. "Reno, can you hear me?" Repeatedly, she said his name, talking to him, imploring him.

The flannel of his shirt seemed to check the flow of blood from his chest, and Katie dared not remove it to look at the wound. The gash on his head still oozed, but didn't look dangerously deep, though what kind of blow he took, she had no idea. She lifted up her sweater and tried to tear a piece of cotton from her shirt, but it was too strong. Remembering Reno's knife, she removed it from its leather case attached to his belt and slashed a square from her shirt. Carefully, she pressed the cotton gently to the wound, letting it stick there. The low insistent roar of the chain saw grated on her nerves, but she couldn't reach it to turn it off and refused to leave Reno's side.

"Reno, you're going to be fine. Sonny's gone for the truck. He'll be here any minute. Reno, please hear me." *What was taking Sonny so long?* Why didn't she hear a truck start up? Reno's body quivered. Jerking her sweater over her head, Katie laid it across his chest, heedless of the blood.

Sam licked again at Reno's hand and Reno moaned, jerking his hand away.

"Reno, I love you. Please hang on."

Katie finally heard the loud gunning of a truck engine. Minutes later, Sonny broke through the branches of the fallen tree, dragging a large rectangular sheet of plywood. Dropping the plywood near Reno, Sonny grabbed up the chain saw and within minutes, cut a somewhat clear path to the truck.

"We'll get him on this board; use it as a stretcher. Take his feet," Sonny commanded. "Gently. We don't know what may be broken."

Shifting his body rather than lifting, they laid Reno the length of the board. Then Sonny lifted one end and Katie the other. Reno was dead weight. The rough edges of the plywood ripped her hands and Katie's grip began to slip.

"Sonny!" she cried out.

"Hold on, Katie, just a few more steps," Sonny urged.

They made the truck. Sonny rested his end of the board on the tailgate and stepped to help Katie just when her hands and arms were giving out.

"Blankets?" Katie looked to Sonny. Could he possibly have thought of them? Wonder of wonders, he had.

Grabbing two horse blankets from the cab, Sonny tossed them to Katie, who spread them over Reno, trying to tuck them tightly around his body from where she sat cradling his head in her lap as Sonny drove the pickup bouncing over the rough ground.

"Sonny, take it easy," Katie cried as Reno winced, then moaned.

Sonny slowed in the barnyard. Katie saw Maggie waving, scurrying to meet them, hampered by her stiff leg. Maggie's steps faltered, her chest heaving from the exertion.

"What's happened?" she called.

"Reno. An accident," Katie said. "Joey..."

Katie didn't have time or need for more. She watched Maggie nod in understanding as Sonny hit the pedal and sped the truck down the drive. Joey, Katie thought. He would be home in less than half an hour. Thank God for Maggie.

With the pickup flying across the blacktop, Katie bent low over Reno, shielding him from the battering wind, talking to him all the while. Over and over she said his name and repeated, "I love you. You're going to be all right." She wasn't sure if her words were to convince Reno or herself. The hospital seemed an eternity away.

Sonny leaned on the horn as he pulled the truck into the emergency entrance. Immediately, two nurses and a tall orderly appeared. Seconds later another man wheeled out a stretcher. Reno was transferred to the hospital bed and rolled inside. Katie never let go of her firm hold on his hand.

As they wheeled Reno into the examining room, Katie walked beside him. "Reno, can you hear me? We're at the hospital. You're going to be fine."

A nurse touched Katie's arm. "You'll have to wait out here," she said.

Katie shook the woman away, never taking her eyes from Reno's face.

"I'm sorry," the nurse said more firmly, fastening a restraining hand on Katie's arm. Katie raised her eyes, piercing the woman with her gaze. The nurse relented, stepping back to allow Katie entrance.

The examining room came alive with activity, nurses murmuring, running to and fro for equipment, repeatedly checking Reno's vital signs.

"Reno. Reno, I love you. Please don't leave me."

"You his wife?" the doctor shot at Katie.

She nodded and watched the doctor finger the area of Reno's scalp around the gash.

"He's at least got a concussion. Keep talking to him," the doctor ordered.

"Reno," Katie murmured again and again.

A nurse passed the doctor a pair of scissors, and he slit the front of Reno's shirt, revealing a chest matted with blood. Taking a sponge, the doctor wiped at the blood, his plastic-gloved fingers gently probing the area. Reno groaned.

"What happened?" the doctor asked.

"He was felling a tree." Katie heard Sonny answer and for the first time realized he stood at her elbow. "The trunk splintered and kicked back at him."

The doctor grunted and, satisfied with his inspection of Reno's chest, raised his eyes to Katie. Gently, he said, "You've done well. The bleeding is checked, but we have to do tests to ascertain the extent of injury. You'll have to leave him for now, but I'll get back to you as soon as I can."

Realizing there was nothing else she could do, Katie nodded, her eyes registering the doctor's competent expression, the concern in his eyes. She took strength from these things, allowing Sonny to lead her to the waiting room.

The emergency waiting area was quiet. Katie wearily sank to a worn and patched blue vinyl couch. Sonny brought her a cup of coffee from the machine, and Katie took it with shaking hands she was unable to still. After several sips of the coffee, Katie sat back and forced herself to relax. There was absolutely nothing else she could do, but wait. All was in the doctors', and God's hands now. She clung to the vision of Reno smiling and pushed all worry aside. *He would be all right.* He had to.

Lifting her gaze to Sonny, who leaned against the wall, staring into space, she was surprised to find him smoking.

"I didn't know you smoked," she said.

"I haven't for two years." He gave a bitter grin. "Damn Reno for making me start again."

Taking in Sonny's pale, strained features, Katie went to him, putting an arm around his neck, and leaned against his shoulder. "He'll be all right, Sonny. We have to believe that."

Sonny let out a choked sound and moved to stab the cigarette into the sand of an ashtray. "I should have gone with him. It's never safe to cut alone. It's just that he's been so distant lately. I figured he didn't want me around."

A tear slipped from Katie's eye. She grabbed him roughly. "Don't you blame yourself. Blaming never helped anyone. It was an accident. He's going to be all right."

Sonny wrapped an arm about her shoulders and she held to his waist for what seemed a long time. Then Katie said, "I'd best phone Maggie." Looking down, she realized what a state she was in. Her blouse hung loose, a large patch torn away. Her face was smudged and her hair was tangled wildly. And she didn't have any money.

Sonny dug into his jeans and handed her some coins. Katie reached Maggie at the house, explaining as best she could to Joey herself.

A little over an hour later, the doctor came out to talk to them. "Mrs. Martin," he said. "I'm Phillip Moore. Your husband is going to be fine. It looked worse than it is. He has three broken ribs, several more bruised. He is suffering from a concussion, but I do believe it's a mild one. He's not fully conscious, though. I'll need to keep an eye on him until he comes around, and for a few days after that."

"Can I see him now?" Katie asked anxiously.

"It will be a few minutes. The nurses are finishing up. You'll need to go to admitting anyway. You can see him when he's been moved to a room upstairs."

"Will you go and get Summer from school?" Katie asked Sonny after the doctor left. "Explain things to her and take her home. Joey will feel better with her there."

"Yeah," Sonny said. "Want me to bring you back a change of clothes?"

"Thanks...just a sweater. Summer can find one for me," Katie said. "And take time for a meal and a beer. I'm not leaving here until Reno wakes up."

When finally allowed to see Reno, Katie stood at his bedside, staring into his face a long while, giving thanks. "Reno, I love you," she whispered.

Pulling up a chair, Katie took his hand and stroked it with her fingers. After a while she rested her head against the mattress and slept.

Quietly a nurse rustled by, checking Reno. Groggily, Katie raised her head.

"I'm sorry, Mrs. Martin," the young nurse said. "I didn't mean to wake you."

"That's okay," Katie said, checking Reno's face for any change.

"He's still out, I'm afraid," the nurse said. "But he should wake soon."

Katie waited as the hours ticked by. Several times Dr. Moore came in, and each time his expression seemed to grow more intense, but he didn't say anything and Katie didn't ask. They were waiting.

At dusk, Sonny returned with a totebag for Katie.

"Summer packed this for you," he said.

"Thanks."

Sonny looked at her closely. "Have you eaten anything yet?"

Katie shook her head. "I'm not hungry."

"I'll get you a sandwich from the cafeteria while you change," Sonny said and left.

Using the adjoining bathroom, Katie changed clothes, grateful to see Summer had sent fresh jeans along with a sweater and a hairbrush. She washed her hands and face and brushed her hair thoroughly. The actions bolstered her spirits and made her feel stronger.

Sonny returned with a sandwich and a soft drink, commanding her to eat and watching as she nibbled obediently. Except for a dim light over Reno's bed, the room grew dark.

"Why don't you go home, Sonny? Borrow a car from Ted Carter and leave me the truck. I'll be home later," Katie said. "There's no need in us both sitting here."

"I'll just wait," Sonny said, slouching down in the chair, resting his hat over his eyes.

Once more Katie rested her cheek against Reno's hand, praying desperately for him to wake up, knowing the longer he remained unconscious, the more serious his head injury was bound to be. She slept.

"Katie." In her sleep she heard someone call her name. Whether it was a dream or real, she wasn't sure. "Katie." She heard it again, barely a whisper. It was Reno.

Katie lifted her head. "Reno? Reno, I'm here," Katie said, rising to her feet to peer into his face.

Reno's eyes opened and focused onto her own. Fringed by sable lashes, his dark brown eyes regarded her warmly, full of love. Katie stared into the depths of those eyes, her spirit returning the love, knowing for certain that these were the eyes from her dream of months ago.

"I love you," Reno said, giving a grin, lopsided at best, before once more closing his eyes.

Katie continued to hold his hand and gaze down at his face for a long time. Then, turning, she tapped Sonny's boot.

"Okay, let's go home," she said.

"What?" Sonny started, looking around. "Reno okay? Did he wake up?"

"Yes, for just a minute. But that was enough." Katie smiled. "Let's go home," she repeated.

Chapter Seventeen

Katie walked to the living-room window for the third time in twenty minutes. Reno was coming home today. Anxiously, her eyes scanned the drive and her ears listened intently for the sound of a truck. Still nothing.

She walked back into the kitchen and checked the coffee-maker. Reno loved his coffee, would want a cup immediately.

Running her fingers over the ripples and bumps of a stoneware coffee mug, Katie set it beside its mate, remembering the day Reno had bought the two. It was the day after they were married and were traveling here, to what was to be her new home. They had stopped for lunch and Katie had spied the mugs on the dusty shelf along with other curios for sale in the café. Reno had said to her, "If we can't be traveling together in the same vehicle, at least we can drink coffee from matching mugs." It was such a silly little thing, but the small act had made her feel very much a part of him.

All the months since, he had done many similar things to make her feel wanted, to feel a part of him and his life. He'd not grumbled, not much at least, about all the books, the Garrett rocker, the dishes and other special pieces Katie had wanted to bring from home. He'd encouraged her to bring these things and even suggested places to put them around the house.

Together they rearranged the bedroom so the rocker had a place of honor, and Reno drew up plans for a cherry-wood desk he wanted to build her in there for her writing.

From the very beginning, Reno included her in dealing with the children, deferring to her judgment many times when Katie knew it was hard for him. And twice the past summer, he even asked her advice about men he had hired to work the ranch and who were giving him trouble.

But blind to all this, she had only focused on the times she felt shut out from his life: the money disagreement, the problems of running the ranch and the situation with Millicent.

It had taken the accident to open her eyes and to make her see that by focusing on all the things she didn't have, all the things she felt were wrong with her marriage, she was overlooking the true wealth she possessed.

Reno loved her; she was his wife. Joey and Summer loved her and she them. Katie was blessed with a family of her own, a home of her own.

Katie allowed her eyes to flow around the room, touching on the bright yellow-and-orange curtains, curtains she had made. The teal-blue teapot, which had belonged to her mother, now graced a small shelf, and her typewriter, along with a jumble of papers, was stacked, none too neatly, at the very edge of the counter. Joey's kindergarten artwork, with

"Katie" and "Reno" printed in his childish beginner's scrawl, adorned the refrigerator doors. On one paper he had struggled with "To Mom."

Mom. Summer called her that for the first time last night. Katie wondered if Summer even realized she'd said it.

Katie thought of precious minutes in the night darkness spent quietly in the Garrett rocker with Reno. Or by herself of an afternoon. The new afghan she had crocheted for two months and which now lay across the foot of the bed. The front-porch climbing roses and the pleasure she derived from digging and fertilizing, trimming and cutting, bringing their crimson beauty into the house to enjoy.

All this time, gradually, she had formed a place in Reno's life, in this family, in his home, and not even seen.

For the past three days Katie had looked on everything with new eyes, a new understanding. And was grateful, thrilled. With wonder, she hugged her newfound treasure to her heart.

"Ah, Katie girl, you've been a fool," she said aloud.

The last four of the season's roses standing in a crystal vase caught her attention, and in a moment of whimsy, she plucked one from its place, snipped the stem with a knife and tucked it above her ear.

Yes, she'd been a fool. How hard it must have been for Reno to go against the patterns he'd built over the years, a way of living his life as a loner. Yet, he'd tried—for her. And for every time he'd been unable to share, for everything she didn't understand about him, instead of loving, she'd blamed him. And the blame had gone deep, fuel to fire the bricks that built the barrier between them.

A sort of chuckle rumbled from her throat, and she shook back her head. What a shock she must have been to his life, storming in, so to speak, wanting to give love and be loved.

At the sound of a familiar engine coming up the drive, Katie peered out the kitchen window, her heart thumping rapidly. Reno's truck, Sonny at the wheel, pulled into the yard. Sonny and the children had gone to the hospital to get Reno; Katie had chosen to wait at home. She wasn't sure why. Only that she wanted to be here when Reno came home.

Maybe it was because she was frightened. During the days Reno had spent in the hospital, a newfound love and understanding seemed to exist between them. Katie spent every possible minute with him. He seemed to look at her with a new awareness, and Katie sensed none of the invisible barriers that had plagued their last months. They didn't talk much; they were content just to be together. Often Reno reached for her hand, holding it in the entire visiting time. Did he sense the change within her? Or had he experienced a change, too?

Or was this new understanding, this bond, simply a mirage that would fade once Reno returned home?

Shaking the thought away, Katie stepped slowly out the back door and down the stairs. Joey and Summer alighted from the truck calling and waving in their excitement.

Katie's peripheral vision took in Sonny getting from beneath the wheel, but her eyes remained riveted on Reno's shadow behind the tinted windshield. Stiffly he slid from the seat and out into the sun.

Katie ran several rapid steps toward him, then stopped, hesitating, studying him. He bent slightly to the left and kept his arm close. A large white bandage remained above his temple and on his forehead. The sunlight touched his hair, bringing out varying shades of sable amongst the deep brown. His eyes fastened on her, moving slowly from her head to her toes and back again. Katie looked deep into their velvet depths, seeing again the warmth, the promises of love.

Meeting her halfway, Reno pulled her to him, so roughly that he winced, but he didn't let her go. She felt the stiff tape beneath his shirt where she gently lay her cheek. Placing a hand beneath her chin and tilting her head, he kissed her deeply. His lips were warm and sweet, softly sensual. Katie's blood raced, a spark of desire teased deep in her stomach.

The children giggled and Maggie said, "Reno, I walked all the way down from my cottage, and I didn't do it to stand here in the bright sun while you spend all day kissing your wife."

"Hello, Maggie," Reno said, bending with some effort to hug the older woman.

"Hello, my boy," Maggie said, her breath raspy after the exertion of the rapid walk, her eyes bright with unshed tears.

The children were playing upstairs in the loft, Maggie had gone home, and Sonny had taken the day to spend with a woman.

"You being laid up kept me pretty busy, Reno," Sonny had said. "I'm in need of female companionship."

Katie lay with Reno across the bed, talking and laughing while Reno was supposed to be resting. At least by lying down, he was easing the pain in his ribs a bit.

"The flower added a nice touch, Miss Katie." Reno gave a teasing grin.

With a start, Katie blushed and reached up to touch the rose still tucked above her ear. "I forgot about it," she said sheepishly.

Reno's eyes burned into hers. "I missed you, Katie," he said.

"And I missed you. Terribly." Katie raised her hand and stroked the hair over his forehead.

They stared at each other. Katie saw the hunger grow in Reno's eyes, felt the burning flame of desire ignite low within her own body.

"Reno." Katie laughed. "Stop that. The doctor wanted you to stay quiet for two weeks—to stay in the hospital at least a week—and here you are home after three days. You have to think of your ribs." She laughed again, tossing back her long hair. "And you know what you're doing to me, Reno Martin."

"Come here," Reno commanded, his voice low and husky.

Bending her face to his, Katie kissed his lips. He brought a hand to the back of her neck, and she moaned at the touch. She broke away. "Reno, I'm afraid we'll hurt you."

Smiling slowly, Reno said, "Let's go on a picnic."

"What?" Katie looked at him, incredulous.

"Let's go on a picnic—to the east pasture. Take the kids and get out in the sun. I nearly went crazy cooped up in that hospital." His expression turned more serious. "Besides, I have something I need to say to you, to explain, and I can do it better there."

"What is it, honey?" Katie asked, searching his eyes.

"Never mind," Reno said, playfully slapping at her rear. "Get the makings of a picnic. I'll get the kids." He sat up, grimacing from the effort.

"Reno, you don't have any business going anywhere."

"Getting out in the sun, the air, feeling the earth beneath my feet will do me a world more good than lying in a stupid bed."

Giving him a skeptical look, Katie walked to the kitchen, trying to remember in which cupboard she'd seen the picnic basket, her mind racing on to the sliced ham for sandwiches and Joey's usual peanut butter and jelly.

Her spirits soared and she whistled gaily as she prepared the lunch. Reno was home. What in the world did he need to discuss with her? He'd already said the most important thing: I love you. What else could there be? It was something good, something wonderful, she could tell.

Reaching for soft drinks in the refrigerator, Katie spied the bottle of sparkling Burgundy she'd bought yesterday. She'd intended it for a private celebration with Reno tonight. Now was better, she thought, tucking a linen cloth around the bottle and placing it in the basket. Way back in the cabinet, she found two stemmed glasses and included these, too.

"We're all ready," Summer said, coming into the kitchen. She'd changed to worn jeans, a sweater and a faded denim jacket. "Can I help?"

"Grab some paper cups, and I'll get the chips. That's it," Katie said, tossing the bag of chips into the basket. "And a good thing, too. Nothing else will fit. Let's go."

Reno insisted on walking, but Katie wouldn't let him carry the basket. "It's heavy. Summer and I can change off," she said.

"Me too," Joey added.

"Yes, you too," Katie said, ruffling the top of his hair before he sprinted off after Sam.

They walked along the edge of the wood and over to where Reno had had the accident. Stepping around the tree, Reno inspected the scene carefully.

"Gee, Dad, that sure was a big ol' tree," Joey said.

"Yes, son," Reno agreed solemnly. His eyes went from the tree to Katie. Putting an arm around her shoulders, he said, "I was a fool to come cutting alone. A fool about many things."

They walked from the shadow of the trees back out into the open sun. "Me too," Katie said. "I'm just glad you're okay. I'm glad to have you again." Katie caressed his profile with her eyes, enjoying the feel of his arm about her as they walked up the sloping hill.

Just over the rise, on the downside, where the hill could break the west breeze and they could still be out in the open sun, they stopped. Summer and Joey tromped the tall tufts of winter-dry grasses to make a somewhat flat place for Katie to spread the vinyl checked picnic cloth. The children ran on down the slope, Summer to tackle the climb of a large elm tree and Joey to scamper with Sam.

Katie sat cross-legged on the cloth with Reno stretched in front of her, resting his head in her lap. "Wine, sir?" she asked.

He raised an eyebrow. "Wine? My, you did pack a special picnic, Miss Katie. But how do you think I can drink wine in this position?"

"If you can walk all the way out here in your condition, you can sit up to drink wine."

"It's not the walking, it's the getting up and down. Besides, that's no way to talk to an injured man."

"Okay," Katie said, nonchalantly, sipping at the wine.

"Give me a glass," Reno said. "I'd like to make a toast." Stiffly, with a bit of effort, Reno raised himself to a sitting position. Katie handed him a glass of the amber liquid, and he raised it in the air. "To us—our marriage and our life."

Something in his tone brought tears to Katie's eyes.

"I love you, Katie." Reno said earnestly. Taking a sip of the wine, he paused as if unsure of his next words. Then, "Katie, I need to explain about the past few months. I know I've been acting like an ass." He took a deep breath. "The accident—it made me realize I've been so afraid of losing you to something, sometime, that I haven't been able to see the beauty of today, of what we have." He looked at her with a wry grin. "And my fear was causing exactly what I was afraid of. I was pushing you away."

His brown eyes appraised her, drawing her close.

"I wanted you to have your own bank account in case that day should come...the day when you would need to leave," he said, watching her carefully. "And I didn't want you to get involved with any dealing with Millicent because I couldn't stand you taking her abuse, abuse she really meant for me."

"There's no need for explanations, Reno," Katie said. "I know now all you did was for me. I couldn't see it then, and I'm sorry I didn't help matters a great deal. The accident has opened my eyes quite a bit, too. None of it matters now."

"I just wanted to tell you that I know I'm pretty used to doing things by myself, my way, but I've been trying, and I'm going to try harder to include you. Hell, I need you, Katie. I couldn't do without you now, even if I wanted to. And I don't." Taking her hand, he looked down and rubbed his thumb over her knuckles. "Summer's birthday is Saturday. We can speak to Millicent tomorrow."

Katie nodded in answer, unable to speak.

"And I thought maybe I would charge the saddle at Heath's. We can squeeze it out."

Katie sniffed, swallowing the lump in her throat. "Let's wait until spring for the saddle. She can have it as a 'just-for-nothing-day' present. There's a sweater-and-skirt set the same shade of blue as her eyes also at Heath's. She's going to be twelve. A dash of perfume might also be nice."

"Thank you, Katie," Reno whispered hoarsely. "Thank you for loving my children. For giving so much to them."

"I love you, Reno Martin."

Reno tossed the glass to the grass and reached out for Katie, drawing her to him.

"Reno, your ribs..." Katie began.

"Shut up, woman," he growled, and kissed her hard.

Katie swayed against him, the blood pounding in her temples, the heat beginning between her legs. She clung to him. Dragging his lips away, he rubbed his cheek roughly against hers. Katie moved her lips to his ear, then to his neck, kissing and nibbling softly, enjoying the low moan that came from his throat. Reno, fumbling with her sweater, slipped his hand beneath the wool and stroked the small of her back. Shivers of delight shook Katie, and she pressed toward him. Reno flinched.

"Oh, honey, I forgot," Katie said, trying to move from his embrace.

"Don't worry about it," Reno said huskily. "Come here." With one hand clamped to her wrist, the other hand sought to move to her breasts, and again Katie shivered, but still pulled away, struggling for control.

"Reno... the children," she reminded him, and took a deep breath, trying to quiet her thumping heart.

He looked at her with heavy-lidded eyes. "Okay. You're right... for now. But just wait until I get you alone tonight," he said with a playfully wicked grin. "And I'm starving, woman. Break out the food and I'll go for the kids." Getting to his feet, Reno drew in a quick breath, muffling a cry.

"Reno." Katie said sharply. "I'll call them. You lie back down."

"No, I need to walk. To feel and look at the ranch."

Nodding, she watched him walk slowly down the hill, then turned to set out the food. After several minutes, she rose and saw Reno, a child holding to each hand, slowly ascending the slope toward her. As she watched, the children broke from his hands and ran, playing a game of tag on their way up the hill. Squinting in the brightness, Katie felt with pleasure the warm sun upon the back of her head. Sparse tall prairie grass blew at her knees.

The dream...it flooded back with full force. Katie watched Reno approach, taking in the familiar set of his body and the leisurely pace of his stride. Closer and closer he came, until at last he stood only several feet away. Katie searched the depths of his eyes. There she found the promise of the dream: the vibrant look of life, and the welcoming warmth of love.

*   *   *   *   *